W9-ACQ-836

THE
ANGLE
OF VISION

THE

ANGLE

OF VISION

THOMAS R. COLEMAN

VANTAGE PRESS

New York Washington Hollywood

FIRST EDITION

Published by Vantage Press, Inc.
120 West 31st Street, New York, N.Y. 10001

Manufactured in the United States of America

TO
MY MOTHER AND FATHER

CHAPTER I

"Looks like it's going to be a great day for hunting," exclaimed Jesse as he directed the car down the winding road and it darted over a knoll. A stone shot from under the wheel of the trailer and crashed into a tree.

"Yes, I hope there will be a lot of shooting," returned Simon.

—oh it's really cold out—I hate the cold—sure hope Jess doesn't get mad at me this time like he did last time we camped out—he yelled and threw a pan at me—hate it when he gets mad . . . (Sometimes I almost think you're normal, then you act so stupid. What's the matter with you?) —no, Jesse—no, don't hit me—don't, I promise I'll think—won't goof up again—Jesse is good to me—he really never hit me hard and he didn't really throw the pan to hurt me—he is the only one who is good to me— why do I feel this way—how can feeling this way . . .

"Did you hear what I said, Simon?" Jesse exclaimed, as the wind whistled around and over the car.

"Oh, I'm sorry," Simon replied, "what did you say?"

"I said that we'll pitch camp later tonight and go hunting as soon as we get there."

The tall trees shot past and the car slowed as it swung into a curve.

"OK," Simon replied.

—wish he would quit calling me Simon—hate that name— Simple Simon met a pieman . . .

"Next time, listen to me when I say something," Jess added, "and don't be off in your little world—you know it gets you in trouble when you don't pay attention. Remember when you weren't watching and that car ran into you? It's lucky you didn't get hurt. You see, if the driver hadn't been paying attention you would be dead now."

The motor pulsated in Simon's ear like many faraway drums. He swallowed and his ears felt funny; they popped and the hum of the engine came closer as he focused his attention on

9

the loud rattle in the trunk. Suddenly he gave a jerk and shook his head.

—come on—I must pay attention to Jess—if he says something to me—I must—I must—don't want him to get mad at me again—really hate the musty smell of the car—wish I was outside in the fresh air—the cold air.

The tires squealed slightly as the vehicle turned a corner and shot down the narrow highway pushing Simon against the door. As he straightened himself up his mind buzzed.

—Simple Simon met a pieman going to the fair—wish we would get there—the sun's starting to come out maybe it'll warm the outside up and . . .

The car sped past a truck that was slowing on a grade and Simon reached over and grabbed his own right hand and held it firmly with his left.

—I must not fall out of the car . . .

He held his hand tighter.

—what if the door should accidentally open or I should accidentally open the door and I fell out and that truck ran over me—blood—my face smashed in—clothes torn—an eye out of his head—poor Mister Abel is so dead that he didn't know that the truck had killed him—with his leg forced under his back—the concrete got all black from his blood after they took him away. . .

Simon's eyes looked at Jesse.

—hope he hasn't said anything to me that I didn't hear—looks as if he is frowning—hope he isn't mad at me—better ask him something to see if he is mad. . .

"Jesse, when will we get to where we're going to hunt?"

Jesse looked at him with squinted eyes. "Now look, Simon," he said sternly, "try and use your head. I said just a few seconds ago that we would be there very shortly."

—now I've done it—got Jesse really mad at me by asking another stupid question—why can't I be like him—I'm twenty-five years old and he is only three years older—why can't I be like him? Mother used to say to me. . . (Why can't you be like your brother? You must try hard to be like your brother. You must do what you're told!)—I don't know what I would do without Jesse to help me but I'll bet if I really tried I could really show them all and make my own place—after all I can dig a hole faster than most people and chop up logs fast—can even drive a car well—there isn't much I can't do when I'm paying attention—all I need to do is pay attention and there ain't nothing I can't do—Jesse has been good to me though and he is a very good brother—he has helped me out many times when I was in trouble—hope he can't tell—hope he doesn't know about this stupid feeling that I have—wish I could get rid of it—I will ignore it and maybe it will go away—Jesse is pretty smart though—if he could tell that I had this stupid feeling he would probably hate me—what's the matter with me—why do I feel like this. . .

Simon clenched his hands together tightly. A shudder crept slowly up his spine, then faster and faster until it shook his whole body. Opening his mouth, he took a deep breath, held it and let it out slowly. Clenching his hands even more tightly, he went on thinking.

—what's the matter with me—I must not touch the steering wheel—it's stupid—I must not— I must relax—yes that's what I'll do—relax and keep my hands under control. . .

Sitting back in the seat, he let his arms drop and closed his eyes.

—that's better—I can feel myself sinking into the seat—deeper and deeper through the springs and the floor—the road is unwinding under me—what would it be like if I dragged my ass on the road— I would wear it bloody—the road would be black there—I'll put wheels under me. . .

He could feel himself relaxing and opening his eyes. He gazed straight ahead.

—what if I had to get down on my hands and knees and lick the center of the road for a mile with my tongue—I would get dirt and germs in my mouth and puke and get very sick and my mouth would be sore and black. . .

Simon felt the auto slowing, glancing at Jesse he noticed that he had a slight smile in his face.

"Are we here, Jesse, are we here?" Simon inquired excitedly.

Jesse didn't answer. The car slowed as the driver flicked on the turning signal and turned onto a very narrow rough dirt road. There were no houses for miles and the trees hung over the road forming a gray wire tunnel. Dead leaves darted across and spread themselves in their path and Simon could hear stones hurling themselves at the bottom of the car.

—it's a beautiful day even though it is cold—it's going to be

11

great to get out into the wide woods with no houses and nobody to bother us—we will be as free as birds. . .

The car and trailer bounded like two adjacent pistons. Looking to the side, Simon saw the shadows of the tree branches gaily prancing in the wind, sweeping leaves back and forth, back and forth like an inefficient housewife with her broom. Looking directly at the sun, he saw the tree branches melt into its bright body and then reappear on the other side of the blinding ball. Simon then closed his painful eyes and looked at the sun imprinted on his eyelids. It faded to a dark circle. Opening his eyes again, he caught a glimpse of a crow lumbering along, waving his feathery arms slowly and sliding with the breeze. The wind slipped over the vehicle and a small cloud of dust welled from the cold earth under the car and swirled like pipe smoke.

—it's wonderful to be alive and free—I love it out here—the trees are so tough and strong—the air is so fresh that I can't wait till we stop— I know we're going to have a good time—I just know it. . .

The car leaped over the crest of a small hill into a valley, blowing aside clouds of dust which expanded into an ever larger mass, and eventually thinned out to mingle with the sky and the leaves, to nest with the squirrels and sink into the deep fur.

Jumping up again, Simon pictured the car coming closer as it parted the breeze and set it to tumbling. He bounced and swayed back and forth to the rhythm of the auto.

—why can't I feel great all of the time and fully enjoy things that I look forward to for a long time—I want to get out of this stagnant car and yet I don't want it to stop—want it to go and go forever—it makes me feel sick and cooped up and yet it can't stop bouncing—things won't stop going by—my eyelids must not stop being heavy—this heater feels good on my legs—just so my feet are warm—I don't care if my hands get cold—you must keep going, Jesse. . .

"What did you say?" retorted Jesse.

"Wha—but I didn't say anything," Simon replied defensively.

"Yes, I distinctly heard you say that I must keep going. Just what did you mean by that statement?"

"I'm only kidding," Simon said, his face flaming. "You know how I am."

"Yes, I sure do," affirmed Jesse.

—why can't I keep my big mouth shut—I always get myself into trouble—big mouth—fat mouth—black teeth—rotten taste—taste haste waste paste maste caste shased—crap—shut my big crappy mouth—tongue tongue—slimy tongue—slimy tongue tongue tongue tongue tongue. . .

"Well here we are," exclaimed Jesse, "this looks as good a place as any."

The car turned sharply off of the road and came to a halt.

—wonder how cold it is out—I'll bet it's cold cold cold. . .

He could feel a chill run through him as the ignition turned off. Waving ceased to bounce and have things pass and the last blast of warm air from the heater caused a panic to grip his stomach and brain. It was intense for an instant.

I need it—I need it—I must have it—we must keep going must must must—Simon pieman rotten stomach painful brain—must learn to ignore the cold and quit minding it so much—if I don't think it's there it won't be—I won't be cold—cold ears —frozen feet—cut off bloody black ear. . .

Leaning forward, Simon tugged once at his eyebrows with both hands.

After reaching into the back seat, getting his gun, and climbing out of the car, Jesse placed his firearm on the hood and slipped his arm into his heavy hunting jacket. The cold rushed through the open driver's door and across the seat, gripping Simon so that a shiver shook him. Sitting straight, Simon reached for the remaining weapon, crawled out of the auto, put his gun on the hood, and with his eyes on his brother, put his arm into his coat.

—why can't I be like Jesse—he's so strong and always does everything right and here I am a stupid ninny—I'll show him by getting a deer—sure is cold out here—wish I could take the cold like Jesse—bet he never even notices it—he could run naked in a blizzard and live. . .

Simon zipped his coat and pulled up his collar so that the cold afternoon air would not penetrate. Turning toward the bright sun which was smiling at him through a small clearing, he raised his arms up and out toward it to gather in more of its rays.

—wish I could concentrate the sun on me—it's so cold and the sun is so bright— wish Jesse would say more but wish he would say nice things and only nice things. . .

As he watched the steam pour out of his nostrils, Simon sucked at a piece of beef that was imbedded in a large black cavity of his molar. Then he clamped his teeth on his tongue.

—it's great to be alive—the day is so beautiful—the trees are so straight and tall and the chipmunk sounds cheerful— I could kill him. . .

He was looking at two of the animals that were inserting their noses under the dry leaves and scampering over the roots of a thorny apple tree. The tree had no leaves, but several wrinkly yellow apples still clung to it.

—all I would have to do is raise my gun, aim and shoot—it would be so easy and yet so horrible because they are such beautiful animals—wonder if those two furry animals are married —wonder if they cuddle together on cold nights or if they fight— wish I could—I could touch one and run my fingers through its coat without having to kill it—I love them—they are so beautiful and quick—they seem as if. . .

"Well, are you ready?" demanded Jesse impatiently.

"Yes, yes, Jess, I'm ready!" Simon exclaimed breathily as he hastily put his red cap on his bushy head and threw his firearm over his right shoulder. With quickened step he hurried after Jesse who had already started into the thick wood. Catching up, he followed a few steps behind, imitating his brother's stride. The incline became steeper and his breath came deeper and faster. The sound of the ground crunching under his feet came to his ears.

—leaves, leaves and more leaves—roots trees bushes and more leaves for miles and miles on hills and in valleys—they all grew and died probably without anybody around to see them and nobody to help them grow—nobody cares for these dried up things—nobody watched while they grew—wish I could go around the woods and look at each leaf and bush and then they would matter and yet they did grow and die without anybody to see and they did grow well and die without crying—when it gets warm and wet again they will get black and rot and the worms will crawl through them and hide in the black pieces they make—wonder why it is that leaves and trees don't hide and yet worms do—they never come out into the sunlight and enjoy it they don't like people to look at them—remember on the warm nice summer night when we were little we used to gather nightcrawlers—they would lie there in the warm damp grass sticking partly out of their holes and we would creep up on them and quickly pull them out of their holes and put them into cans—they were very slimy and skummy and many times slipped through our fingers into their dark dingy holes—they seem to sense that we were ready to get them —remember when Snakey and I were out playing in the back yard and it was very dark that night and I couldn't tell Snakey pushed me and I fell down and fell on my hands—the skin of my hands began to move slimy scaring me—it was a weird feeling because I didn't remember that night that the worms were out covering the ground all over and when my hands fell on them they started to go into their holes—horrible feeling to know they are there and yet can't be seen and sometimes it scares me to suddenly realize that they are there—we used to play in the back yard many nights and usually never remembered that the worms were out. . .

—we stamped and ran around the grass and must have killed and bruised thousands of poor worms without knowing it—this hill is getting steep—wish Jesse would slow down—he walks so fast and I always get that dull feeling that tingling feeling all over whenever I walk hard and it makes me feel that I want to sit down just when I've started to do something—it makes me feel like I can't do anything strenuous like other people because I'm too weak and get so tired fast. . .

They mounted the hill higher and higher bracing their feet against trees and rocks in their ascent. Then Jesse stopped suddenly and turned to face Simon, looking him squarely in the eyes. Simon shyly dropped his head and looked at the rifle that was cradled in his arms.

"Simon," said Jesse in half a whisper, "You stay here. This stump will make a good seat and I will circle up and around to the top of the ridge and work back this way. You keep an eye open for any deer that I chase this way."

Simon nodded meekly and Jesse turned to leave. His heart gave a jump as he remembered.

"Jesse," he whispered in a loud crackly voice for Jesse to hear.

"You forgot to give me any shells. I can't get you a deer without shells."

"Oh, yes," said Jesse, "so I did. Now you must remember to be very careful if I give you any shells. I taught you how to shoot, but make sure you have a good target before you start blasting, or you will waste the shells. And hold very still if any hunters come so that they don't see you; but I don't think you will have to worry about that."

As he handed him three shells, Simon's whole being shook in ecstasy.

"OK." his brother whispered, "Make your shots good. We only have the rest of today and tomorrow to get deer and I don't want to go home empty handed."

Turning around, Jesse strode forward silently and disappeared behind the scatter of trees as Simon turned the magnificent brass projectiles over and over in his hand and marked every minute detail. The shells wiggled and wriggled in his palm, seeming to contract and expand because of the power that was forced inside of them. It was as if they would explode at any moment without waiting for a target.

—what if they should go off in my hand—wonder if it would kill me or just make me bloody—they're beautiful—lovely—they would go through my hand if they went off. . .

Concentrating his whole being, Simon gingerly forced the cartridges into the clip. Then he pushed the clip into the gun and, pulling back the bolt, watched the bronze shaft click up into the chamber. For a few seconds he eyed it in awe. Pressing the mechanism forward, he watched the brass disappear into the barrel while the impression of the splendid cartridge remained implanted in his mind.

—now I have power—nothing in the world is as powerful as I am—wonder how well I could hold off a force of Commies. . .

He pictured an army charging up the hill at him while he gallantly dropped them one by one.

—kill them or they will kill me. . .

He could see them lying on the hillside, bleeding from their newly inflicted wounds.

—they would bleed and their blood is dripping onto the dry leaves and being soaked up by them—the bloody leaves are turning dark from the blood just like the blood did that was on my hands when Jesse and I went rabbit hunting— I would

16

clean out the guts of the animal with my bare hands and put dead leaves inside of its chest so it would keep until we got home— the guts were long and slippery like worms—long worms— but they were not cold like worms they were very warm—I would take my cold gloves off and put my freezing hand inside rabbits guts to pull them out and it would be warm—it is very cold out and still the rabbit guts are warm—the cold does not leak inside of him—I love blood on my hands and the smell of rabbit blood is good— I can show the world my hands and tell them to see what I have done and let everybody know that I have killed a rabbit and I would have proof when I put the dead rabbits into my coat's game bag—they are heavy and yet I love it heavy the heavier the better—that is why I love to carry both of our rabbits because I love my game bag to be heavy and the rabbits in my bag are warm they warm the bottom of my back and the more warm and the more heavier it is the better I like it—it seems as if—if there was at least one rabbit in my bag I would have more energy and could hunt all day— and some of the blood would leak out of the rabbit and sink into my coat and turn black and my coat sleeve—my hands are getting cold. . .

A shiver ran through him.

—where are my mittens—did I forget them—yes, I forgot my mittens. . .

"Doggone it," he mumbled to himself. "Why did I have to go and forget my gloves?"

—oh well—I'm tough—I don't need them—Jesse rarely uses his unless it gets real cold—where did he tell me to sit and wait. . .

Looking around, Simon located the stump. Rising onto his tiptoes, he slid his backside onto the high pedestal and sat with his legs dangling.

—this stump is sure rough—the sharp parts are jabbing me— why can't I walk around—want to walk around and sneak up on the deer and shoot it—why can't I do that—I feel so much like walking around—feel like I need to walk but I will stay here—wonder if my gun is clogged while I was walking through the forest—I wasn't paying attention to set if a twig got stuck inside the barrel—if there is something in the barrel the gun will blow up when I shoot it and will kill me. . .

Pulling the bolt of the gun back, he caught the ejected shell in his hand and then put it in his pocket. Grasping the cold barrel of the weapon, he swung it around so that the barrel was pointing at him. He looked down the barrel and saw the curls imbedded into the side of the shining barrel. At the other end of the tube he could see the shell that was ready to be inserted into the barrel. The point of the cartridge was aiming his way and Simon thought of its going off and driving through his eye and head. Simon's right eye began to hurt as he thought of the damage such an accident would inflict. The gun was not clogged so he turned it around and pushed the bolt closed, forcing the projectile into the barrel. Simon gave a start as he realized that he had just rested the gun pointing downward and that it was aiming at his foot.

—is the safety latch on—oh no, it isn't—I could have shot my foot off—what's the matter with me—why can't I watch what I'm doing—this stump is sure rough—wish it were smooth and wouldn't jab me like it does. . .

Shifting his weight, he got into a more comfortable position and attempted to relax with all of his might.

—there—can feel myself getting limper and limper—the stump is moving—it's shooting upward higher and higher trying to shake me off—it makes me dizzy—remember when we were little I used to lay on my back under the big tree in our back yard—the sun was hot—so very nice and hot and I used to look up at the sky and the clouds and it would make me dizzy to lay on my back looking at the clouds—it seemed as if the tree and I were moving that we were floating along and the clouds were standing still—the tree and I would float over the earth so smoothly and easily and it would make me dizzy and confused and then I would relax even more and float peacefully but then I would sit up and look around and see that I had not moved at all and that I was in the same place from which I had started—then I would look up and see that it was the clouds that were moving and not the big tree and me—the clouds were moving in the opposite direction and leaving me behind but there are no clouds today and I am moving but this is different because I am moving upward and back and forth and it is trying to shake me off as if I don't belong on this stump and yet I feel very at ease now and want to sit here and move with the stump—what if I had to sit here a long time and what if limbs started to grow out of the stump

18

and it began to grow upward—they would grow up through me and grow through my warm guts and a branch would grow out of my mouth and leaves grow on the branches—the tree would grow up through me and I wouldn't be able to move and I would be trapped here forever and I would bite my teeth down hard and my teeth would sink into the tree and would wear the bark off of the tree and my tongue would always have to lick the limb because it would always be on my tongue— my stomach feels rotten and full of roots and I nod my head and the leaves would fall off of the tree in the fall and the leaves. . .

A cold gust of wind blew against his face and Simon didn't feel it. A splinter from the stump dug into his flesh and he did not notice it, but an impulse wound its way from his right index finger up through his body and concentrated its power on the back of his eyes. Suddenly he squinted and felt the cold, and a compulsion then ruled his body. It was a feeling that made him tense again. His hands knew what to do; they proceeded to release the safety latch and pull back the bolt which ejected a shell while snapping another into its place. Placing the shell into his pocket a certain way, he carefully turned the gun around, placing his hands exactly where he knew they must go. Then he looked down the barrel again to check for any obstructions. He knew that he must do it right or he would have to do it again and again until he did do it correctly; however, he did not know why he had to check the barrel again. He just knew that he must. After looking down the barrel again, he carefully turned the firearm around, closed the bolt, pointed the gun at his foot, and put on the safety latch. He had done it, but he did not feel he had done it quite correctly; so he repeated the process again, very carefully, so as to do it exactly right. As he pushed on the gun's safety latch, he suddenly felt he had done it the way it should be done this time, and a feeling of relaxation crept over him again. Pulling his collar higher and hunching his neck closer to his shoulders, he continued his vigil for game.

—wouldn't Jesse be proud of me if I got a deer—must pay attention and I bet I get one—the winds starting to blow harder —wish the sun would shine brighter in here—love the sun— wish it would never go away—isn't it funny how the sun can shine and yet it is freezing outside—hands are starting to get numb—

better put them into my pocket—gun's slipping—there—now it won't fall off my lap this way—this tree stump is sure uncomfortable—love it when I am here in the woods alone—don't feel so queer as I do when people are around— wish I knew why I have all those queer feelings—those ugly feelings when people are around so that I never feel at ease—I don't even feel at ease with Jesse any more—here in the woods I feel all right—relaxed— can touch a tree anywhere and it won't scream and tear a limb off and it won't hit me—I don't have to worry about where my arms are or where my eyes are looking—when people are around I feel so tense and I have to be very careful every minute so that the feeling won't overcome me and I will do something terrible—Jesse would let me drive but it scares me—I would go down the road very fast and would get that terrible feeling that all I would have to do was jerk the wheel suddenly and it would be over—I remember the time that I was watching a painter and I was eating an ice cream cone and I felt like I would throw the ice cream cone at the painting he was doing and ruin it—seems like when I want to do my very best I goof up the most and get these feelings—why do I always get these feelings I don't like and do what I don't want to do—sometimes it is almost as if people know what I'm thinking —I can tell by the way they look at me and that is why they don't like me and yet Jesse still takes care of me and is so good to me—wonder just how much he really does know about these feelings that I have—why can't I be like other people and not have these terrible feelings and never do or think bad—I must try harder to fight it—must must. . .

—the gun is clogged—did I check to see if it was clogged—it could kill me if it were clogged—must check it—it's possible something got clogged in it while I wasn't noticing a twig or something and it could make the gun blow up and kill me— no I will not check the gun—it's all right—must fight this feeling and it will go away because the gun is all right I know it is— this tree is awfully uncomfortable—maybe if I sit on this side— there that's better. . .

Sliding his tongue over his teeth, Simon inserted it into the large black cavity and sucked at the morsel of meat still wedged there, he finally dislodged it and felt it floating over his palate. Swallowing loudly, it disappeared into the mysterious depth of his insides. Still turning his head slowly, Simon's mind considered his mouth.

—it's like a cave and when I shut my lips it must be very dark inside like the inside of the refrigerator when the door is closed—remember trying to find out if the light really did go off when I closed the refrigerator door, but it was on as far as I could see—the refrigerator is cold inside and warm outside but my mouth is cold outside and warm inside—dark warm and wet wiggly tongue . . . (A snake slithers from the rocks.)—it is slimy and looks bad—hate to see a person's tongue—it hides there in their warm mouth but when it comes out it looks bad—hate to see it or know that they have one—they look so awful—it hides in the warm mouth and never gets cold but my lips and nose are getting cold—can't stand it much longer—hands are getting too cold and I'm hungry—it probably won't be for several hours until Jesse comes back and my hands will be frozen stiff then and I will die of hunger—put hands inside of my warm mouth or inside of me through my bellybutton to keep them warm—remember that story of a man who was caught in a blizzard and killed a moose, took out its guts and crawled inside to keep warm—wish I could kill a deer so I could pull out his warm guts and get my hands warm—must do something to get my hands warm and still be able to shoot fast when a deer comes—will go back to the car and get my mittens—it won't take long and I will be more comfortable—Jesse isn't like me, he doesn't understand but it won't take long to fetch my mittens and get something to eat and then I can pay better attention and get a deer. . .

He descended from his perch, determined the direction he must take, and proceeded to stride and slide down the wooded slope in the direction of the car.

—I will hurry just in case Jesse comes back soon—my hands are really getting numb—can hardly hold onto the gun with my fingers now—oops that branch could have poked my eye out—better be more careful—is the safety closed on the gun— don't want to shoot myself—hope I can find the way without getting lost—it would be terrible if I would get lost—Jesse would never forgive me for that—my nose is wet. . .

He felt snot hanging from his nostrils. Shifting the rifle to his left hand and slowing his pace, he squeezed the point of his nose firmly with his right thumb and index finger and exhaled forcefully. A long string of mucus streamed down and he leaned forward so as not to have it attach itself to his jacket. With a sweeping motion he threw his right arm down and outward, flinging the slimy substance aside. Then he heartily ran the canvas sleeve over his dripping nostril and rubbed his hand on his pants.

—snot—snot—buggers—wet snot—gummy chewy . . . (Keep your fingers out of your nose. You'll pick your nose bloody and it just isn't proper to pick your nose. Always use your handkerchief.)—always forget to carry a rag—anyway there is nobody around here to notice that I didn't use my handkerchief . . . (If you go to sleep like all little boys should, then I will have a surprise for you after your nap.)—could always hear Mother's footsteps coming to check and see if I was asleep and closed my eyes—she always knew that I wasn't asleep but gave me a surprise anyway. . . (You always squinted your eyes when you were pretending to be asleep. That's how I could tell.)— I don't think there is anybody watching me but I get that weird feeling a lot of the time that someone is watching me and then sometimes it goes away—the trees are alive—they have no eyes but they are supposed to be alive and I can feel it—they really are alive and they don't like me today—they are thicker today and want to stop me and fall over me and hold me— can't stand to be caught especially caught in a black room and with nobody to help me— love the sun—love it when it is bright and it makes me squint and it shines on everything and I can see in every corner and nothing is there that can hurt me—love it today because the sun is so bright and I can see so that the trees and ground will not hurt me—if I should sink into the ground and be caught there forever and not be able to move my arms or legs and see nothing but black forever I would fight and fight and nobody would help me and I would fight and not be able to get out of the ground but it is a nice day and the sun is bright and nothing can kill me or stop me from moving— wish Jesse knew that I wasn't stupid and that I am smarter than I act most of the time—if he could see in my brain some of the time he could tell that I am smart but then again sometimes I am stupid and I always get these terrible thoughts—somehow someway I will be better and I will show them that I don't need anyone and that I can do it without any-

22

one—(You are such a darling child, but just do as you're told and you will do all right.)—I don't need any help and I will prove it—which way is the car—oh yes this way— better hurry or Jesse will come back and get mad—why do the trees seem to be so alive today—they were always so happy to me before but today they don't like me— don't care I have my rifle and nothing can hurt me—nothing can hold me and the sun will see me while I am alone—the car. . .

Approaching the waiting vehicle, he opened the back door and while still scanning the landscape, steadily thrust his arm into the sedan and slowly drew out a large pair of three fingered mittens. Pulling them on, he surveyed the trailer that contained the nutrients that he desired.

—I will have to move much of the camping equipment to get to the place where the food is—that will take time and Jesse will find out by seeing that the stuff is put in differently from what he and I did, but I must get something to eat—I must. . .

He started for the trailer with his arm outstretched, but suddenly he was stopped by a peripheral awareness that caused him to jerk his head to that side and focus on the apple tree under which he had previously seen the tiny animals scampering. Swollen with realization his intellect regurgitated an idea.

—the tree is small and has no leaves but there are still apples— yes the apples—yellow apples they look juicy maybe I can eat them and not bother the trailer. . .

This new thought preoccupied his mind. It was a good thought. He walked a new line now, toward the tree, to pluck the fruit from its precarious ledge. Reaching up high, he tore down two of the hard golden offerings and dropped them into his left jacket pocket.

—I must wait to eat them because Jesse could come back to the stump at any time and he will be mad if I am not there. . .

With the rifle trailing, he scampered back into the forest and disappeared like a foolish Indian pursuing a fleeing deer. Darting over stump, around trees and under branches, he quickly ascended the hill, loudly crushing the sticks and leaves under foot as he went. A rhythm revolved in his mind, and with each fast breath he repeated words to himself.

—Hurry—hurry—hurry—hurry—hurry—hurry. . .

His whole body called after him.

—you're tired—want to sit down—lay down and sleep (Jesse is

frowning.)—stomach feels empty, rotten—eat bark— dirt—anything—those apples—hurry to eat those apples. . .

All the way up the hill he scurried. Clinging, gripping, slipping, at last he reached his destination and with the steam furiously puffing out of his nostrils, mounted his pillar anew.

"Now I can eat," he whispered to himself aloud between choking breaths. A shivering girlish glee shook him as he plunged his fist into his pocket. His head jerked up and his eyes opened wide as he became fully aware of the message he was receiving from the hand buried in his coat pocket.

"The shells, the shells are in my pocket and not in the gun. What's the matter with me? I put the shells in the gun."

Gripping the firearm firmly with both hands, he inspected its content and found it empty. Becoming furious with himself, he began to sputter from the mouth and, raising the gun into the air, he brought the butt down squarely on his left shin, causing intense pain to shoot up his leg. Gritting his teeth tightly he muttered stiffly through his lips:

"What's the matter with me? I am always doing these stupid things."—they're right I'm crazy crazy crazy crazy. . .

The word echoed in his head bouncing from side to side and becoming louder and louder until they reached a deafening roar. In the meantime he yanked the three brass cylinders from their abode and hastily rammed them into the clip and crammed the clip into place; then, throwing the bolt open, he forced the shells into the barrel.

—crazy crazy. . .

The words echoed in his head bouncing from side to side drawing back and rushing into the tree tops, then gathering up its forces anew, to throw its full weight again. It was as if the tempestuous air wanted to flatten everything in sight. The sun still shone brightly, but the cold winds fought its rays and negated its warmth. A billowing wall of clouds peeked over the horizon and rolled slowly and steadily toward the ball of fire, like the unimpeded flood waters from a broken mountain dam bearing down on the unsuspecting population of a bustling city below. The gusts rose steadily, drawing the fluffy mass across the heavens. The opaque body of clouds triumphantly neared the illuminous daystar with open mouth and began slowly to consume its power, reducing it to a faint glimmer.

The larger trees groaned under the weight of the gale and small dead branches were struck to the ground by the incessant flood of air. Two dry leaves hung tenaciously to the same branch, side by side. One had lasted only to early summer and the other had borne the summer's heat into autumn. They smote each other furiously while the branch shook its skinny fingers to be rid of them both. In a sudden gust, the more feeble of the two lost its last hold to be rocked away on the breeze and fall to rest in the myriad pile of leaves below.

Snow began to fall. Large flakes, white flakes, everywhere they flew. They blew into the tree bark, into the squirrels' nest and melted on the deer fur deep in the forest. Landing on the bare tree stump, they covered it with a white film. Some circled the stump and came to rest on the surrounding ground and on Simon's canvas jacket and wool hat. Simon fought off the cold. It was getting dark and Jesse had not returned. He huddled up in a ball, his whole body shivering with his every heart beat. In his pocket was one apple; he had eaten the other to placate his demanding stomach and he was keeping the smaller one as an offering in case the wrath of his brother should fall upon him for some reason. It was snowing and getting dark and Jesse had still not returned. The outer fringes of his mind longed for Jesse's return and release from the torturing cold and threatening approach of night. Gazing inward, he concentrated intently on scenes from his childhood; about the time when it was dark, very dark. The car had broken down on the lonely road home and his father could not get it started so they were walking through the darkness.

"Father, I'm scared," little Simon exclaimed.

"Don't worry, son, there is nothing that can hurt you," his father returned comfortingly.

"But there's wolves, Dad."

"It's not much farther," his father answered sharply, "and anyway I have my pistol. So shut up and do as I tell you."

"Can we go back to the car and try and make it go? Please, Father!" he implored, feeling his legs weaken.

"Will you hush your mouth," retorted his father.

"But," Simon began. Then he hesitated because he knew it was no use, this was the only way it could be done.

—it's so dark out here. . . (Simon clenched his father's hand more tightly.)—what if a bunch of wolves should attack us or we get lost—father is big and strong though— he has never failed me and why should he now. . .

Simon's father suddenly stopped short, startling the little boy.

"Wait right here, and don't you move," he ordered, drawing his pistol and quietly striding forward down the path.

—no no! father has left me—scared—I'm so scared—it's so dark out and the wild animals will kill me —they won't see me over here. . .

He ambled off of the path and squatted down beside a large tree. Clenching the cold tree tightly and looking around himself, he repeated over and over, "Nothing can happen to me; nothing can happen to me; nothing can. . ."

He saw the faint outlines of the enormous trees that hovered over him and looking in back, he perceived more rocketing vegetation and an oblong black rock beneath one of the trees about fifteen feet away.

It was chilly in his short sleeve shirt, so Simon wrapped his arms around his knees and drew himself into a smaller bundle while he stared intently ahead, waiting for his father's return. A strange magnetic force suddenly seized his chin, causing his head to turn. His eyes opened wide and strained until they hurt. Staggering backward and almost losing his balance, he continued thinking.

—the rock—it is closer—it can touch me. . .

"A wolf! Help, Father!"

"Help, wolf!" Simon yelled, leaping up and looking around. "What's the matter with me?" he asked himself out loud as he suddenly caught himself.

—they told me I was attacked by a wolf long ago and that's how I got the scars, but I never really remembered it. Hope Jesse didn't hear me when I said that— he will really be mad.

Shaking profusely, Simon forgot about the cold; his head was pounding with the thought of what he had just remembered.

—simple Simon met a pieman—you moron what's happened to you—ever since that night you have never been the same—sometimes you seem almost normal to me—said Simple Simon to the pieman—help a wolf father help—what's the matter with me—this feeling is terrible—Jesse will be mad—must shoot a deer and keep an eye open for wolves so Jesse won't be mad. . .

Grabbing his gun and concentrating all his attention on his immediate environment, he became very tense and jumpy. Things began to move around. He was becoming dizzy—no, he wasn't. Looking to one side, he caught sight of something moving out of the corner of his eye.

—a wolf—it's a wolf running down the creek bed behind the bank—must get it as soon as it comes into sight or it will get me. . .

He raised his gun and fingered the safety latch. It was already off. Maddened by this discovery, he calculated and aimed and pulled the trigger stiffly. A shot rang through the forest.

—oh no—I think I missed it —he will surely be proud of me if I did hit it—better make sure or it will sneak up on me if it is not dead. . .

Half sliding, half running, Simon worked his way down the hill toward the gully. Coming to the edge of the bank to where he had aimed, he looked down. Suddenly his eyes focused on only one thing, the object that lay in the gully; the peripheral areas became completely blocked out. Simon's lips moved, but not a sound came from them as he took a step to the side to look down at a different angle. Then he put his hands over his eyes and, with his mouth still moving silently to the sound of "no, no, no," which throbbed in his brain, peeked through the fingers and said:

"Jesse, what's happened? Come on, Jesse, I didn't hurt you, did I?"

The snow danced around Jesse's body which lay over the uncovered roots of a giant oak tree in the frozen creek bed. Jesse did not move and Simon could see that he was bleeding from his left side.

"Oh no, what will happen to me?" Simon asked in a quivering voice. "What have I done? Jesse, are you all right? Oh, please Jesse don't be dead. Please, 'cause I need you, please, Jesse, please." Simon kept standing on the creek bank, leaning over the edge to yell words of encouragement into the space below. "Jesse, wake up! Are you hurt bad? Did I hurt you?"

Suddenly a realization shook him, radiating throughout his body. He squinted his eyes firmly in their sockets as the terrible feeling rocked him. It came again and again. He was aware of a dreadful dull feeling in his heart and a sinking acid sensation in his stomach.

With his lips still forming noes, he leapt over the breach of the bank and stumbled to his brother's side.

"Oh no. He's dead. Poor Jesse is not moving. He is dead and I killed him. What will become of me? I killed him. What will I do?"

Simon was shocked by the defiant realization that he had made a good shot. He wrestled this reaction back down and forgot it. Contemplating what he should do, his mind buzzed with random thoughts.

—I will be killed for this. . .

He thought about being hung by the neck. Unable to cry, he could only dwell on the consequences: the gas chamber; the electric chair. He had not had this awareness of death before and his mind reflected on the animals that he had killed.

—they are made of flesh and blood and yet it is all right to kill rabbits and yet it is a terrible thing to kill your brother— why is it that I don't feel like this when I kill a rabbit. . .

—a man shows no emotion and I don't feel like I'm going to cry but I must do something—let's see what would Jesse do. . .

Simon was not unhappy. Simon was not happy as he picked up his brother's body and walked toward the car.

—must keep a cool head and do the right thing and not let my face show anything . . .

Feelings were not a part of Simon; he could feel neither remorse nor the cold. He only knew that he must do something because he was now alone and in charge.

—must make the decisions and must be right—this is an unfortunate happening but must be a man and show the world I can handle myself—dead man—man's dead—dead—never touched a dead man before, but this is my brother and guess that makes it different—more dreadful. . .

It was getting darker and Simon knew that it would soon be completely dark, black, and it made him nervous. The dark was something he hated when he was alone so he knew that he must get out of there before the night engulfed him. He was seized by a fear which made his body rigid as he realized that he would be alone in the woods at night.

—what is death—am I alone—Jesse has never left me alone for long—I am alone. . .

His pace quickened. Slipping off an icy log, his left ankle drove itself into a sharp rock and his leg bled from the gash.

He knew what had happened, but did not look down. The pointed thorns of bushes pricked his flesh, but his eyes remained fixed ahead. The body of his brother was heavy and he staggered a few times. But he went onward with his burden because he knew what he must do.

—it's getting too dark—must hurry faster—car's ahead and will be able to get into it and drive— will be safe then—safe from the night and the animals—must hurry faster. . .

Stepping up his pace, he stumbled onward through the woods. The wind threw cold icy snowflakes at him while the trees poked their sharp grey fingers at his eyes, as he passed. Simon felt his eyes begin to oscillate quickly from right to left.

—there are wolves all around—must get to the car before they get me—there's one—it just ran behind that tree—and another and there's another. . .

Bathump, bathump, bathump . . . Simon's heart pounded in his ears but he did not drop the weight that hung precariously over his shoulder because he knew what must be done and Jesse would do the same for him.

—wolves are hiding in the shadows—coming closer—must hurry—faster, faster—they are closing in— will kill me and chew on my ribs—must hurry faster—the car is only a short way— must get there before they kill me and chew on my ribs—those sharp teeth—terrible eyes are following me—Jesse help me—no— Jesse's dead—I killed him and now the wolves will kill me— must hurry—must hurry—bloody rib . . .

Simon's breath came in sharp deep gasps as he staggered forward, brushing against trees and running through thorn thickets. The trees bent into his way and the wolves gathered thicker and closer.

—the car—the car—oh, Jesse, there's the car. . .

With a new burst of energy, Simon bounded forward. Rocks and leaves flew from under his feet as he threw himself into and across the clearing toward the machine. His heart expanded with exuberance as he bore down on the auto and safety. Throwing upon the back door of the vehicle, he thrust his brother onto the back seat. Then getting in himself, he slammed the door with all of his power. Crunch went the door as it bounced open again.

"What happened?" Simon exclaimed excitedly. "Oh! Jesse's foot is in the way."

Pulling back his brother's projecting leg, he slammed the door anew. It closed. A feeling of momentary joy shot through him as he hastily climbed into the front seat behind the steering wheel. He flicked on the headlights and their beam blazed into the forest melting the obstacles directly ahead. Glancing around, he noticed that it had suddenly become black and that the woods in other directions were frightfully dark. He could feel somebody staring at him through the back window of the car. Looking down, he saw that his brother was frowning. The lights flooded into his eyes as he turned forward again. He jabbed his fingers into his right pocket in search of the car keys. He must get the keys before something dreadful happened.

"Must find the keys and get out of here," he breathed heavily to himself.

His hands vibrated with his whole body because he could not discover the keys; then a thought hit him.

"Jesse has them," he breathed heavily.

Leaning right and throwing his elbow over the back of the seat he leaped across and fell stiffly into the back seat where he began to rummage through his brother's pockets.

"Jesse, what did you do with the keys?" he pleaded.

Coins and shells came flying out of his brother's pants as he yanked his hands out of each successive pocket.

"Jesse, please! Where are the keys?" he implored whiningly. Then he thrust his fingers into his brother's shirt pocket and rejoiced:

"The keys, Oh Jesse, I found the keys!"

Diving roughly again into the front of the car, he fumbled with the ignition and pressed the gas pedal to the floor.

"Start, please start!" he prayed.

Suddenly the engine roared to life. Simon threw the gear shift into reverse and feverishly let out the clutch. The sedan leaped backward toward the road with the tires whining. Then the car came to a resounding and crashing halt as the trailer jackknifed. Throwing the wheel and whipping the shift into first gear, Simon spun the car around, up onto the bank and then directed it loudly spitting dirt, down the highway. The sides of the road blurred and darted past as the driver zoomed along, faster and faster. Stones thumped and bashed themselves against the bottom of the vehicle and still it accelerated onward through the night. Driving in a heated frenzy from the area of danger, Simon became obsessed with the darkness behind him. He must catch up to the light. But the pursuing darkness dogged his heels and threatened to choke him from the rear. Flashes of snow threw themselves against the windshield in powerful attempts to penetrate.

After driving for many minutes, Simon came to an open place where he could see fields on each side and where there were no trees close enough to hide an enemy. He slammed on the car brakes and stopped. Nervously he glanced back at his brother.

—must do something with him—he will choke me to death— I killed him—Jesse don't kill me— it was an accident. . .

Looking carefully around, he got out of the sedan. He opened the back door and eyed his brother's face. The door was left hanging open as he went back to the trailer which was full of camping equipment. Throwing back the canvas cover, he hurriedly began to scatter the bedrolls, pots, silverware and all of the other contents of the trailer onto the road. Once more aware of the weather, he knew it was cold, very cold. Looking up, he saw the snow dancing around him and felt the impact of a million eyes looking at him. This feeling caused him to work more frantically.

—must hurry—eyes—cold—hurry—very fast—faster faster. . .

When he had emptied the trailer, he went to the car and quickly drew his brother out.

—I must remember that he is dead—horribly dead—he's dead and stiffer than he was before—that's because he is dead—not as limp. . .

Gingerly he slid the body into the trailer floor and covered it with the canvas. The heavy material roughly outlined the bulk of the cadaver.

—must remember that he is dead—he can't choke me here and get the back seat bloody and kill me with his smell— they say that the smell of a dead man kills a person— I don't need Jesse any more—I can make it alone and can prove it—will prove it—he'll see that I don't need him and go away—my name is Jud and I am no Simple Simon and they'll see that I don't need anybody—the cold is stiffening my skin—must hurry—wish the sun would come out and stay out all of the time—love the sun— the canvas is moving—Jesse is mad at me—he will kill me but I really didn't mean to kill you, Jesse. . .

31

"Jesse I really didn't mean to kill you. Please don't be mad at me," he pleaded.

—Jesse don't come into my mind—please Jesse—I really mean it really, really, Jesse, so please don't look at my brain because it doesn't know—I better get into the car it is cold out here all of a sudden—so very cold—I could run naked—they must not get me—must get into the car and close the doors quick—there now they can't get at me—better lock the doors—now I am safe and they can't chew my stomach—why do I attract wolves—evil wolves—they're almost here—better drive fast because I don't want them to get at me or to eat Jesse's feet—but they won't eat his toes—I know they won't. . .

Off zoomed the auto. After proceeding for a mile, Simon felt more secure and for the first time sat back in the seat.

—I am powerful now—will tie a rope to the sun and pull it after me for all to see but they will see the shells blood and will hate me—if I'm moving they can't get me—I love to move— I can move faster than their hate—the car smells musty and nice —musty and—no, it will choke me—the smell of the blood will choke me—will open the window to let cold fresh air in. . .

Reaching back, he opened the window behind him slightly so that the wind whistled into the speeding vehicle.

—there can breathe better now and will be able to breathe deeper and the dark will blow out the blood through the window. . .

The sweat had begun to bead on his chest and his heavy woolen shirt was soaking up the body moisture. Opening the window made Simon realize just how warm it was in the car. A dull but delightful chill ran through him as he snuggled in the seat and thought about the cold outside.

—I love you heat—heater feels warm—love the warm—could ride like this forever and sweat forever or do anything to get out of the cold—would do anything to stay warm and get away from the cold so I can have warm air on my legs—my leg hurts. . .

He drew a deep breath between his clenched teeth as he thought of his hurting ankle. Reaching down he felt a damp sock and a swollen bleeding ankle but somehow it felt good that he was hurt. It meant he had paid. He had paid some.

—see, Jesse, I'm hurt—my body is torn and aching and I'm paying attention to what I'm doing—I'm driving carefully and

32

don't feel like turning the wheel into a tree any more and I bet if you were alive, I would not have the same terrible feeling that I hate—you would be proud of me now—I can pay attention—are you dead, Jesse—are you really dead—the gun shot at a wolf, a dangerous wolf not at you— a wolf—a wolf must have jumped in front of you or you must have attracted the bullet because I really didn't kill you—there is a wolf in the trailer— a big black wolf and I killed it and Jesse will be proud of me— the gun just went off, Jesse— I couldn't make it listen to me and it shot you I didn't shoot you—Jesse is a wolf—no—he is naked and it is a blizzard but I am naked and it is cold and I am living and the wolf is dead or I am alive but the wolf is alive and running in the cold—am I a wolf—no I am paying attention and you are proud of me because I am me and not— Simple Simon scrimple dimple running round the cold trees a pie in my face—burning dimples—burning flesh is better than rotten flesh—burning means heat—a person's skin blisters and sometimes you don't die right away—they shave my head and are strapping me in and turning on the juice and you burn and get warm and die. . .

A cold sweat began to form on Simon's brow as he saw his end. Then suddenly, with a jump of his heart, the full impact of death leaped screaming into his consciousness.

—*death*—in a cold stuffy coffin stinking and no warm air—not able to get out and get warmth and I can't bear to be without warmth—I would die—oh no, what have I done—I have killed the wolf and now I will be cold forever. . .

A dull, sour, heavy sensation expanded in his stomach as he deliberately moved his swollen ankle. The pain stung like broken glass driven into the flesh but he continued to move his foot.

—I can't die—no, I must not die—don't let me die. . .

Suddenly he looked down at the car hood as it plowed over the road, then at the steering wheel, then at his hands. As he looked at them, he felt he had come to full realization of them and could understand them deeply, and yet his hand didn't respond correctly. The auto slowed to a rolling pace as he looked up.

—my right hand doesn't work it just sticks to the wheel but my left is doing the steering—what's the matter with it—it must be asleep. . .

He bent his right elbow, and his right hand came limply up

to his open mouth. He bit down hard on the back of it so that red teeth marks remained.

—can't feel anything—my hand is dead but still it feels sticky —there is something on my fingers—must wash off whatever is on them and then it will be all right. . .

He brushed the hand against his pants to wipe off some of the residue of blood and dirt that clung there. The car sped up and onward. A ribbon of road appeared ahead lit by the headlights; it seemed to be moving rapidly as the auto approached, darting under the car and into the darkness again.

—I don't know the way home—Jesse made his way here, but I don't know whether the road will take me home—the world is in this light and it might not make my way home for me— home—home is where we live but they were not my friends— they were Jesse's friends and if I brought Jesse home stiff and black they would be mad at me and not like me—I can't go home because they will bury me—wish the sun would make tomorrow's world now so I could see and the wolves would quit following me but maybe because I am a murderer the sun will not rise and I will have to make the road but I can't make the road and it might stop and I would go off the end and get lost in the dark end space. . .

Simon imagined the car and trailer going off the end of the earth and revolving through space, throwing him around the car forever.

—just so the headlights work—they make the road and if they work they will save me from the dark and from falling over and over. . .

The car parted the darkness as it sped through the night; Simon was hunched over the wheel in a trance; his eyelids were becoming very heavy. All at once Simon felt the side of his heart expand. Then with tremendous force it contracted, as if it were ejecting a large clogging lump of mud. This reaction was touched off by the recurrent and intensely disconcerting realization that he was a killer. Simon shook his head sharply in order to try and clear it, but it also seemed clogged and dim. But this dull, recurrent cognition that he couldn't get used to caused him to panic this time, and swerving to a jolting stop, he leaped out of the car to escape the feeling which continued to plague him. Throwing his arms violently into the cold air, he danced and contorted his body in a futile attempt to wring the feeling from his flesh, but it screamed even louder in his mind.

*—murderer killer killer murderer killer—*kill the wolf or the wolf will kill you—he is dead and accident is dead—you killed—wolves kill—black ribs—the wolves are coming to kill you and get revenge—can't stand this feeling any longer—must escape—must kill wolves—must kill—*kill—kill me I don't care— kill me—I want to die—you are crazy—eat ribs.* . .

Throwing his arms around wildly, he lost his balance, fell down on the cold dirt road and rolled convulsively around, yelling at the top of his lungs.

"Kill me, kill me, kill me. I can't stand it any longer. I can't," he pleaded.

The wind blew and the snow flew, in mingled profusion, striking each other, the twigs fought their eternal duels as the leaves began to get soggy. The snow melted slowly after it had fallen on the tree stumps, the ground and on Simon's canvas jacket. A faint glow shone in the east and the darkness began to recede as the shades faded away in the hills, in the woods, and on the road. Drops of water began to form on the stalled auto as it stared down the road with its beams becoming dimmer and dimmer with approaching day. Life began to move Simon again; a faint glow expanded to fill his whole being and he slowly began to move his dirty, damp body. First his eyes moved, then his mouth closed, and then different muscles in his body stirred slowly as he gradually came to life, and to realization.

—shiver cold—very cold—I am frozen to death—close dirt—wet —that stone—it's brown—cold brown—I am cold brown—wet—where am I—father, where am I—not in my cold warm bed and brown rock—cold me—very cold but the car is someplace—body is aching cold—must wake—I am where the sun is coming up and I feel black and stiff cold, but Jesse sits—where am I—the dark and cold and light and guns we were to get and be out hunting but is Jesse here and why do I live so close to the cold earth and Jesse is mad because I lay in bed too long—must have kicked the covers off last night but it is light all over and no window so the out of doors is here and no tent. . .

Lifting his cheek from the soil, Simon raised sluggishly to his elbows and looked around.

—the woods are near and we were going hunting and the car is in back of me with the trailer—how did I get here and why is it so cold—must find Jesse and find out what happened—hope I didn't get myself in trouble this time. . .

"Jesse, Jesse," he called as he slowly clambered to his feet. "Jesse, where are you?" he demanded, looking around. Inspecting the car and trailer, he began to remember and with memory came an impulse that shot up his spine and shattered at the top of his skull, causing him to flinch with the ever increasing horror at what he had done.

—I have a terrible feeling of being alone but how can I be alone if Jesse came along to save me from the wolves—I feel black—my ankle feels black hurting—where has Jesse gone—wonder if he is mad at me and left me lying in the road but he never would do that. . .

He stared at the trailer and perceived the faint outline of his brother under the canvas inside.

—wonder where the camping equipment is because the trailer looks empty—maybe the camp is somewhere and he is there but I took the car. . .

Sauntering over to the trailer he looked at the canvas and the contours that it made.

—I feel bad—dirty—I feel I have been had but don't know what it is—must find the wolf or deer or where is Jesse. . .

He lifted the covering in the trailer and it hit him in the back of his eyes.

—Jesse, you are in the trailer—what did you do—was I bad and are you trying to punish me—are you playing a joke on me. . .

"Jesse, get up! Please get up," he pleaded.

Jesse did not stir.

—Jesse looks different—he is cold and white looking— I know what happened to him—he is dead—a wolf killed him and made him black and look that way—the gun went off and the wolf —missed and killed and Jesse jumped into the bullet and he is dead and I am free but they will blame me—I know they will but I can't take him home because they will kill me cold and I will be cold and black and freeze—Jesse doesn't like the cold and death but the cold will kill me and I will hate it and it is bad for me because I can't stand it but for—but I was holding holding the gun—but I was holding the gun and I will be blamed for killing him because I was holding the gun but I can't help

36

it if the gun went off and missed the wolf . . . (You killed Jesse!)—no I didn't—it was an accident and the shell killed him and the wolf ran away and ran after me and the wolf is Jesse and Jesse must be mad at me because it was not my fault but the sun is coming up and the wolves won't kill me now because I can see them coming—must do something and get this feeling from me—must show the world—my stomach is hungry—must get food before I die and get colder—must find a place to eat and find a place for people and so I can eat. . .

Turning his head, he saw that he was alone and that there was nothing around except deep wood and hills. He went to the car and attempted to start it. The battery was dead. Getting nervous thinking that he was stranded, he squashed the gas pedal against the floor board in a futile attempt to start the motor.

—must think—must get the car started or I will be left here forever and I have committed an unforgivable sin—must escape this cold forest before it grows over me and I am buried with the worms—but I should be buried with the worms but it would be monotonous and unbearable to live in the cold ground—I will never be forgiven for what I have done—I am not worthy to live but must get this car started—I must move so I can get some food and then think—I will be able to think then what I should do and will make the right decisions and when I eat it will come to me what I shall do. . .

The glow of the sun could be seen through the thick clouds as it rose over the horizon. Simon again climbed out of the car and pondered as to his course of action. His heart beat rapidly in nervous expectation of an answer. Then suddenly the solution leaped at him.

—there is a slight hill ahead—maybe if I get the car going fast enough I can start it. . .

Leaning his shoulder against the door frame, with his left hand on the open door and his right on the steering wheel, he began to push firmly into the sockets of his shoulders and legs, and the supporting muscle groups tensed strenuously. Pain from his injured ankle riddled his leg but he pushed even more frantically. The auto did not move.

—what's the matter—why isn't it moving—it moved before when I pushed it this hard—oh I left it in gear. . .

Extending his arm to the gear shift, he drew the steel arm

down to neutral and then resumed his previous stance. Slowly, ever so slowly, the auto began to roll forward over the stones and down the dirt road. Then it began to speed up and go faster. Simon was running and his right shin hit the car several times in his progress, but he did not bother to ponder on it, but thrust his body ahead even more forcefully.

—I think it is going fast enough. . .

With a long stride he threw himself behind the wheel bumping his head on the roof as he entered. Forcing the stick into second gear, he let out the clutch. The engine came to life with a splat and sputter. The dashboard lit up and a red light told Simon that the headlights were still on. He turned them off and roared away toward the horizon.

—must find people and food and then think and do the right thing—I feel that Jesse is dearer now and that he is more horrible but far away. . .

The auto lunged forward down the road and finally came to a tar highway.

—this road must lead to a place to eat—my stomach is rotting away for a place to eat. . .

The road wound around, over and by, like a long serpent slowly devouring everything in its path: trees, stones and sides of hills. The sky was overcast but it was a clear morning. Simon pulled over, got out, and walked around the car in long strides. He had run out of gas and was straining his intellect with this new problem.

—must get food and feed the car so it will go. . .

Finally he remembered and went to the trunk of the auto. He opened it, took out a five gallon can of gas, and was pouring it into the tank as he watched a car come up the road. The moisture spattered from under its tires as it sped by.

—wonder if they saw the trailer and Jesse's feet—he makes kind of a large bump—hope they don't know that he is under there—but how could they know—but maybe they could just tell. . .

After slamming the trunk door, he climbed carefully into the driver's seat.

—hope that the engine will start with the battery so low . . .

The engine ground and whined for what seemed an eternity and the starter sounded like it was giving way when the motor revived again. The car roared anew as it gained momentum.

—the morning is good terrible—oh, I hate to think—wish I could stop thinking and having bad dreams and feeling sick and getting looked at and run after—hate it all hate it hate the world and everything—I don't deserve to live—have done a terrible thing and should be punished for it—wish I could just stop the hurt in my head and stomach and not have to worry about thinking and forget about everything and keep warm and—darn it, I must get away but I can't wish I never had to eat or drink—this hunger for a glass of water will kill me if I don't hurry . . .

He stepped harder on the accelerator.

—maybe I should make myself die and not eat anything but I must eat so I can think and then I will know what to do . . .

As he sped down the road past trees and scattered houses, his mind whirled with distaste. With every breath his stomach released a ravenous growl that became so loud as time passed that he could clearly hear it.

—food and then will be able . . .

Not noticing a curve in the road ahead, he kept the auto at a constant rapid speed. Suddenly he noticed over the wet pavement the sharp, tree-lined curve and slammed on the brakes as he began to slide on to it. The auto slipped sideways and Simon frantically revolved the wheel in an attempt to get it in his power again. The thick gray trees at the side of the road leaped out at him as the screaming wheels left the road and sank into the soft shoulder of the highway. The car stood up on its two outside wheels as dirt flew from the furrows the tires were plowing in the soft clay. Simon clung tightly to the wheel as the auto heaved up, and his mind blurred and swam with fright. The trailer followed innocently, like a cock boat in a storm, as the vehicle plunged directly toward a large tree. Frightened, Simon threw the wheel toward the road. The tree slid by as the trailer flew sideways. With a resounding crunch and jolt the auto came to a halt. The rear of the trailer had hit the tall oak. The canvas in the trailer shifted with the bulk of the body that it held. After the trailer recoiled from the tree, the cadaver slid out on the ground. As Simon leaned nervously over the wheel, hugging it close, a cold sweat began to pour down his face. He reviewed the happenings of the previous few seconds.

39

—curvefalloverkilledtreetrailerhit savercurve manytreesrunintokilledsteering wheel . . .

His heart pounded like a hammer against his ribs, as if it wanted to escape his body, and his whole body was shuddering with every gasping breath. Looking into the rear view mirror, he choked as he saw the body of his brother lying sprawled face down across the road. Rolling quickly out of the car, he staggered weak-kneed to where his brother lay and spread his fingers wide in the horrible expectation that he would have to pick up this bulk. He stood bent over and looking downward.

—Jesse, you jinxed me—you tried to kill me for the horrible thing I've done—you're the one who's taken my mind and now you want to destroy me—you haunt me—I should leave you here to rot but I must think so I'll know what to do—must do the right thing because I have done a terrible thing and I'm not to be forgiven but must try to think and see what I'll do—Jesse, you're all black on the back of your head and neck and your face is pale—you don't look like my brother—you look terrible—guess I must touch him and put him back—hope it is my brother but my brother would never look like this . . .

Leaning over, he gingerly lifted his brother and began to drag him toward the trailer.

—you're all stiff, Jesse—you've gotten all hard and cold but you could stand the cold—wonder if he really knew that he fell out of the trailer—wonder where he really is—the trailer is kinda smashed in on one side but not too bad—guess it'll still go—must get water and food—my stomach feels awful . . .

Hearing a car coming, he quickly turned the body on its back again and slid it under the canvas. A truck rolled around the curve and passed by. Starting to feel very numb after this ordeal, Simon climbed wearily back into the auto and resumed his journey.

—why does everything have to happen to me and why do I get all of the bad luck . . .

His stomach gurgled loudly as he ran his tongue over the top of his mouth in an attempt to wring saliva from it.

—my mouth is very dry—it will get black—I hate the word black—hate anything black—I could drink muddy brown water now and like it—brown is better—it is not as bad as black—better pay attention so I don't have any more close calls—must get my mind to think—there will be a place to eat here some-where 'cause I saw a sign for a town back there somewhere—here comes a car—must be careful to stay on my side of the road—wonder if somebody who drove up behind me to pass could see him under the canvas 'cause it is blowing in the wind—I don't care—they won't see . . .

He slid his tongue into the black cavity and tasted the peculiar taste that the rotting decay produced.

—maybe there is food in the cavity—Jesse is made of meat—that's stupid—I sure do think of the stupidest things—anyway I am very thirsty, more than I am hungry . . .

Suddenly he sat up in the seat and stared intently forward.

—that man is going to run across the road in front of me—he will be killed—it is Jesse but it can't be—Jesse is dead—the brakes . . .

He fumbled for the brake as Jesse leaped into his path. The tires squealed again as he came to a stop.

—Jesse was dead but I just ran over him—he was really alive but now I've really killed him . . .

Staring back to where the body should be, he saw nothing but empty road. He visualized Jesse slithering under the greasy bottom of the car and trailer and then getting under the canvas into the empty body that lay there. Simon slowly acceler-ated the car as he glared intently into the rear view mirror at the highway behind. The road was empty. Then suddenly he saw Jesse rolling around the road laughing. He was laughing at Simon. Simon jerked his head around to look and saw that the road was empty. The car came to a sudden halt against several wooden guard rails, denting the fender and shattering the right headlight.

—Jesse was laughing at me but he disappeared—am I going out of my mind or was he really there—yes I saw him—he is punishing me for the terrible thing that I have done—maybe I can get away—hope the car will work now—maybe it is hurt bad—put the gear in reverse—let out the clutch—it's working—now forward gear the clutch—yes—it works—faster—faster. . .

The engine hummed in his ears as he pressed the accelerator. A voice was saying something to him. It was Jesse's voice com-ing out of the engine.

"Kill yourself. You are evil and not worthy to live and I

41

will destroy you. Kill yourself, Simon. Kill yourself. Kill yourself, you are not good enough to live."

"Yes, I killed you, Jesse, and I am sorry, you know that I didn't mean to kill you," Simon replied in horror.

Someplace in the back of his head, Simon was unrepentant. He wanted to say truthfully that he was sorry for killing his brother, but couldn't. He couldn't make his mind conform, no matter how much he tensed his neck muscles. Even though he wanted to purge his brain of this eternal blackness, he could not.

—I am bad and not worthy to live—wonder if Jesse knows how I really feel—if he knows how I feel. . .

"Yes, Simon, I know what you are thinking and that is why I say you are no good. That is why I say go kill yourself. Hang yourself. You are not worthy to live another minute. Drive into that tree. You are forsaken for what you have done and never will be forgiven for it," Jesse called out of the engine in a monotone.

"Yes, yes, you are right, Jesse. I must kill myself. I am not worthy to live. If I could only get something to eat, then I will be all right and know," Simon replied.

"Kill yourself now, now, Simon. Drive off of the road," Jesse commanded.

"Yes, Jesse, I will, I will. I am not worthy to live. I am not good enough to be even a cold worm."

Suddenly Simon saw a flashing red sign up the road that said Potter's Diner. Saliva began to flow in his mouth as he thought of food.

—I will eat and then I will be able to think and know what Jesse is really saying to me—will be able to eat listen and see and then I will do the right thing—maybe I should get rid of Jesse but I must eat and then I will know. . .

Turning off the highway, he looked at the deep wood that the sun could not penetrate. He drove around to the rear of the diner and stopped the vehicle so that the trailer was next to the back window of the eating establishment. Slowly, carefully, he climbed out of the auto and walked around a path to the door of the diner; he did not want to get too near the engine of the car in which Jesse's ghost was lurking. Self-consciously, he strode into the diner, bumping his forehead on the door frame as he entered. He looked around to see if anybody had noticed and then quietly tiptoed over to a table and sat down. Picking up the menu, he pretended to look it over with his eyes, but his peripheral vision was scanning the room to see if people were looking at him. Yes, they were. There were several men sitting silently at the counter and a woman dressed in white behind it and from time to time the men glanced one by one over their shoulders to look at him. Simon became very tense and felt out of place. Looking out the window at the trailer, he could see the canvas and a foot projecting from under it. He was nervous. The woman in white came over to him and placed silverware, bread and a glass of water in front of him. She stood looking at him for a moment and then said, "Are you ready to order?"

Simon opened his mouth and was going to say that he was not ready yet but he could not make his vocal cords work. Finally, looking intently at the print on the white page, he managed to shake his head no, and the woman went away.

—is she mad at me—I don't feel right here—they are looking at me—wonder if they can tell that I am a killer but I must have something to eat so I can think and then I will. . .

Suddenly Simon's heart leapt in his mouth. A policeman had entered the diner. He moved his head slowly as he looked around and stopped momentarily to survey Simon. Then he went to a table by the window and sat down. At the sight of the cop, Simon's attention became fixed on the officer's head; the window and all other visual remnants of Simons environment melted to nothingness. He saw a head framed against the window as though suspended in space, and nothing else. Simon wanted to walk over to this new visitor and shake his hand and make friends. No, he wanted to throw the table at him and destroy him. Suddenly this man lifted his head from the menu he was studying and glared out of the window. At the same time, Simon's vision dimmed fuzzily, coating his eyes. Then his sight came into brilliant, narrow focus.

—does he see—yes, he must see—I am not afraid—storm cold naked—must think—must eat and then. . .

Eyeing the table in front of him, Simon saw the water and bread. Hastily he gulped the liquid and then forced two slices of bread into his mouth.

—must get out—the place is smothering me and that man will kill me. . .

His cheeks bulging with bread, Simon stood jerkily, almost overturning the table in his urgency. Thinking about paying for the food he had eaten, he dug into his pockets for money and found thirty cents that he had gotten from Jesse. Casting the money on the table, he plunged for the door and ran to the car with great haste while the man at the window watched. The auto drove off.

—is he coming—Jesse killed him—wolves got him—he's not coming—still can't think—wait and it will come—stay on the road—must get away—my head hurts—thick forest full of wolves —feel so tired—town ahead—must know what to do and then I will be all right—will wait for the food to get into me better and then I'll know—maybe it did me no good.

"Why didn't you let the policeman get you?" Jesse demanded above the hum of the engine.

"He didn't, Jesse. He just didn't," Simon replied.

"Simon, you are such a scatterbrain. Listen to me and you will be. . ."

"No, Jesse, no. I can't. I won't any more. No! No!" Simon yelled and screamed at the top of his lungs, trying to drown out the commanding voice. Swinging his head feverishly, he looked around the interior of the auto, his brain still repeating loud noes.

—not in here—Jesse will kill me—maybe the motor will burn him away—open the window some to get air—that's better—need gas—will run out soon. . .

Trying to ignore the sounds that he heard arising from the engine, Simon concentrated his attention on looking for a gas station. Before long he spotted one, and drove into it. As he stopped the car by the pumps, a short young man walked up to him. Fatigue glided over and through Simon and he felt so sinful and black that he didn't answer the attendant's question.

The man leaned impatiently closer to the window and called into Simon's ear, "Hey, look, buddy, do you want me to fill it up or what?" Then he began thinking.

—what a creep this guy is—he is a monster—he must be all of six foot seven or eight—he really fills the driver's seat—wouldn't like to meet him in a dark alley 'cause he looks real mean with those big scars on his face—he is just sitting there looking forward—he doesn't even seem to hear me or know I am here—gives me the creeps—yell louder in his ear. . .

The attendant took a deep breath to call louder at the man behind the wheel, but just as he was about to repeat his question, the big guy nodded his head slowly. He went to the job of filling the tank.

Simon turned his head slightly and looked at the young man in the rear view mirror as he filled the tank.

—he doesn't realize how lucky he is I have to fight all of these black feelings and he is free—maybe I should give in but I don't think that is the right thing to do yet. . .

The fuel gurgled into the depths of the empty tank and the fumes pierced the nose of the station attendant as he went on thinking.

—what a real weirdo—wish he would stand up so I could see just how big he really is— I could even stand that face if I were that big and husky instead of being so low-slung with this damn boyish face—he doesn't know how good he has it to be so big—if I had a body like that I could take on the whole town with one fell swoop and she would really fall for me then and not snub me so—wonder what he does—probably a mean lumberjack—that trailer is sure battered and—he is watching me in the mirror—better not look that way—sure would hate to meet him in a dark alley—if I had a mean face like that people would really stand up and listen to me. . .

Simon sat meanwhile hunched at the wheel.

—he's looking at the trailer—now at me and again at the trailer—he sees Jesse—can tell by the look on his face—he will have me killed before I can do it—he will kill me and I will be cold—I can't—must get out of here—the clutch—gear—gas pedal —must hurry before he kills me. . .

The engine roared and the car lurched as Simon threw the idling motor into action. The tires squealed as the attendant leaped back from the wheels of the trailer.

"You dirty bastard, come back here," yelled the attendant after the fleeing auto.

—what's the matter with that bastard—he could have run over me with that blasted trailer. . .

Dashing through the station house door, he grabbed the telephone and gave the operator a number, pleading with her to hurry.

"Hello, hello, George," he screamed into the phone. "Some crazy bastard came into the station here to get gas and. . ."

After relaying his message to the police, the attendant sat down to try to calm himself.

—at least he won't get too far with no gas cap on the tank—think I will press charges that will give that big son-of-a-bitch a fine that will make his hair stand on end. . .

He was still sitting there when a police car zoomed by down the wet road and up the hill.

—they are really going to have to make time to catch up with him but they are sure going fast enough—hope that guy doesn't think of revenge after I press charges but he did almost kill me—maybe I better not press charges but just make him sweat and be grateful that I didn't throw the book at him. . .

Many minutes passed. The attendant was standing beside the auto of another customer, telling him every detail of what had happened, when he heard a siren screaming down the hill. By the sound of the noise the police car was traveling very fast. On edge because of the noise, the attendant exclaimed to the customer, "Guess I got that guy into a real pack of trouble. Hope the cops aren't too rough on him."

"He could have killed you," answered the customer, turning around in the direction of the sound. "Guys like that should be locked up until they cool down."

They watched as the police car sped by on its return journey.

"He didn't stop. I wonder why he didn't stop?" he asked the attendant as he watched the auto blur by. Simon had been looking out the window while a policeman sat watching him.

CHAPTER II

—I shouldn't sit so slouched because my shoulders will get rounded and I won't look right but it looks more in to sit this way—ouch this darn knee—why is it when I turn it only a certain way that it pains me so—who's perfect—guess I will always have this thorn in my side—a bum knee misery loves company so throw in Byron—Maugham and ol' Iris Joyce—baby why do you torment me so—can't you see that you are beautiful—so beautiful—and that I can not have you—why do you set me burning—now I know what hell is like and I love it—I can't turn away—can't say no—would prescribe you for a fat boy—then after knowing you he could reduce because of lack of appetite and you're better than Nodoz except that you demand the mind as well as the consciousness—I would be great but we couldn't share it together because I know that it would never last because I must wear the pants in the family and be the one to be renowned and not a second fiddle—you will blind me if I don't get out and yet I am powerless—pride what of pride—it's just a word—let me touch it and I will show you that it doesn't exist—the tribes of Judah would have destroyed themselves for your favor and the Levites would have blackened their temples with the smoke of offerings for a smile from your lips and I must study this book but it is more than my mind can handle—you are enough you are selfish you take all or nothing and I am a caged animal and no better since I met you. . .

Joe bent over his notebook, looking industrious. His hand was writing slowly and carefully on the white page. He wrote her name over and over again. That was all he could squeeze out of his cerebrum. D-E-L-I-L-A-H, over and over, the point of the pen left the letters.

—guess I really am a fool because I am rushing in ahead of the pack—they say that it is a good feeling and yet I feel contaminated and yet this feeling of mental masturbation over-

47

whelms me and makes me frightened and stopping is out of the question because I can't—I am being taken over—yes that's it the name of this story is *The Possessing* and I am a twig in a stream being roiled by the current—well, got a lot of work done tonight. Let's see—two cans of beer—nine cigarettes—forty-seven Delilah's and a quarter of a mile of doodles—well, guess I better get set to see my lover—I'll put on that new bottle of lime cologne—that should do the trick. . .

Rising from his chair, Joe removed his clothes and piled the articles one by one on the chair from which he had arisen. With two ballet leaps he found himself in the bathroom of his small apartment, turning on the shower.

—water water everywhere and plenty of it to drink—it washes all your cares and dirt gaily down the drink—no—that's bad—oh yes—it rids you of your cares and woe before you can give a blink. . .

—try again. . .

"Once upon a time—
I wanted to make a rhyme—
but as you can see it's as surface as can be—
but I shall not fret at least until my diapers get wet—
so I will shower now and think of Moo cows. . ."

—oops better take my diapers off before I get into the shower—when will I wise up now my knee is really hurting—maybe it will atone for some of the guilt that I have been storing up—oh oh look out Josephine there is a cloud of seriousness passing over you—you know what happens when you start to get serious you get depressed—a manic-depressive all of the way that's what you are—why do they have to make rusty water in this ratty hole—isn't bad heating enough for the rent that I have to pay. . .

Glaring stupidly at the bottom of the bathtub, Joe looked at the rusty water collecting there; the inefficient drain hadn't captured it yet.

—ah yes I recognize you—Lake Lucerne—no come to think of it—you look more like the dead sea—may I sink my feet into your buoyant depths—thank you. . .

After thanking the gurgling drain, he stepped under the shower and scrubbed himself while muttering melodiously broken bars.

"Oh, the cannibal king with the brass nose ring fell in love

48

with a lovely dame. And every night in the pale moonlight, glub gurgle burble the bay he came. . .

"He hugged and kissed his pretty liglubblelugglub.

"And in the pale moon light every night. . ."

All this time Joe's mind was concentrated on the face of his lover. He tried to dissect her beauty, to find a flaw that he could cling to, but there was nothing and he was hopelessly hers.

—hers is loveliness that will increase and mellow until old age because the bone structure of her face will always give her the symmetry that she has now and her self discipline and cool brilliance will always help her keep and even polish that lustre —I love you—you must be mine—and yet I hate you and with a bloody passion—oh are you mine—are you really mine—can I flatter myself that the conquest is mutual but you are not as torn as I or at least you cover it up well—if you only knew what I really am would you love me the way you say you do—I am so afraid that you wouldn't but you are a luxury that I cannot afford—I know that and yet I keep trying to right it in my mind somehow—I want you so much and can't have you and just as Byron was haunted so maybe that is the way it will be with me—I have this feeling of greatness that I know will be spoiled because there is no room in it for you—for I can not take a back seat to a mission and yet they call this love but I don't feel that feeling of warmth that they say comes with—all I feel is a demon tearing at my soul and eating it with luscious gulps —if you only knew that medical school was now out of my reach and that I don't stand a chance of having a practice because of my marks for the past year—but you couldn't understand it because learning came too easily for you—you can sit down concentrate and learn while I am now struggling to sink my mind into—what has happened to me—I have gone from a scholar to a bum and my future has become so dim but I must not give up because that's not the way to conquer—I have fallen but I will get up and run harder—yes harder—even with a bad knee I will run and will win. . .

Stepping out of the shower, he rubbed himself vigorously with a slightly soiled hand towel and then threw it over the rack. Glancing up he looked at himself in the mirror.

—sure do have a mean looking face—I will have to quit frowning so much and laugh hysterically more—to look at me you would think I was a high school dropout plus a sex fiend—if I

49

had my choice I would like to be a raving hebephrenic and laugh until the back of my head hurt—yes I would like that for it could be no worse of a prison that I am in now—*Ich liebe dich* or is it *Ich liebe der*—oh well what does it matter I will just have to speak English in Germantown tonight—will have only a couple of drinks tonight for my mind could not be any cloudier than it is now—let's see what will the high school dropout wear tonight for his beautiful Theodora—yes I will wear my loud red and white seersucker jacket—that should do nicely —that's good enough for fighting bears at the hippodrome tonight.

He laid his neatly pressed clothes on his bed and slipped into them being careful not to get any dirt from the floor on them.

—dirt dirt—I need a woman around here to clean up after me—maybe I would be better off if I were married and more settled but only with a wife that would tease me and excite me, but give in fully to my commands—there should be no children until I have found my mission and then at least half a dozen and several girls because girls are the ones who rule this world with their looks and smiles—yes I must have at least three beautiful girls and if one is ugly I will spend hours with her to teach her literature and math so that she can become a university professor and all of the things that I am not and rise above the mediocrity of her father—I am such an egoist and yet such a masochist and a confused one at that—wonder what would happen if. . .

He finished dressing and then looked at the clock.

—oh no it's six bells—better get going. . .

Running around the room in a hurried frenzy, Joe did different little things in preparation for his lover. He collected his money, put on his tieclip and when it was all done, glanced at himself in the mirror.

—not bad—I will be a real lady killer tonight—I will put on a disarming air tonight and play hard to get at first. . .

Looking around to see if he had forgotten anything, he gave a few short shuffles and skip and was out of the door and up the steps from the basement apartment.

"Well, Delilah, here comes your Samson," he exclaimed as his feet suddenly met the sidewalk. With a slight limp, he turned down Bedford Street and then up Barrow.

—why can't they make concrete a little softer—put a little

50

latex or something in it so that it is not so hard on the feet
and this knee—the world is so cold and impersonal—think I will
bid the next lady a good evening and catch the reaction—here
comes a nice looking customer now. . .

"And a good day to you," he exclaimed wide eyed while tipping an imaginary hat. The woman glanced sharply at him, but
kept her head set straight ahead. Then she withdrew her look
quickly and walked on down the street, but with a more self-
conscious gait.

—well that wasn't too bad—at least she didn't call the cops—
she looked like some dish—maybe I will go back and pursue
her and ask her to marry me—hope she is a high school dropout
—no I better not because I have a date with an angel. . .

He glanced at his watch.

—it's getting late better hurry. . .

Quickening his step he made his way through the winding
streets past the brick townhouses, and drew a deep breath as he
finally came to Washington Square Park. Traversing diagonally
and cutting across the grass, he made his way up Fifth Avenue
past the skyscrapers. Crossing the street against the light, he
dodged a forceful cab driver.

—those guys are really out to kill—wonder how many points
they get for running over old ladies. . .

Striding past a large window, he glanced at his reflection
to see if he would be acceptable in his lover's eyes.

—still not bad—she better be entranced by me tonight or we
won't get along—she dresses so elegantly every time we go out
—wish I could wear a different jacket every time I see her,
but that's life—guess I will have to put up with being a poor ol'
college student—Byron had a coachman pet bear and mistress
but all I can afford is a dingy dungeon and that's the story of
my life—an inaccurate mind and a foolhardy soul—ouch this
leg is really bothersome today—it must be the humidity—better
quit the dancing around too and besides people will think I
am crazy—oh well just so I am hebephrenic—love it out tonight
it's so cool and springy—there is nothing like spring in New
York with the leaves green in every blasted flowerpot and the
near riots in the park on a Sunday afternoon—sometimes I wish
that those people would start a real big riot but all their foolish
minds can think of is calling the poor sucker cops names—they
displace all of their frustrations on the cops or the negroes—

why don't they all try a little masochism and it will be aimed in the right direction. . .

Walking closer to the buildings, he looked slightly upward.
—it's so exciting to walk so close to buildings because you never know what may slip off of a window sill and come crashing down on your head—wonder if a penny thrown from the top of this building would crash through my skull and into my cerebrum—at least it would hurt plenty but that's the excitement of it—oh insanity what would I do without insanity to amuse me—my love you are insanity to me and that's why I cannot get you out of my blood—you contaminate my corpuscles and lymph nodes—you say things that I long to hear and I love it and you know it I love it—you throw a net over me and I cannot fight—my legs get weak and I am your sheep dog but what can I do but obey your command—I would like to have a mind of my own but it doesn't fit in your plan so I will steal you away with me tonight from all of those other grubby hands and we will be alone in a place far away from your habitat —Dear Sigmund Freud to what tribe do you belong—why must you band together so can't you see you are in a country of melting pots and pot ash—why do you keep your identity—why does anyone keep their last name—we should all be known by the last name of the town of our birth and not cling to ancient custom but that is the way it is and that is the way it must be so I am a slave and that is the way I undoubtedly will remain— we must be known by our genius and not by our extraction but so often it is not the case because the latter often creeps in so what can I do but join—join—join—a world of joiners that is what it is and it is awful—I will start a new reformation but it would be a real comedy to see me running around and doing nothing around and around and turn into butter—maybe I should just give up and get carried by the current like I have been but then I would have to give up my delusion and the world would stop revolving around me and I don't think I could give that up—this knee is really bad today— I hope she won't notice it—that would be fatal to let anybody know that I am human—human—human—that word sounds funny to my ears—I hate that word—it ought to be banished from the human vocabulary and then nobody would be the wiser when it is referred to —wonder what it is in German—maybe it's *Das Human* or some stupid thing—ouch this darn knee—better not dance

too many polkas tonight—never could do the horah tonight—
thank goodness that they don't play that there. . .

Joe glanced at his watch: "Six thirty; I'm late; better move
it. Oh well, it will do her good to wait and wonder if I am
coming."

—she won't wonder because she knows me—she knows that
I will come—the ol' reliable sheep dog will come to get his
back scratched—why do I have to be so human and run by my
emotions all of the time—I am no better than a car—all you
have to do is know where to put the key and how to step on the
accelerator and there I am a captive of the driver—the name
of this story is *The Cab Driver*—I would make a good cab—so
reliable with a little gas and oil and watch me beat traffic—a
few dents here and there but that's the kicks of the race—this
leg—maybe I would be better if I had a wooden leg at least
it wouldn't hurt—let's see, shall I make her walk to the subway
with me or go in style and take a cab—better take a cab 'cause
I don't want her to notice this knee—we will come back by
subway 'cause then I will have a few drinks and won't feel it
and then I will be able to walk straight without all of this pain—
that's me—a real walking two-legged circus—why do I have to
get so frisky and start it hurting—that man doesn't know how
lucky he is to be able to walk straight like that—looks like he
is walking a little bowlegged though he is either a Texan or he
has piles—can imagine it now—a big burly Texan riding painfully down a dusty main street of El Paso because he has piles
—that's more interesting than a bum knee but it must be awful
though to have to use suppositories and be afraid of taking a
healthy crap—wouldn't like to be a cripple though—oh here we
go again Josephine with the depression—can see that cloud
coming again—better stop feeling sorry for yourself and quit
thinking of yourself as a lame mule—mules are such interesting animals and so determined—wish I had some of their
spunk—can picture it now—me riding into her hotel lobby on
a mule and asking at the desk to page her room and all of a
sudden Mr. Mulie lets out a big mulepie right on the floor—
splatt—and the manager comes out pulling his hair and screaming and people gathering around to see—yes that would be at
least half a laugh but so much for my fantasy world for here
I am before stark reality this enormous structure which con-
tains my loved one—better hurry for I am late. . .

53

Stepping through the revolving door, Joe found himself in an expensive lobby. He started to proceed to the elevator when he caught sight of Della, sitting on one of the thick sofas. Pretending not to see her, he turned and proceeded in the general direction of where she was, with his head slightly turned and looking down.

—now play it cool Joe—pretend—don't act too overjoyed to see her—here comes that excited feeling—try not to let it disconcert you—she is sitting there calmly looking at me as she always does—she is always so poised and sophisticated—it is so natural for her but I must act—an idiot strutting and fretting his hour upon the stage and here I come—here comes that sinking feeling—she looks so dazzling tonight—beautiful—utterly perfect—a red dress and hair flowing down her back—will I be able to stand it—yes I must baby—I love you so—mustn't look at her yet. . .

Walking over to the sofa, he pretended he was going to walk nonchalantly by. Then he stood a few feet away with his back to her and slowly looked over his shoulder.

"Hi baby, you're beautiful. How about you and me stepping out on the town?" he said in a slow, careful voice.

"You entertain my eyes, too," she replied in that low sexy voice of hers. "I might think about it."

—aw tear me up—there she goes breaking down my resistance again—better sit down and get my strength back. . .

Carefully he moved toward her and sat down beside her. He put his arm along the back of the couch being careful not to touch her.

"Nice weather we're having. Think it will rain?"

"It might," she replied, staring straight ahead.

"Did anybody ever tell you that you have beautiful eyes?" he whispered softly in her ear, still being careful not to touch her.

Slowly she brought her big brown eyes around and looked at him.

—don't look at me yet—I haven't gotten my adrenalin back to normal yet—you are simply gorgeous. . .

"And did anyone ever tell you that your lips were softer than the finest silk," he said, bringing his face close to hers as if to kiss her and then withdrawing.

—there that should tease her a little—let's see what she says. . .

During the ensuing silence, Joe surveyed the smooth symmetry of her features. She looked off at an angle over his shoulder; she reminded him of a precious diamond that never shows you all of its color at once. Neither spoke, and just before the silence became embarrassing she replied,

"OK, you win. Where shall we go, handsome?"

—oh, oh there she goes scratching my back again—ah but it feels so gooooood. . .

"I was thinking in terms of the Hapsburg on Eighty-sixth Street—if that cuts ice with you."

"Whatever you say, darling," she replied.

"And we're off," he said, standing up and facing the door to see if she would follow the lead.

—she's getting up—this leg—shouldn't have gotten up so fast—did I bring my pipe—yes—good—light it. . .

By the time they reached the street he had his pipe lit; the aroma, among other things, made his head swim. He turned his head in search of a taxi.

—she isn't saying much tonight—wonder what's the matter—there's a cab. . .

Waving his arm into the air, he stepped off the curb in an attempt to flag the cab down. It drove past without stopping, followed by two others.

"Doesn't seem as if I am having any luck. Maybe you'd better take over. You know, just look distressed and lift your skirt a little and watch them come flying. Did you notice we match tonight? My jacket and your dress."

"Look a little closer, honey, we clash. My dress is more an ocher color," she said seriously.

"Hey, what are you trying to do, pick a fight?" he exclaimed happily. A smile started to light her face as she looked at him.

"Because if you are, you are picking on the right fellow. There's another cab." He waved his arm and the taxi pulled over.

"*Entrez,*" he commanded, holding the door. "The Hapsburg on East Eighty Sixth, please," he said to the driver as he sat down on the seat.

—well, we're off to a mediocre start—let's try to pick things up—can't get over how nice she looks tonight and she has been told it so many times that she can't help but have it go to her head. . .

55

"That perfume of your really turns me on, baby, you picked the right one tonight. You're enough to make even Calvin sit up in his grave and breathe in the air with pleasure; and I bet his eyes would bug out, too."

—oops better leave religion out of this—these taxis sure like to rob poor people of their coins. . .

"Isn't it nice out tonight, darling? Spring is such a gay time of the year and it won't be long until you graduate and go to medical school and I can call you doctor. Then I can lay on your couch and you can psychoanalyze me," she whispered softly as if daydreaming.

—oh no there she goes again off into her fantasy world contemplating things that will never be. . .

Turning to him she asked, "Did you hear from Columbia yet? You should be hearing from them very soon, shouldn't you?"

"Not yet," he said, trying to sound cheerful. "You know how those big universities are, nobody can hurry them. They just take their good ol' time. Sometimes it takes until summer before you hear from them."

—isn't life just one big bowl of mud and I am stirring it up with a stick by not telling her of my rejections from Michigan Syracuse and Columbia—maybe I should tell her that I don't want to go to medical school or maybe I should tell her the truth but I can't bear to find out that she is a Hedda Gabler—no that would kill me—I love her so—I will strut and fret some more—besides I can't throw water on those starry eyes—they're too beautiful or is it my eyes that will be watery. . .

"Isn't it beautiful out tonight with all of the lights?" she remarked leaning toward him.

"It sure is, honey, but not half as beautiful as the light reflected in your eyes," he affirmed, gently putting his arm around her and drawing her close to him. She pressed her weight against his ribs and lay back on his arm. Turning his head, he softly caressed her cheek with his nose and then looked forward.

—I sure am laying it on thick tonight, but I can't let my guard down for a moment even though I have known her this long—there are so many grubby hands that would do anything to hold her like I am now—I must make this moment last forever—forever—oh must it all end—I must find a way—there must be a way—maybe if I—no that's a horrible thought—can't even

56

consider it—her father would go into a wild rampage if he couldn't throw a big wedding for his only daughter and anyway she wouldn't even think of doing such a terrible thing and what would I do with a child right away—I can't live off of her father's cash and I don't have the money to keep her the way she is used to—this moment must never end—she is so warm and soft—she is just made for my arms—I can tell—if only it could be—say something. . .

"Do you know what the most beautiful word in the English language is?" he said seriously.

Thinking for a moment she said, "I don't know, What is it?"

"Cellar door," he responded earnestly.

"Cellar door?"

"Yes, cellar door. According to what I read somewhere, the word 'cellar door' is supposed to be the most beautiful word in the English language, that is phonetically. Say it, see how easily it flows out when you say it," he added, still seriously.

"Cellar door, cellar door," she repeated softly with her eyes closed as if to get the full impact of the sound.

He watched her velvet mouth form the words and he shivered with delight at her naïveté. It was this that made him feel important, as if he were the boss.

—she is so good at it—she should be an actress—if she went to Hollywood all they would need to do is take one glance. . .

"Yes, it does flow nicely. I shall remember that," she whispered, smiling.

Silence ensued, an uncommon silence that spoke to Joe.

—seems that now we have known each other all these months we have run out of things to say—words words words—whoever invented words must have been dumb—what do they mean—what do they say—do people talk or is it pseudo-communication—do people really hear what someone else has said or do they just pretend to—it's all mechanics—hot air—lungs—larynx—vocal cords—nasal cavity—teeth—tongue—condensation—rarefraction—external auditory meatus—tympanic membrane malleus—incus staples or is it staplus—oval window and a round one—cochlea—scala media—scala vestibuli and tympani—cochlear nerve—goooh—goooh—goooh—blah—blah—jabberjabberboobooboo—the more complicated it gets the simpler it seems—she's probably a little angry because I was a little late—and then comes the dawn—it is not I who is the superb conversationalist—she is the one who makes the conversation by listening and thinking ahead—she draws the adjectives and adverbs from between these central incisors—if she feels like listening she lets me talk and up goes my thirsty ego—catharsis and all of that stuff—baby you are my cause cure and pleasure combined—my jailer and my liberator—Sixty Eighth Street already—why is it that 'when I want time to go slow it speeds even faster—guess I had better quit enjoying life—insanity all is insanity—well better probe and do some reality testing. . .

"How is school going, honey?" Joe asked softly drawing her closer.

"O.K., I guess. Fine Arts class has been marvelous lately. We are studying Van Gogh, Matisse, Picasso and some of the more modern painters lately. What modern artist do you enjoy the most?"

—that confirms it—she really does lead with the questions (Joe decided)—guess I will bite. . .

"Really get a jab out of Pollock," Joe exclaimed, recollecting. "You remember the painting in the Museum of Modern Art with the splashed-on color? It was entitled *Number One*."

"Oh yes, I think I do," she returned with a little excitement in her voice as if she were a little girl who had found a beautiful new stone. "What did you enjoy most about it?"

—there she goes again—ooh how I live that immaturish attention she bestows upon me—she probably knows the painting better than I—well here goes. . .

"Well, I liked the concert of textures he worked on the canvas and the different densities of paints employed. It's fun to study the angles at which he cast the oil onto the surface, and see how they flowed down and finally dried with some of the drops having a wrinkled appearance. But the real thrill of it is standing back and casting your eyes on the whole work with its symphonic blending," he explained as if deep in thought.

From the corner of his eye he could see her looking at him attentively with the youthful exuberance of a student who is deeply involved in the lecture of a beloved teacher.

"Ah, yes, but we are only children," he exclaimed cheerfully.

"What do you mean?" she asked puzzled.

"I was thinking that here is a big wide world with so much in it, all forms of art, and nature the most perfect form of art, and a whole world of it to see and enjoy. We should all act like children and before long we will be children, discovering all of the new delightful things that life has to offer. But too often people walk around looking at the floor and declaring their woes to themselves and don't even realize that there is a world outside of their heads. Did I ever tell you I was a scared kid in a big world?"

"Why, no, you never have. What do you mean?" she replied.

"I just mean that the world frightens me—yes, a male *homo sapiens* who is supposed to be fearless, ruthless and aggressive. But that is the thrill of it, discovering the new, different and dangerous. Do you like to live dangerously?"

—I I I I I—garsh am I getting carried away—better get my head out of the clouds before. . .

"I do in some ways. Guess we all do in some ways," she replied puzzled.

—drop the bomb—test—test. . .

"Let's live dangerously, then," he said.

"What are you saying? You talking in riddles," she replied cautiously.

"Let's live dangerously for a few moments."

—riddles—riddles—she thinks I mean one thing and I mean another—she would never do what she thinks I mean and that's one of the reasons I love her so much—test on. . .

"There is a fountain just below the bottom of Central Park. I think it's next to Fifth Avenue. Let's go wading in it," he said earnestly.

"But darling," she replied, spying him quizzically. "We have good clothes on. We will get all wet and probably get arrested. Are you feeling well?"

Suddenly he could feel a coldness growing between them. She was warm against his body, but a coldness was creeping between them. Her eyes looked at him like light shining through an icicle; or were they warm?

—confusion—life is one big wading pool that nobody will wade into—confusion is life and life is bad and yet good— good and bad and love is life and love is torment and torment is love and love is deep and deep is surface. . .

"Yes," he said, "I will ask the driver to go there and we will go wading on a chilly spring evening."

"You can't be serious," she responded, trying to stay calm.

"Yes, I am serious! Dead serious, but never mind!"

—the explosion and what have I done—I have dropped my cool and myself has shown through—a poor idiot. . .

The cab came to a halt in front of the Hapsburg and the cabby turned around and surveyed Joe.

—oops the ride is over and we are here—it was nice while it lasted—oh yes he wants money—be extravagant. . .

Reaching into his pocket, he found a couple of bills, and handing them to the driver, he exclaimed, "Keep the change."

The driver gave him another peculiar look, and as soon as they had gotten out, sped off.

—wonder what's the matter with him—maybe he has family problems or could be that I didn't pay him enough—should have looked at what the meter said—the cool air feels great—we're early. . .

"Shall we proceed inside, baby?" he inquired, turning to her.

"Anything you say, darling," she replied.

Starting across the sidewalk to the door, Joe extended his arm around her back and guided her with his hand on her right hip.

—poetry sheer poetry in motion—wish we were snow bound or caught on a desert island with no one around—wish I could just hold her in my arms all night instead of having to endure other eyes looking at her—people are turning and staring now—wish they would leave me alone with her but she is reserved with her charms and quite conservative in the things that count and that's one reason why I love her so. . .

Shifting his fingers slightly, his mind began whirling.

—sooo soft and yet so firm under my finger tips she would be the envy of Hera, Aphrodite and all of the Greek godesses and she has been mine all mine for these months—here is a step down—must be careful not to put too much pressure on my knee—we are early—the band isn't playing. . .

They walked through the entrance and a waiter greeted them and led them to a table. Some men watched from the bar and snatches of German phrases could be heard here and there.

—there is an awful lot of guys here tonight—maybe I picked the wrong night—maybe Friday is stag night—they always have a good band and we're here so we'll stay—just let those vultures try to get her away. . .

Stopping at a table against the wall, the waiter seated them across from each other on the outside. *"Ein Bier und ein seben und seben,"* Joe told the waiter. He nodded and went off to bring the order. Glancing down, Joe noticed that he was grasping his pipe in his left hand. He emptied it into the ash tray and lifted it again. Then, watching the wandering eyes of his lover, he struck a match, lit his pipe, and began puffing it.

—what would I do without this need to orally fixate—wonder what she is looking at—she is just looking at the place nervously —her brown eyes are so big and bright—she is so gorgeous—I must have a drink. . .

He could feel an excited sensation in the lower extremities of his abdomen as he looked at his jewel.

"Aren't we talkative tonight, honey? You look as if you have something on your mind. Do you want to tell big daddy?" he inquired suddenly.

Looking at him as if startled, she replied, "Oh, I am just happy tonight. Why?"

—she is lying—have known her long enough to tell. . .

"Just wondering. You look like Einstein about to conjure up the theory of relativity."

Her eyes brightened as she peered deeply into his.

"Say something very unintellectual," he continued.

Thinking a moment, she replied, "Everything is relative."

"Very good," he said gaily. "Did you know that there are three levels of conversation?"

Shaking her head no, she looked at him inquiringly.

—ooh she is going to make me destroy myself if she keeps up that passionate look. . .

"Yes. The first level is talking about people, the second is talking about things, and the third is talking about ideas. Come on, let's gossip."

She smiled with her eyes and asked, "Who shall we gossip about?"

"How about your roommate," he exclaimed, cupping his hand over his ear and leaning across the table.

After thinking a moment she pulled herself closer to him and, holding her hands daintily over her mouth as if to direct all the sound his way and exclude an imaginary listener, said, "Yesterday she forgot to get her clean clothes from the laundry, so she had to go to classes without a bra."

Joe roared with laughter and then, aware of the noise he

had made, inspected his surroundings to see if anyone had heard him.

"I'll have to remember that the next time I see her," he exclaimed heartily.

She pleaded with him not to mention it and then said, "Now you give me a bit of gossip."

Sitting back in his chair, Joe thought deeply. Two long clouds of smoke streamed from his mouth.

—quickly think of something—something cool even if you have to make it up. . .

"I don't know if I could ever think of something to match that one," he replied, "but did you hear about Joe Rosen last weekend?"

She shook her head.

"He came into the dorm last Friday night drunk as a skunk and got off on the wrong floor so that he wandered into the wrong room and got into a bed that wasn't his. It happened that there was some other guy in the same bed cutting Z's who was also out of it. The roommate woke up the next morning and found them in bed with the door to the room wide open. It's going to take a long time before Joe lives this one down."

"You mean that neither of them realized that somebody else was in the bed?"

"Let's hope they didn't," Joe replied. "Joe keeps insisting that he didn't remember a thing."

The waiter came with a beer for Joe and a seven and seven for his companion. They continued to converse for several minutes; after they had ordered another round of drinks, the band started playing German music and the dance floor began to fill.

—what's the matter with her tonight—she seems agitated underneath—maybe she doesn't like this place—there do seem to be only a few couples here tonight—I'll try to help her forget whatever is on her mind. . .

"Would you like to dance, darling?" he asked softly.

"No, thank you, not right now," she replied as though repulsed.

—I am smitten—that is enough to make a guy steam—she just talked as if I were one of those wolves asking her to dance—she could have at least declined nicely—baby don't act as if I am getting on your nerves or I won't be able to stand it— I feel so false tonight—so pseudo—I must try and be my poor sucker self and if the world doesn't like it they can lump it—I'm getting tired of this mask and tired of being manipulated by the whim of the moment—I must find the truth but I am not sure of what the truth is—if she talks to me that way she must not love me nearly as much as I love her—O unrequited love how bitter is your taste. . .

"Waiter, another drink here," he called.

Sitting quietly, Joe inspected the girls in the room.

—she is by far the most beautiful creature here, but this passion that burns me is only idolatry and nothing good can come of it but I can't overcome this yearning in my heart—this attachment that I have for her is hopeless—test on before you start sobbing like a baby and be yourself—what does it matter. . .

"Do you have any skeletons in your closets?" he inquired.

"You mean relatives that you don't talk about?"

"Precisely," he replied.

—got to cool down—I am prostrate right now but that doesn't mean that I have to kiss feet. . .

"I have a great-grandfather on my father's side who was a robber and was sent to jail at thirty for robbing a bank and killing a bank guard. They never found the money he stole," Joe said, trying to cheer up the atmosphere with lively conversation.

"I had an aunt who was a prostitute, and from what I remember, she was very beautiful and wealthy," Della related, "and you want to know where she lived?"

"Yes."

"In Boston. She was the talk of Boston's high society, so they tell me."

"By the way," Joe remarked, "you never did get around to telling me how you got such a seductive name as Delilah."

"My father's brother named me. My parents were having a difficult time during the depression and my uncle helped my father keep his business going so my parents told him that he could name their next child. He was going to name me Aaron, after him, but since I turned out to be a girl, he gave me the name I have. I have no idea why he picked such a name," she said.

Joe nodded at her words.

—I must touch her—must hold her one more time before giving up—it's a slow one. . .

63

"Would you like to dance this time?" Joe inquired.

Studying the dance floor, she finally nodded in agreement.

—that's better—whew. . .

Taking her hand, Joe led her up the crowded aisle. They began to dance slowly and smoothly.

—conversation is so tiring—I just want to hold you like I am now—you follow so beautifully and you're so soft and shapely. . .

Holding her closer, he caressed her forehead with his chin. He closed his eyes as they danced on.

—wonder if she feels as I do—at least a little of the fire that consumes me—does she enjoy touching me—wonder if her eyes are closed or she is making eyes at someone on the floor—I feel so unsure of myself as if I could lose all of my composure and maybe lose my balance and clumsily step on her dainty foot or something—come on pull yourself together—wish she would act like the Della that I first came to know—feel as if I am dancing with a stranger tonight. . .

After the music stopped they went back to their seats and sat down. Then Joe asked her to dance again and again she accepted.

—what's the matter with her—she wants to stay seated—if she would only sit by me instead of across the table—where has that smile gone that I used to see. . .

When the music stopped, she immediately turned to make her way back to the table. Joe caught her at her chair and gently grasped her arm.

"Come on, baby, sit on my side of the table. You'll give those playboys the idea that you can be made and then you will be pestered by them all night."

Without a word she sat into a chair next to the wall and he placed himself beside her. Examining her deeply, he finally asked earnestly, "Come on, baby, you can trust me, spit it out. Why aren't we moving tonight?"

She gazed expressionlessly ahead as if she had not heard. While gulping his drink, the sound of the "Beer Barrel Polka" came to his ears.

—my knee doesn't hurt anymore and I feel like dancing—must dance. . .

Grabbing Delilah's hand he made for the floor saying, "Let's do a polka."

She followed. Joe felt great as he swung around and around

and watched the dim lights becoming oblong. The thick pine beams of the ceiling bent as he turned and the people around him became one large circular mass as if he were in a whirlpool.

—I feel so great nothing is going to spoil it—nothing will ruin this evening. . .

The floor moved like the ocean in a soft breeze. Suddenly the music stopped and Joe found himself being led back to the table. Glancing up, he noticed that two girls were seated in the chairs opposite theirs. Stopping before his seat, he whispered in Della's ear—

"Nature is calling. I will be right back." With those words he was off through the crowd. He heard the music starting again.

—better hurry—those greasy grubby hands will be after her. . .

More forcefully he made his way through the standing men. A few minutes later he returned; as he approached he saw two men bending over Della. Walking up and throwing back his shoulders, he asked, "Are those guys bothering you, darling?"

Looking up coldly, but as if relieved, she replied, "Sit down."

"Those guys are really friendly, aren't they?" he exclaimed with a desperate, breathy laugh.

She made no reply.

"You must tell me. What's the matter with you tonight?" he pleaded as she continued to gaze coldly ahead.

The two girls returned from the dance floor jabbering to each other in German. They were still talking as Joe sat studying Della's sculptured profile.

"What's the matter? Are you becoming a catatonic schizo tonight?" he begged desperately.

—she is changing—what is happening to me—I am being smitten—eternally bruised—it had to come sometime—guess I will have to take it on the chin—but I can't really resign myself —no never. . .

He stared silently at her like a puppy who has just been punished by its master and doesn't know why. The band started to play another polka and men began to gather around the two girls across from them. Suddenly Della turned to Joe and begged him to take her home.

—well this is the end of a wonderful affair and she will step out of heart forever leaving an eternally bleeding scar—she looks scared—very undone. . .

"Waiter, *die Rechnung bitte,*" Joe called, trying to keep his emotions from falling into a pit of depression.

The waiter approached quickly and scribbled on his tab. Joe examined the check as he reached for his wallet.

—wow the check is eleven fifty—hope I have—oh no I only have ten and seventy five cents—my checkbook. . .

Reaching into his pocket, he slapped his checkbook on the table.

"I hope you will take a check because I don't have enough."

"Sorry, sir, but we cannot take checks. It is impossible," the waiter replied.

—I better be careful or I will be washing glasses tonight—Della. . .

"How much money do you have?" he asked, turning to Della. Groping through her purse, she replied "I only have a dollar and fifteen cents."

"Let's see," he said to himself, completely sober now. "That makes enough." He sighed with relief as he took the money. "I'm sorry, but I don't have enough money to give you a tip."

"That's all right," the waiter replied taking the cash. "You can remember me the next time you come here."

"What's your name?" Joe inquired.

"Just ask for Jacobson," replied the waiter as he left the table.

"Jacobson, Jacobson, I will remember that name," said Joe as he stood up to leave. "That was too close for comfort," he said to Delilah as they made their exit. "We now have just enough for the subway," he added looking at the coins in his hand.

They walked out onto the sidewalk and headed toward the subway. The air cooled Joe's sweating forehead as he watched his companion from the corner of his eye.

—this deafening silence—people talk together as they walk but I am afraid to say a word for fear it will be thrown back into my face and then my ego will be completely demolished but nevertheless here goes. . .

"What's the matter with you tonight? I never have known you to be like this. Was it the night club?"

"I'm not exactly sure myself what got into me, but I felt as if everybody was against me," she replied.

—well I have a paranoid companion. . .

"You see," she continued, "I was raised for many years by

66

my aunt who was in a German concentration camp during the war. She lost her husband and many of her relatives, and she used to tell me stories that would keep me awake nights from fear. I am not sure whether that has something to do with it or what, but I just know that I couldn't stand it any longer and had to escape."

"So that's it. You associated being in a German establishment, hearing German being spoken and hearing German songs with the atrocities of the Second World War. Why didn't you tell me this before? I would have understood," he said.

"I couldn't really put my finger on it before," she replied.

—now I feel better to know that maybe it wasn't all my fault —wonder if she still wants to go home—she probably does 'cause she never backs down on what she says—I will wait and see— she has shown me that she is human—some things can shake her up—she has lowered her guard but watch her drop me tonight—I can feel it now that I have seen a weak spot in her personality she will not want me around to remind her of it.

"Are you all right now?" he asked. "You know that feeling you had was irrational and that nobody was out to harm you."

"Yes, I know," she replied in an irritated tone.

—well I guess that tells me what I wanted to know—yes I am expendible like any other guy and she is surely the one who will and can expend me. . .

The remainder of the way to the subway everything seemed silent to Joe except frantic buzzing in his head.

As he was exchanging the coins for tokens he heard the train pull in. Deciding to try and make that train, he quickly flipped a token into his companion's hand and buzzing through the turnstile, stood holding the door and laughing at Delilah hurried after.

—I must laugh—I will laugh and maybe I'll feel happy inside and be able to escape the world—yes maybe life as a hebephrenic would suit me fine—I could construct a world that would really revolve around me and laugh hysterically at everything that I want to happen in it—I could snigger at love chuckle at death and guffaw at tragedy and life would be one big joke—she seems to be brightening up. . .

He released the door and the train jerked forward as they sat side by side.

—bounce jounce bumpity bump—these trains sure do like to

make a lot of noise—remember when I was little and took my first ride—thought that the train would bounce off of the track —not much sense in making a joke or something 'cause she wouldn't hear all of what I have to say anyway—think I will slide a little closer and push her with my shoulder—ah she's pushing back but gently ever so gently—people are watching— we make a handsome couple—I don't mind if they look—they don't bother me now—look everybody—look at the most beautiful creature in the world—she has a flaw but that has just made her human where I had figured her for a goddess—somehow the realization that she is not a flawless masterpiece detracts from my image of her—I must be truly immature to look for perfection—perfection is not of this life and yet I look diligently for it and I don't even know what it is—bumpity bump gathump gathump the train is jumping bumpity bump—the rails are steel and hardly move but when the train stops we get off my luv. . .

Joe sat entertaining himself with these thoughts as the train pulled into the Fourteenth Street station. Suddenly he got to his feet and dashed out on the platform. Della, stunned because he had gotten off one stop before their planned exit, gained her feet and looked through the window as the doors closed. Sitting back down, but partly turned and gazing out of the window, she searched the platform for signs of Joe. The train was in the dark tunnel when she glanced around and saw him standing before her, grinning.

"You thought I took off, didn't you?" he asked, half laughing.

"I should have known you were going to pull some kind of gag," she replied, perturbed.

"I almost didn't make it through the door in the next car. The laugh was almost on me. Picture me running six blocks to meet you," he yelled over the sound of the train.

"Yes, picture that," she answered in a half mocking low voice.

—she is still in a bad mood—wish I knew how to cheer her up—I can't stand it when she is like this—why has she changed so—or is it I who have changed—I must try to hang loose and be myself and take the future on the chin—wish I could figure her out. . .

The subway soon pulled into the Astor Place station. Joe took his companion's arm and they stepped onto the deserted platform. Then he dropped his hands to his sides.

—better not touch—keep my hands to home because she

seems to have withdrawn the permission to let me fondle her so I must learn better self control and try to be gay and not mopey—my leg doesn't hurt too much now but I bet it will really be sore tomorrow—tomorrow and tomorrow and tomorrow that word strikes me funny for some reason—well better put my mask of wit and see how joyful I can sound— I will try to keep my voice subdued though. . .

"What can multiply, but can't add or divide?" he asked.

"I don't know. What?"

"Rabbits," he replied, trying to sound serious.

Thinking for a moment, he added. "You know what my walking encyclopedia says? Well, even if you don't want to know, I will tell you," he exclaimed without stopping. "You take two rabbits and a little multiplication and in three years that there will be enough rabbits to fill all of the subway platforms in New York."

"I'll have to remember that," she replied, looking at *him* with a new sparkle in her eye. "You never know when you will need facts like those."

"But can't you just picture it," he said, sounding deep, "trying to beat a pack of rabbits for a subway seat?"

"Yes, and I can picture a rabbit carrying a briefcase and wearing size twelve shoes," she said, starting through the tall, steel turnstile gate.

"And a rabbit with glasses on a subway seat, crossing his legs and studying the *Daily News*," he said with wonderment in his voice as he stepped through the barrier beside her.

She gave a delighted gasp that sent a burst of joy shooting through Joe.

—life is just one big balance first the arm goes one way and then another but maybe I am just a blindfolded mortal stumbling in the heart of darkness—life is so cruel and exciting—my conversation has been very unskillful tonight as well as my thought—I jump from one idea to another and my sentences are not as long winded to say nothing of hers—flight of ideas but there is a central theme to this—the unrequited one—I should have been a philosophy major instead of a mediocre pre-med student—think think—the parietal bones connected to the temporal bone—the temporal bones connected to the mastoid bone—the mastoid connected to the cervical vertebrae bones—the cervical connected to the thoracic vertebrae bones

—then comes the lumbar vertebrae—ilium—pubis—femur—tibia and fibula—then come the tarsal bones and the tarsal bone's connected to the phalanges bones with a few in between—that's it start from the top and work your way down—it's easier that way—I should have stayed home and sat on my gluteus maximus and studied. . .

"You know," Joe remarked as they walked up Eight Street, "I love the names tibia and fibula."

"What brought that on?" she asked.

"Oh, I was just thinking about bones. If I ever have boys I will name one tibia and the other fibula," he said.

—oh there I go again thinking about—my subconscious must be working overtime tonight—oh what the heck follow it through—it is kind of amusing and it makes me feel better—I bet she would have beautiful kids and smart. . .

"Or how about having a kid named phalanges or one called clavicle," he continued. "Aren't they exotic names?"

"Exotic to be sure," she responded.

"I can see them in school with the teacher taking roll: George, Peter, Norman, Clavicle, Mandible, Metacarpal."

"That would surely add spice to a teacher's life," she remarked.

"Wouldn't it though," he returned.

—I love her—she is the only one who can talk my lauguage—she understands me better than I do myself. . .

"Or getting down to the flesh, dig this: how about a girl with first and last names, Miss Superior Vena Cava or Miss Hepatic O'Flexure."

"Now we're really getting carried away," she replied, brightening.

"I can see it now: a handsome little boy named Johnny Jones coming shyly up to a cute little girl and asking her name and she responds innocently, 'My name is Delores Duodenum.'"

Joe looked at her out of the corner of his eye and saw that she had that amused look that he loved.

—my lucky charm is working—at least for tonight—wish I knew the exact words to say and what to do but non-omnipotence is my fate—maybe I am better off that way knowing the future would be sad and unexciting—why didn't she say something—oops—better watch out for those fire hydrants or I will really break my knee and then. . .

"Joe, look," she said, breaking his train of thought.

Turning his head, Joe noticed that she was examining, through a break in the fence, a gigantic crater in the ground, where a building would stand some day.

"Well, how do you like that!" he exclaimed, "They sure do like to get carried away in digging basements, don't they?"

"What are those things in the bottom of the ditch?" she asked innocently.

"Those are I-beams driven straight into the ground by that crane over there. See, the crane has driven that one partly into the ground with its pile driver. That big weight is lifted into the air and acts as a hammer to pound the beam into the ground. You see, the ground is made of sand and to get a tall building to stand without crumbling they have to drive those long beams into the ground. That way the foundation will be secure."

—the house built upon the sand and the flood came and the wind blew and the house fell—sand is broken stone but one is strong and the other is weak. . .

"That must account for the loud noises I have heard during the past few weeks while I was walking to class," she said.

"That's right, the vibrating sound of the steel and the crashing of the pile driver can be heard for blocks," he answered.

They continued walking west on Eighth Street as Joe continued to explain how the building would be constructed from its concrete foundation; a steel skeleton would rise on top of it, soon to be covered by more concrete; or else floors of concrete would be molded one upon the other. Delilah listened intently as they walked along the sidewalk. The conversation flowed freely now as they turned up University Place. After traversing a block and a half Della said, "It's still early yet. Please don't take me home."

Joe stopped and looked aside. As he stared at the display in a store window he asked, "Where do you want to go?"

—she knows I cannot say no to her request if only I could stand up and say an empathic no—she would desire me more —I am sure of it but I cannot so I will be my meek reliable self —I do not want to stay with her forever—I have no money. . .

"I'm sorry," he said and then asked, "What did you say?"

"Let's just walk around. It's so nice out tonight."

—oooh—aah—that did it—I love the way she said that—it

71

sends me into ecstasy—if only I could stand here and dwell on that heavenly sound—pure rapture—speak please speak your voice hypnotizes me but my own sounds like a foghorn next to a harp and it tears me from my revery—I must stay with you—forever—yes it is true but why do my thoughts have this muffled note of irony—now I understand—possibly it is a buffer so that I will be able to recoil and not become completely devastated —I must get some money—the delicatessen. . .

"Yes, let's," he replied hastily after a short silence. "Come on while I cash a check for tomorrow. I know the proprietor of this delicatessen."

Taking her hand, he pulled her into the small store and left her in the front while he talked in a low voice with the man behind the crowded counter. Della stood looking over the profuse collection of boxes and cans until Joe approached her with a bag under his arm.

"Did you get that much money that you need to carry it all in a paper bag?" she asked in wonderment.

"Oh, you're really on the ball tonight. Come on!" he exclaimed enthusiastically. "Let's go climb trees in the park, Jane."

"O.K., let's," she answered with bright eyes as she followed him out the door.

"What's in the bag?" she inquired as they strode down the street toward Washington Square.

"You know what curiosity did to the cat," he said happily. "I just felt like buying something because they were good enough to cash one of my bouncy checks," he continued in a cheerful voice.

Silence ensued while his companion realized that she would not find out what Joe had until he was ready to reveal it.

"I don't know how girls can wear high heeled shoes," Joe said seriously. "Those sharp toes must really hurt your feet."

"You get used to them. You ought to see what kind of torture girls have to go through to look nice," she exclaimed ironically.

—She couldn't find herself qualified to make such a statement if she went through all kinds of torture to look nice for me—if only she knew the torture and sleepless nights that I lose because of her—I should have a penny for each one and I would be a rich man instead of a struggling idiot with no goals. . . .

"You seem to be thinking very deep tonight. Now what is it

72

that you are thinking about?" she asked, reversing the tables.

"Oh, it's nothing," he said, trying to mimic her previous words; then pulling in his chin, he let out a gasping laugh while glancing to see if she was amused.

"OK, Admiral Byrd, lead on," she answered to his imitation.

Joe was just becoming aware of his environment. He had seen it many times before, but it was as if he were discovering it for the first time; he had not noticed the steak house, drycleaners, or sweet shop, although he had been in the restaurant on the other corner. It was as if, when he passed before, there had only been blank scenery, but now the establishments all had functions. His mind then sprang back to the gorgeous creature following him, and he experienced the same emotion of discovery as he thought of her.

They walked across Eighth Street again and followed University Place until they came to the north-east corner of Washington Square. It was darker there away from the bright street and shop lights. Turning and walking toward the Washington Square arch, they looked about them at the scattered people conversing or making love on the benches that lined the walk. Joe was regaining courage with great rapidity and he tenderly placed his arm on Della's hip as they strolled along. Joe's heart gave a sigh as he beheld two lovers entwined in each other's arms. Tugging softly with his hand, he communicated that they should sit in the shadows. Setting the bag on the bench beside him, he put his arm around Della's neck and sat looking up through the leafless trees at the looming monument.

"I love this place," he said as if in a revery. "It has such a history and many of the great men of the world have come here at one time or another to hallow this ground."

"What does MDCCLXXXIX mean?" he asked, playing stupid this time.

"I'm not sure but doesn't M mean a thousand and probably D means five hundred and. . ."

"Oh yes, I remember now," he interrupted quickly, not wanting to play too obtuse. "You add the two C's, which mean a hundred each, to the five hundred and get seven hundred; then you add the X's to the L, which is fifty. Let's see, doesn't it mean 1789?" he said after a quick calculation.

"That sounds right," she said softly. "Where did you see that?"

"Up there," he said, pointing to the top of the monolith.

"Wonder what happened in 1789?" she asked dumbly. "Is the monument that old?"

"I don't see how it could be. Maybe that's when Washington's inauguration was or something. I don't know my American history that well."

She nodded.

—why do I always start talking about things that are farthest from my mind—all I want to do is sit here and enjoy her company for it won't last forever—I want to kiss you and yet I dare not but maybe I will anyway. . .

Tightening his grip on her shoulder he pulled her to him. She gave in easily and leaned her shoulder against his chest.

—Oh heavenly ecstasy—this is a reward for all of the agony that I have endured—I must kiss her . . .

Reaching with his right arm, he caught her small waist and drew her even closer. His head was bent as he caressed her neck in back of her ear with his nose. Then he ran his lips there while his every breath drew wisps of soft fragrant hair against his nostrils. His head swam with euphoric delight.

oh ecstasy—lust—the spirit is willing but the flesh rules—she is acting as if she were putty in my hands—as if I could do anything . . .

The word "anything" echoed in Joe's mind as he considered certain images.

—if she would she would do it only for me and nobody else— here I am being driven again but I don't care what happens will happen. . . .

Drawing his face back, he fixed his eyes on her countenance. She looked up as if she were a kitten wanting to be petted, and his eyes absorbed all of her features. Yes, she was better than the Mona Lisa. She was an eternal masterpiece which Joe wanted to possess, but he knew that the price would be great, if, in fact, there were a price.

—but never mind live for now—she has captured you and only green lights follow for as far as the eye can see—it is true I am driven. . .

Cocking his head to one side, he continued to examine her beautiful complexion and the dazzling way the lights and shadows accented her face. Parting his lips slightly, he was about to continue when the thought came to him:

74

—she has acted exactly like this and then refused to let me kiss her—I must wait and make sure for now it would drive me too hard—she can not toy with me tonight for I am sure tonight would be my breaking point and I would surely become that raving hebephrenic—she seems as if she will let me but I must be sure—why does she refuse one day and consent another while her preceding actions are indistinguishible—I will give her a taste of her own medicine. . .

Turning his face away, he gazed absently at the strong stone memorial as if to reorient himself in his environment.

"Would you like a beer?" he asked softly.

"Whatever you say, Where shall we go?" she inquired in a half whisper.

"Right here," he said gayly.

"What?" she asked in wonderment.

"Right here at the Washington Square Bar. Now what would you like, lady?" he asked, sounding like a big, burly bartender. "We have beer, beer and beer." He held up the paper bag for her to see.

"Well, in that case I guess I will have beer," she exclaimed as if considering deeply.

"There," he said, drawing one quart of the brew from his bag and keeping the other for himself.

After presenting it to her, she looked at him wonderingly and then broke the silence by saying, "Do you mean that we should drink it here? We'll be arrested." But she was laughing.

"Not if the cops don't know what it is. Here is the remedy to that," he answered happily, holding up another paper sack, putting her bottle into it, and presenting it back to her. "Keep it covered with the bag and only we will be the wiser."

Giving a short gasp, she continued to look at him questioningly and then as she held the bag up to him, "Mr. Bartender, I can't drink it if the cap is on."

Clearing his throat, he looked at her as if she were stupid and said in a deep voice, "You poor misled girl. You mean your daddy never showed you how to open a beer bottle? That's the first thing you learn in survival training. It's done this way." He held the neck of the bottle up to his mouth, pretending that he was removing it with his teeth, and then he feigned spitting the bottle cap out.

"Oh yes, I see," she exclaimed with a laugh.

75

"Actually, my ingenious mind must find a way to release those tenacious pieces of metal," he said looking around. "Of course, I know," he said, grabbing her bottle and reaching over the back of the bench on which they were sitting. After forcing the caps off by pressing them against the steel frame of the back of the bench, he handed one back to his companion.

—but I love the way she looks at me and goes along with whatever I innovate—this is saving me much more money than if we had gone to a bar—better keep an eye out for cops—remember when the group of us used to frolic around the park and turn cartwheels swing on swings and play on the jungle jim—this place has so many pleasant memories for me and a few unpleasant but that makes it even that more poignant—we used to enjoy climbing the dirty sooty trees and the girls would watch in wonderment at the way we would swing on the limbs and the chicken fights by the fountain were always so. . .

They sat close and watched the autos glide around the square, looked at the clear sky and studied the few people who happened by.

—the sound of the city and brushing of the breeze against my ears is like dinner music—it covers the annoying sound of gulping as music makes the sound of chewing inaudible. . .

Tipping the bottle, he looked around and saw a policeman walking down the path.

"Here comes a cop," he whispered. "Shall I offer him a swig?"

She replied in the negative as they concealed the bottles and the officer passed.

Soon after, Joe finished his bottle.

"Are you finished?" he asked as he set the empty bottle down.

"No, I'm not," she replied. "Here, will you finish it for me?"

"Are you sure you don't want any more?" he asked.

"I'm positive," she replied, handing it to him.

"Just call me a lush," he exclaimed as he tipped the bottle to his lips.

After emptying it, he got up and threw both of the empty bottles into a trash basket and again sat down beside Della.

"There, you can't say I didn't do my part in keeping New York clean. Chalk up another Brownie point for me," he exclaimed as he turned to her.

—now where were we—oh yes I remember. . .

76

He gently drew Delilah to him until her head came to rest on his partly turned chest. Gazing downward, he saw the reflection of the light shimmering from Della's smooth long hair. As he bent his head down, she responded by slowly raising her face. Parting his lips, he pressed his mouth on hers and stole a short kiss. Noticing that she was responding to this show of affection, Joe strengthened his grip and embraced her firmly, attaching his lips tightly to hers. After some time, he drew back his head and began to feverishly caress her neck and face. He could feel her fingers digging into his back.

—sooo soft and smooth—wonderful—I must make it last forever—I could never live without her and if she truly loves me she will not care if I am a bum or the president of U.S. Steel but I have this horrible feeling that this is all a reflection in a bubble and it will disappear when the bubble meets turbulance—I need help—what will the poor helpless idiot do now. . .

In the next few minutes Joe's metabolism rose. He embraced Della tightly so that she wouldn't escape and he could hear the increased breath from his lover's responsive lips.

—she is willing—so willing tonight—she seems to be giving me her all but how long will it last. . .

They had remained entwined in each other's arms for an indefinite period of time, when silently and slowly Delilah drew herself from Joe's arms and fixing her hair said, "It's getting late. I'd better get back to the hotel."

Joe looked at his watch and then gazed heavily at her.

—if she really truly loved me she would have stayed with me longer—she has nobody checking up on her—why does she care to tear herself away—she can't love me as much as I do her but I can't change the way I feel and I won't . . .

The image came to his mind of them hiking over wide meadows into deep forests, the country a dazzling color as they walked forever hand in hand enjoying the works of Mother Nature. He pictured himself sitting before a roaring fire engrossed in a book with her by his side, waiting to do his every command.

—but no it will not be like that—I know her too well— it will be I who will be at the arm of the chair to do her bidding but I do not care—she has taken my sense and just to look at her is enough for me. . .

Joe got up and held his hand to help Della gain her feet.

Then he pulled her to him and held her so that he could feel every contour of her body pressing against his.

—yes she has a truly magnificent figure and her personality is just as overwhelming as her body. . .

Della pulled herself away and slowly looked up to him.

"You have such a serious look on your face, darling," she said gayly.

—games—games—how can she sound so happy when I'm so serious—she has all of her senses and now mine are completely numb—all right I will play the game I will become happy too. . .

Clearing his throat a little to rid himself of the lump that stuck there, he let go of her and turned toward the monument, saying in as clear a voice as he could muster, "Come on, baby, I'll race you home."

"Don't run," she pleaded, as she stepped beside him and pressed her hand in his.

"I don't want to talk and yet I must—I will show her that two can play the game. . .

"Come on," he said as he grasped her hand tighter and began to advance.

"Don't run!" she exclaimed as she tugged back on his arm.

"I'm not going to," he replied. "Come over here. I want to show you something."

He pulled her rapidly under the high arch of the Washington Square Monument and stood with his arm pointing up Fifth Avenue as she leaned seductively against the inside of the arch.

"Look up there," he exclaimed, pointing up Fifth Avenue. "Don't you feel that you're at the bottom of the world and that the world would just begin for you as you started walking up town? Doesn't this give you the feeling that there is a big conquerable world out there and even though we are at the bottom here, it actually lies at our feet and could even be more magnificent if a person knew how to handle it?"

She nodded, trying to see his point of view.

"Look at those gigantic buildings, the lights and the increasing haze as you look uptown. If a person were to walk up through the world he could study things around him, and, in his own feeble way, attempt to change the world a little. And what is beyond that haze nobody could tell you exactly, but isn't it exciting to know that the world is full of mystery."

Still talking, he walked over to her and held her by the waist; she put her hands on his biceps.

"And just think of what a person could do if he found a side of the street that suited him and promoted his long-run best interests."

"Yes," she replied, "As soon as you become an eminent doctor, you will be able to make great discoveries and show the world the right road to walk."

—she didn't include herself—why didn't she include herself but maybe she senses that I am somehow a failure—why can't I communicate what I mean—I am surely at the bottom of the bottomless pit—this is truly turning out to be a hell. . .

"Darling, do you still work with those barbells that I saw in your room," she asked softly.

"Yes, why do you ask?"

"Your arms feel very big and strong," she replied.

"I enjoy throwing them around, especially when I get mad," he answered.

—she is trying to build up my ego again but it doesn't seem to be working—it is having the reverse effect on me—I wish I could understand myself and rise from this hole of confusion— am I destined to remain forever a misunderstood being—mis- understood by myself and also by others—wish I could take a lover's leap and spread my arms and push on the sides of this temple and I would never have to worry about being tor- mented—but alas I am not strong enough for such a feat. . .

Taking her hand, he began walking with her up Fifth Avenue toward her hotel. Every step gave Joe a strange feeling of imminent foreboding, and the city lights seemed to radiate a happy, yet gloomy haze.

—here I stand at her door—will this be the last time I see her—something is going to happen but I can't tell what it'll be—why was there so much silence between us tonight—why is she standing there holding the door and looking at me like that—why didn't she wait for me to kiss her good night—isn't she going to ask me in—guess I had better go anyway. . .

"I guess I better go," he said hesitantly as he slowly shifted his weight to leave.

"Aren't you going to come in for a few moments?" she asked

—that gives my heart a relief—wish I could understand what is happening between us—I must stand back so that I can see just what is going on and exactly how I stand. . .

Dazed at this surprising invitation, he stepped, like a little boy, into the dimly lit room and stood watching her as she closed the door. Then she sat on the couch and motioned seductively for him to join her. He did so as if he were a stumbling blind man.

—why am I so nervous—something is very strange about her tonight—we must find a way so that we can stay together. . .

Sliding to her side, he took her into his arms and hugged her tightly. His heart flitted like a bat as he felt the exquisite joy of having her close. A fire began to kindle inside of him and he could see his restraint melting in the heat.

—I better leave for I would not want to do something she and I would be sorry for—I don't want to hurt her and I am sure she is not that kind of girl—I know she would not do such a thing. . .

They kissed and caressed even more fiercely. It was as if he could not help himself and was obeying the dictates of his stronger emotions.

Suddenly she buried her face into his shoulder and began to weep. She shook all over with each sob and a deluge of tears streamed down her lovely cheeks.

"What's the matter, darling?" he asked seriously, taking his handkerchief from his pocket and brushing over the moistened eyelids.

As she took his handkerchief from him, she seemed to be crying even harder, but only faint sniffing sounds could be heard in the soft light.

—she looks down at the floor and then at me and then down again—what does it mean—does it mean that she really does love me or is this the end—this isn't like her—what has happened. . .

"Come on, darling, please tell me what is the matter so I can try and help you."

He held her tight to reassure her as she dabbed her eyes.

"What . . .What if," she started, but then broke out into another fit of crying.

"Come on," he said, reassuringly, "you can tell me. Please tell me what is the matter and get it off your chest."

He held her even more firmly. Then her child's voice seemed to change to that of a small unhappy child as she said, "What if a girl loves a guy and is going to marry him and she loves him very much and he gets an apartment where they spend many hours together and. . ."

—she is talking about herself—she couldn't get so upset if it were one of her friends—she had an affair with another man—played house with him. . .

Joe could feel a black fire consuming his heart and the smoke was choking off his wind.

"She goes to bed with him many times," she continued. "and then one day they are supposed to meet at this apartment and when she gets there and opens the door she sees. . ."

Her wailing became even more intense as she became strangled with the words she had blurted out.

Holding her firmly, Joe tried to calm her.

"There, there," he said softly, "everything is going to be all right. It's good if you try to relieve your conscience a little."

"And she went to the apartment one night," she continued, "and found that there were three other guys with him and they took her and threw her on the bed and took her clothes off and as she lay there with one of the guys on her, she could see her fiancé laughing at what was going on, and then she passed out."

"Oh, my God, my God," Joe wailed as the story pierced his ears. He held her face to his shoulder to show that he was there and would give her strength to bear it.

—what has happened to my poor darling—how could God let this happen to anybody—what a horrible experience. . .

"What was his name? Tell me who he was—I will kill him—he's inhuman. A person like that doesn't deserve to live," Joe exclaimed, becoming consumed with a burning hatred as he thought.

"No," she said, becoming more quiet now. "It happened three years ago when I was seventeen."

"Why didn't you call the cops?" he asked, "You could have put those guys away, for at least twenty years."

"I was ashamed. I didn't know what to do. It was all so terrible—so horrible, that I didn't even want to think about it. I have been trying to forget it for a long time, but it doesn't seem to work."

81

"But you should think about it," he said. "You shouldn't try and forget it, because that will only do you more harm. Think about it. Learn from the experience and talk about it, but only with a person whom you know will understand; because only this way will the experience lose its traumatic proportions."

"I just felt I had to tell someone," she said, "and you are so stable and well adjusted. I didn't want to tell you but I felt I had to, because you are always so stable and strong minded. Nothing seems to bother you."

—that's why she has stuck with me this long—she figured I would have all of the answers because I was going to be a psychiatrist and would give her a peaceful mind—it's funny how people can deceive others by their actions and looks—maybe she didn't want me but she wanted what I was going to be and what is out of my reach now—I still love her more than ever—I don't care if she is deflowered—I will take her with me far away and we will live together in peace away from this cruel rat race—we will find a place where that is peace for her and me—a place where we can be alone forever. . .

"Why has that experience seemed to have destroyed me, so that now I am afraid that I am going out of my mind?" she asked.

"I don't have all the answers," he replied hesitantly, "but it has to do with the sex drive which is something that is very strong in a person, and one of the reasons this was such a terrible experience for you was that you undoubtedly had a feeling of ambivalence. You see, your conscience told you that this was a terrible thing that was happening to you by normal standards of human experience, but since you were also being stimulated you had a sensation of pleasure, however repulsive it may have been to you. And so it was those opposite feelings that caused a tearing inside. It is quite a normal reaction and you are no freak. You probably hated yourself for having any sensation of pleasure from such an experience and it is probably this conflict between the grotesque immorality and the pleasurable that caused such a turbulence in you."

"What should I do?" she asked earnestly, "I feel like I am going insane."

"It might be a very good idea to go see a psychiatrist. He doesn't have all the answers, but being the intelligent and sensitive person you are, I am sure he can do you a lot of good. I am certain your father would be glad to let you see one."

"You say that I shouldn't try to forget it?" she questioned, her head still on his shoulder.

"That's right, and if you ever need someone to tell your troubles to, you know I will always be there whenever you need me."

She responded by putting her arms around him. Holding her head up by the chin, Joe kissed her reassuringly.

She embraced him and her lips became warmer and more inviting than Joe had ever known. Her chest heaved furiously to the rhythm of her burning breath as Joe's thoughts turned inward.

—I forgive her—I can do nothing else but forgive her—she needs me more than I know and yet I feel that if I had not put on this façade she would not have wanted me—she is pure in her heart—I better leave before I lead her to do wrong—she is more truthful than I. . .

They embraced violently and she pressed her lips to his fiercely; Joe's head began to swim like a turbulent sea.

"I want you," she said softly after some minutes of silence.

—just what did she mean by that—she couldn't have meant what I heard. . .

"I want you too, darling," he responded.

"I want you now. My roommate will not be home tonight."

—it can't be—I didn't hear what I just heard—she can't mean what I just interpreted her as saying pseudo-communication—I want to—yes yes yes but we must wait but she wants to now—she needs more help than I realized—please stop—please stop. . .

Joe struggled in a sea of confused thought as she dug her fingernails into his back. Joe rapidly began to lose his senses and his self-restraint.

"Please kiss me hard," she pleaded as she leaned back.

Suddenly Joe's thought began to steady above the storm.

—why can't we put off present whim for future satisfaction—I love you so and I would do anything for you but somehow I feel suddenly sober and feel that we must wait . . . were those two men that I saw in your apartment yesterday really to see only your roommate or—no I can't believe it—it's too terrible to think of—please stop—you're hurting me more than you will ever know—it is not purely for sexual gratification that I desired you for it was so much more—you will ruin me for I can never love again. . .

With his mind slowly clearing, Joe leaned forward and kissed her tenderly as she pulled him to her.

—she does need help—I must help her—if I take her away from all of this it will be all right—poor thing I love you too much to make your problem worse—how much truth has she told me—maybe she doesn't really love me—she just desires me—no it isn't true—I can't believe it that all she wants of me is gratification—I must control myself and wait. . .

Joe was aware of a dull frustrated sensation in his lower abdomen as he struggled to keep his senses.

"Please, I want you," she pleaded again as Joe leaned against her in a daze.

—won't somebody please help her—she is not acting like herself and this is not the woman that I know. . .

"Do you have any protection?" she continued.

"No, I don't, darling. I can't. I don't want to hurt you."

"I don't care," she begged. "I want you. I don't care."

"I couldn't give you any gratification. I couldn't last very long," he added, trying to keep his head.

—they say that marriage is a formality and that true agreement is the binding tie but she has only has asserted that she wants me but I am rationalizing a wrong into a right—I must find out if she really loves me—I must see if she will love me no matter what I am. . .

"Darling, there is something I must tell you," he started reluctantly. "I didn't get accepted by any of the med schools to which I applied," he blurted out. "I will never be a psychiatrist or even a doctor," he added.

She looked at him with her wide eyes as if the trance were broken. Finally, she loosened her grip and reality invaded their awareness. They were both silent for a time.

—what does it mean—does it mean that she loves me or that she hates me. . .

"You mean you heard from Columbia?" she asked.

"Yes, they rejected me," he answered sadly. "I would have told you sooner but I couldn't. You seemed to want it for me even more than I."

"It doesn't matter," she said with what sounded like a cold note in her speech as if half stunned.

—does this mean that she really loves me and is sad at my defeat or that she was really in love with the psychiatrist me. . .

"There are other fields to conquer," she added, trying to console him.

—why am I always on the defensive—why can't I take the offense more but maybe I am just offensive tonight. . .

Sitting erect in the soft light, she fixed her hair. He sat as if stunned and stared at her, glassy-eyed, trying to discern what was happening.

"I better go," he said getting up, "because I have to get a lot of work done before we go to the beer blast tomorrow."

She followed him to the door and stood holding it as he gave her a quick kiss on the cheek.

"I'll come by at eight," he said in a low voice.

She stared straight ahead and nodded slowly as her eyes moved to his face. Without another word he made his way down the hall and pushed the elevator button.

—I shouldn't have run away so quickly—should have stayed and tried to discern her reaction—this is a nightmare—I will wake up and find that this is only a bad dream—I'll go back—no—it's better this way—we both made fools of ourselves tonight—whatever comes I will face and know that it will turn out for the best . . . the elevator. . .

Joe did not go straight home but stumbled up and down the quiet streets past the warehouses and down dark alleys. Reality slowly began to seize his mind and with it came the pain from his hurting knee. He watched his legs extend one in front of the other as they propelled him onward over the bright sidewalk under the street light to the shaded pavement away from the illumination. A feeling of extreme fatigue crept over his body as he thought of going to sleep and dreaming pleasant fantasies, but he knew that his mind was too busy buzzing with recent events to be able to relax.

He reviewed his recent experiences over and over. They forced their way into his conscience as he concentrated inwardly. He tried to perceive things in a coherent light, but somehow order evaded him and chaos ordered his conjuring. As he played over the past he came to tender spots which seized him as if they were more vivid now than then, and an inner turbulence welled up through him until it made his face burn in the cool air. He shivered and squinted his eyes and cast the momentary spell from him only to have it return with a slightly new and different emotional tinge.

85

(You shouldn't try to forget it because it will only do you more harm. I was ashamed. Tell me who he was, I will kill him. I'll never be a doctor.)—she needs help—she is not in love with me but with what I was going to be. . . (Dear sir: We regret to inform you that favorable action has not been taken.) —far away faraway with me—I can't stop loving you—my knee is punishing me again better go home if I am going to be able to walk tomorrow. . .

A widening line of light crept across the floor and extended up the opposite wall of his apartment as Joe slowly stepped inside and closed the door. The room was dark.

—darkness cover me—hide me—make me sleep and have peace—cover the sparks in my brain and smother them—I will return to the womb and remain fetal forever—protected—unbothered—unworried—unthinking. . .

Brushing his hand against the wall, Joe hit the switch and light flooded into his eyes, blinding him. Upon regaining his sight, he paced the room.

—wish my roommate were here—I need someone to talk to someone to hear me strut and fret and help me know what to do and which way to go—he would help me for his mind understands her better than me—he's in the in group and would know what to do. . .

After removing his jacket, he threw himself on his back on the bed, drew the sheets over his eyes, and lay staring through the whiteness of the sheet as he hugged the pillow.

—a poor idiot—why isn't darkness creamy white like this— it's just a covering and yet more pure—how many men has she gone to bed with—she is so soft and perfect and I love her too much—white deep white soft lovely white fluffy feathery white . . . (My fiancée was laughing.)—what will my future be—I can't see farther than my nose—a white cloud surrounds me and all of my goals have been destroyed . . . (Some type of great loss is many times a major precipitating cause of manic-depressive psychoses.)—I must do much work tomorrow— she has a magnificent body—how many grubby greasy hands has she let posses her—white soft pillow—feathers—turkeys—pecking turkeys—white sooo soft—soooooo soft and cuddily and sweet and white and relaxed and lovely and confused and no doctor and love—white soft white sooooooooo white—soooooooooooo soft and cudddddddddddily. . .

The loud honking of a car horn pierced the air and Joe rolled over in bed. Suddenly he sat up. He realized that is was day and the electric light was still on.

—oh no it's two o'clock—I slept too long—I have so much work to do—I had a dream—let's see—I was talking to a girl—she climbed into a car and I said I would meet her somewhere—as the car drove off I grabbed a large balloon and with some trouble I got off of the ground and flew through the air—the balloon went where I wanted it to go—over trees, ruins and rivers—then I landed as she was getting out of the car—as she was getting out she hit the horn—that flying dream is similar to a dream I had a couple of years ago when I had discs in each of my hands and I walked off of the balcony of my house—let's see how did that go—oh yes my uncle was standing on the lawn below and said that he didn't know that I could do such a feat as flying like that and I expressed the idea that as long as I concentrated very heard that I could fly wherever I wanted then suddenly I realized that I was far off the ground and lost confidence and fell—wonder if those dreams are related—maybe the balloon means I must rely on someone for success and the other means that alone I can't succeed for long—I could never be an analyst if I can't even understand my own dreams—wonder if Samson dreamt when he was in Delilah's arms—well I better look for my ass's jaw bone for if I don't lick the enemy I will fail all of my courses—somehow my mind is not so amusing today—it really does seem like an enemy to me—well I had better get to work. . .

After rolling out of bed, Joe washed, changed his clothes and grabbed something to eat from the tiny refrigerator; then he talked himself into listening to a few records on his roommate's stereo.

—wish I could listen to this soothing music all day—King Saul had David play music to him to help his nerves but I guess all good thinks must end and—oh no it's three thirty already and I haven't gotten anything done. . .

Sitting at his desk he turned on the lamp and then took a microbiology book from the shelves above his head, opened at a marker, and began to read.

"Antistreptolysin. Streptolysins of Streptococcus pyogenes and related species are of two sorts: (1) streptolysin S, unstable in the presence of heat and acids; (2) streptolysin O, unstable in oxygen. These toxins. . ."

—wonder what she will wear tonight—probably something dazzling but in vogue of course—wish I knew what was happening between us— will it last or—what was I just reading— I have to concentrate on this. . . (In persons infected with Streptococcus pyogenes, antibodies to both streptolysins. . .)— maybe she really does love me and I am imagining this all of the time—I will know tonight—it gives me the creeps to think of how badly we both acted last night—I should have stayed and talked with her a little longer last night instead of running away—it made me look very bad. . . (well over 80% of rheumatic fever patients have considerable titer of antistreptolysin O.)—maybe it's best if I don't become a doctor anyway—some of those diseases give the creeping crawling hebe jebes anyway like this picture of the heart diseased with endocarditis due to Streptococcus viridans—ugh, I can't stand to look at that growth inside the ventricle and auricle—it makes my heart feel like it has that crappy disease—what's the matter with me—I've got to keep my mind on this book. . . (In obstetric cases the hemolytic streptococci may. . .). . .

Joe's eyes followed the words but his mind was far away. After catching himself several times, he began to get very angry and, after what seemed like an eternity of struggling, he became so infuriated that he cast his restraint away and in a wild fury stood up, sending his chair flying on its back. He snatched the library book from the desk and hurled it against the far wall, causing the pages to be dismembered from the cover.

—this is hell—I must talk to her. . .

Grabbing the telephone, he hastily dialed Della's number, but the telephone rang without answer. After some time, he slammed down the receiver, went to the refrigerator, got a beer, turned on the phonograph, and lay on the bed staring at the peeling paint on the ceiling. He alternately paced the room and lay in bed for the rest of the afternoon. By six thirty he decided it was time to get dressed; so he took a shower and donned his black Levi's and a tight, short sleeve shirt; then he threw a can of spaghetti into a pot and watched it as it began to cook on the stove.

"Kettle burn, kettle bubble,
Eradicate my toil and trouble;
help my brain to clear and then
get me back to normal again."
—tonight we will have a great time like we did the last time
and the band will really rock—wish it were time to pick her
up—am I doomed to be a failure in everything that I do—I know
what I will say—after rehearsing all of these hours I must be
able to rehearse something that will change things—let's see
how will it go—darling you know that I love you very much
and that I would do anything for you—please forgive me for
being so dishonest with you—no I can't say that because maybe
it's all over now—I can't ask her to marry me for maybe she
would never do it now—there seems to be a schism growing
between us—the spaghetti is burning. . .

Quickly, he took the pot off of the fire and dumped its contents on a plate; then, washing a fork that lay on the mound
of dirty dishes at the sink, he sat at the table and began to force
the tasteless substance into his mouth.

—hate to eat it's so unsophisticated—guess I would waste
away to nothing if I didn't force this crap into my oral cavity. . .

After eating and listening to a few more records, Joe made
his way out the door and through the streets.

—I'm surprised how good my leg feels today—wonder if
there is really something wrong with it or just a slight pulled
muscle—I should pray but can't seem to—it's been over two
months since I have been to church—will go tomorrow—things
will go all right they will—I will start being happy and not let
myself get depressed—forget about all of the work and sooner
or later it will get done—hope it's not going to be later—think
of something funny—a giant greasy gob of granulated gorilla
grunt—I can feel myself cheering up now—it's that apartment
that depresses me. . .

"Hi," he said as Della opened the door, trying to keep his
face expressionless in order for it not to be inappropriate with
mood.

"Hi," she exclaimed, turning around and putting something
from the desk into her slacks.

"You look beautiful tonight with that fluffy blouse and those
wow slacks," he said in a happy tone.

89

"Thank you," she said, but without smiling, as she walked through the doorway in front of him.

After closing the door, they made their way to the elevator.

—I'm speechless—she seems almost cold tonight and I can't wrangle a word from my lips—I must try to rectify things—the elevator is here—I'll wait so nobody will hear us. . .

"What did you do today? I called you this afternoon," he asked as they stepped onto the elevator.

"Went shopping," she answered curtly.

"Aw, come on," he said in a low voice. "It's going to be a great party tonight. Aren't you in a party mood? I hear they hired a great band tonight, three guitars and a drum."

"Yes, I'm in a party mood," she returned, brightening up a little.

Joe attempted a few more fumbling words, but as they took to the sidewalk outside of the hotel she looked at him questioningly.

"Joe," she asked in a serious voice, "Is it true what you told me last night?"

"Yes, I am afraid it is and I am sorry for having lied to you all of this time."

"You mean that you will never make it into medical school?" she asked.

"It looks that way. I was really just dreaming to think that I could get into those good schools, but even the lesser ones rejected me."

"Why did they reject you?" she inquired.

"What?" he said mechanically.

—I don't know if I can be truthful—I'll be—I'll tell her the exact truth—if she really loves me it won't make any difference unless her father does the thinking for her. . .

"Why did they reject you? You showed me some of your transcripts and you had very high marks. What happened?"

"Yes, you saw some of my transcripts, but last semester and this semester I have had very low grades. Last semester should have been my best semester, but it has been my worst; and besides, I didn't do brilliantly on my med boards. In fact, I did terribly."

"You mean you haven't got a chance now?" she asked.

"It looks that way. All eight of the schools to which I applied were very prompt in sending rejections. One of the reasons, also, was that many of the high marks that I received were not in the required pre-med courses but in liberal arts courses—so that fact didn't help me any. For instance, I got an A in English in my sophomore year, but only a C+ in Comparative Anatomy."

—maybe I should ask her to confirm what she told me last night about herself—no that would be cruel and untactful—I can't believe this is happening to me—does she really love me—maybe she thinks that all that I am really after is her father's money—no how could she believe anything like that. . .

"I should have told you, but I couldn't. Every time I would get around to telling you the truth, you seemed to be dreaming about me being a great psychiatrist, and I couldn't," he exclaimed sadly.

—the dark cloud of depression is coming—change the subject quick before I can't get out of the dark pit. . .

"What was the weather like today? I didn't even look outside the whole day."

"It was fairly nice. I went up to Lord and Taylor's and bought a beautiful summer dress today and. . ."

They walked down the streets and around corners until they reached a small café on Waverly Place.

"Well, here we are," Joe exclaimed. "Looks as if there are a lot of people here already. I hear they really got the basement looking like a real dungeon."

After giving the money to the ticket taker, they made their way down several dimly lit stairs and entered an equally dimly illuminated room. Standing for a few moments on the threshold, they gazed around while their eyes got used to the dark. The room was very rustic and natural looking with large stones protruding from the walls and cement seeping from between; the rough splintery beams of the ceiling hung like heavy weights in the shadows. Scattered around the chamber were many candles and the only other source of light were two small, red light bulbs in oppposite corners of the large basement.

"This is what I call atmosphere," Joe exclaimed delightedly. "Come on, let's go say hello to Joel and Ruth."

"Hi, Joel. Hello, Ruth," Joe said happily as he crossed the room with Della. "Isn't this great down here? This is what I would call atmosphere."

91

"It's right there, isn't it?" Joel returned. "They have about a dozen half kegs of beer and the band is going to get going in a minute."

"Here, try some beer," said Ruth, holding her cup up to him.

"Don't mind if I do," exclaimed Joe, taking the offering. "Hey, that's good."

"Joe, what did you think of that test we had last Friday?" Joel inquired as the girls became engrossed in conversation.

"Wasn't it awful?" returned Joe. "I have been trying to repress it all weekend."

"You really did poorly, then?"

"Poorly isn't the word for it," Joe went on, "What did you think about the question that asked about the . . . "

After talking with Joel and Ruth, Della and Joe wandered around the room chatting with different people that they knew. Then Joe suggested, as the band started to play, "Come on, let's sit down." He motioned to two empty chairs at a table. "I'll go get some of that free beer."

Della seated herself and Joe made his way through the crowd. As he was returning to their table, he saw a boy talking to Della. The intruder was sitting in the chair that he had slated for himself. Joe had seen him before but was not sure where. A feeling of consuming jealous anger welled up in him as he walked up, but seeing him coming, the stranger slowly rose and with a defiant look, slipped into the crowd.

—I hate him—he looks like a real slippery character—if I set my eyes on him talking to her again I will make him sorry. . .

Pretending not to notice, he seated himself in the warmed chair and slid the large paper cup of beer in front of her, keeping two for himself.

"A lot of girls are going to be reducing tomorrow to work this off," he exclaimed cheerfully, holding the cup up as a toast.

She responded to his gesture mechanically with what appeared to be a sad look in her eyes.

—dislike it very much when she looks like that—she seems so beautiful with that face but is so very unresponsive—what has happened to us these past two weeks—where has our love gone—it's just the time of year for budding passion but ours frolicked on the winter and seems to be dying in the spring—I must do something—some heroic feat—something to impress—maybe a fight—no—that would be too barbaric. . .

Taking a gulp of beer, Joe stood up and motioned to dance. Della got to her feet and met him on the floor a step away.

—ooooooow—the band is really good—how I love to dance these fast ones—there's nothing like sublimation—why does she look so serious—wish I could cheer her but I just don't feel up to it—I must try. . .

Leaning over, he spoke above the loud music, saying, "You look so much better with a smile on your face."

—the smile she is presenting to me—it's forced so forced—now even that is fading back to what it was—I feel so hostile tonight—like hitting someone or knocking over a table. . .

The music stopped; standing tall, Joe snatched his drink from the table and stood with his arm around Della's back. He sipped his beer as they waited for the next song.

—shooo depression—say something—anything. . .

"Something just hit me funny," he said whispering into her soft white ear. "Just picture all of the people here as invisible except for their ears. Think of them jumping up and down to the music, but you can see only their ears; or better yet, think of them as only bellybuttons. Can't you just see about three hundred bellybuttons floating around the room and moving to the music. With all of those buttons it's a wonder more people don't belong to the navel reserve."

—she is looking at me with that look that I always loved—maybe I am getting through to her—what else can I say to amuse her—I can't think of a thing—my mind is a blank—why couldn't it be purged like this when I was trying to study—forget about studying and dance. . .

The music started up again and they glided slowly across the dance floor. Joe felt as if they were one and yet. . .

—yes it's true we are growing apart—she is not the same—I have to try and do something but what. . .

The music stopped and immediately Della said, "Let's sit down. I don't feel like dancing right now."

Taking her hand, he led her toward the table. Suddenly Joe glanced back and saw a guy smiling and brushing against Della as she followed him through the thick crowd. Joe burned with fury as he drew her to him and walked behind her the remainder of the way. After sitting down, he took his drink and swallowed it in two long gulps. Della also lifted hers and began to sip at it.

"It's great that they thought of putting the beer in milkshake cups," he exclaimed, trying to cheer himself up. "That saves making a lot of trips back to the tap."

"I'll bet it's crowded at the beer barrels, too," she added.

—she's looking around—there seems to be a lot of guys close by—the wolves can sense that I am done for and are closing in for the kill where I failed—if anybody makes an advance at her I will knock the crap out of him—she seems to be sizing some of them up—maybe I am unwanted tonight—need more beer—keep the wolves off. . .

"Would you like another beer?" Joe asked, taking her cup. She nodded as he got to his feet.

"Would you like to come with me?" he inquired, staring earnestly at her.

"No, I just want to sit here for a while," she answered, turning her head to one side as if to question.

Joe elbowed his way slowly through the thick, buzzing crowd and filled the containers at one of the barrels; then, after casting a few hellos back to different people who recognized him as he passed, he got back to find Della leaning forward and conversing with one of the people collected around the table. The conversation faded as he approached and seated himself again.

—at least she could wait until tonight was over—I wanted to have such a good time tonight and now she is ruining it—she may be planning to meet someone else. . .

After placing a drink before her, Joe brooded in silence.

"Would you like to dance?" he asked sheepishly after a time.

Getting reluctantly from her chair she followed as he forced a way to the dance floor.

"Come on, let's go near the band," he said as he pushed his way forward through the fast surging crowd.

—want to have the music drown out the screaming in my brain—it will move me and make me forget just for tonight—I love this fast sound. . .

They began to dance, but somehow, as Joe peered at Della, he felt a disturbing and frustrating irritation. Closing his eyes, he tried to lose himself in light-headedness and in the depth of auditory stimulation; but his anxiety seemed to become more intense as the reality of his difficult existence focused even more vividly in the dark depths of his mind. After the music stopped, they shuffled back through the ebbing crowd to their

94

table where Joe began to devour more brew.

"You look like a Viking at a big feast," said a friend as Joe wiped suds from his lips with the back of his hand.

"Hi, Moose," Joe exclaimed, glancing up surprised. "Here's to your good health and all of that rot," he yelled above the din in a deep voice as he stood up holding his cup up in toast.

"Having a good time?" asked Moose as his flagon bounced enthusiastically against Joe's.

"Of course, of course," Joe said as he took another swig. "You think I look like a Viking. Well take this in," said Joe as he grabbed a reserve from the table, blew the foam from it, and took a big hearty gulp.

Following his lead, Moose returned in kind; they both vibrated loudly with laughter. After exchanging a few more lively words with Moose which picked spirits up, he seated himself again; his spirits seemed to sink, too. Joe and Della sat together in painful silence and drank.

"Sounds like everybody's having a great time," he said, trying to sound happy.

Della shook her head in affirmation.

The band returned after an intermission and Joe stood up ready to dance as he gazed earnestly at Della. She moved her eyes up to his and pleaded with a glance as if to say that she did not want to dance. Thwarted, Joe slowly resumed his seat, but he felt as if he were sitting on tacks. He had to do something about it.

"Nature's calling again," he mumbled suddenly as he blindly rose and marched through the milling crowd.

As he returned from the men's room, he saw over the heads of the crowd that Delilah was dancing with someone else. Joe's face became scarlet as he clenched his fists and crunched his teeth. Staring downward, he pushed his way through the jostling couples until he found his seat. Throwing himself down, he occupied himself with consuming the drink and pretended not to notice as Della returned.

"Where were you?" he demanded.

"I might ask the same of you," she returned. "I thought you left and so I just danced one dance."

"Oh!" he exclaimed, shaking his head sarcastically.

They sat in a resonant silence, listening to the din of the party and drinking.

Finally Joe demanded, "Do you want to dance now?"

Della followed him to the floor and they moved to the fast beat.

"I feel like a ping pong ball being bounced around in this crowd," Joe threw out as he elbowed another guy who was dancing vigorously.

Della eyed Joe with a look that he could not decipher.

—it doesn't feel so bad now—fun—fun—I will have a good time and nobody will spoil it—feel so relaxed now—the room is bouncing and the ceiling is caving—oooooh better—much better—I can stand the whole world—the whole universe—she is looking at me with a funny look—maybe I am acting drunk but it takes a lot for me to get drunk—maybe she just wants an excuse to—I am not drunk—I just feel more relaxed now—relaxed soooo relaxed—I don't care about anything. . .

The music stopped suddenly and Joe found himself following Della as she led back to the table.

—what's the matter—she doesn't want to dance—just when I feel like dancing—what's the matter with her—if she thinks I am drunk—she isn't doing so badly herself—I can't sit—I don't want to just sit tonight—she is looking at that guy—she seems to know him—I can't stand it any longer—forgot my pipe—will get some cigarettes. . .

"I'll be back in a minute," he muttered in an unintelligible voice as he disappeared into the crowd. Zig-zagging his way, he climbed the stairs and emerged onto the rain soaked street.

—where can I get weeds around here—it rained—the cool air feels great—my mind feels as if it can fly away like the breeze—there's Rockey's—I'll go there. . .

With feet spread apart for support, he seemed to float across the street to a bar.

Returning with the cigarettes in his hand, he hurried to get back to Della's side and to the drink that he had left; for he was beginning to feel depression creeping over him because of the sobering effects of the night air. Upon reaching the gathering, he looked across the room and saw Delilah dancing in the arms of another guy. After going to the tap he walked back and forth aimlessly. Then he stopped to talk absent-mindedly with a guy he knew. When the song was over he cut directly for the table, leaving his conversant in the middle of a sentence. Striding up to where Della was talking with the stranger, he stood beside her gazing hazily into the depths of the shadowy chamber. Finally she noticed that he was near and turned and approached him asking; "Where did you go?"

"I said I would be ah, be right back," he said with a thick tongue.

"You did? Well, I sure didn't hear you," she said with a question mark on her face.

"Well, I did," Joe exclaimed defensively.

—I want to hold you in my own arms—but you are out of reach—what have I done—I am driving you away—I want to touch you but these other crumbs are cramping me—please run away with me—but no it is too late and—but maybe it isn't—maybe it isn't she is staying with me after I left her twice—where's my drink—oh yes, here it is—oh no. . .

He stuck out his arm and clumsily grasped at his drink, but the liquid glided across the table onto the lap of a guy who was engrossed with his girl friend. Feeling the brew flowing onto his lap, the guy jumped up suddenly and with a deep frown, began to stare furiously at Joe.

"Sorry, buddy," Joe exclaimed. "Did I get . . . get you very wet? Look, pal, you look like you want to fight but I did say I was sorry. Here is my handkerchief . . . handkerchief . . . you will accept my apologies because I said I am sorry. What more can I do?"

The boy with the wet lap glared at Joe and then threw several contemptible words at him which Joe could not quite make out because of the noise.

"Whatever you said," said Joe, "the same to you."

At that remark the stranger hurriedly swung around the table and stood nose to nose with Joe.

"What's the matter? Do you want to fight?" Joe asked, smiling.

After a few coarse words were exchanged, Moose who had happened to notice what was going on, stepped in to help break it up.

"Do you want to get arrested?" Moose asked Joe after his antagonist had gone away.

"Where is Delilah?" Joe inquired excitedly.

"I don't know," replied Moose.

Without any farewell, Joe walked off in search of Della. Through a break in the crowd he spied her talking to still another dark headed stranger.

—I'll bet he has a Jaguar and an expensive flat—I'll knock the crap out of him—maybe her father would approve of this guy whereas he would not of me—I need another drink drink drink stink shrink skunk. . .

Roughly, he forced his way to the beer barrels where he began to gulp down another beer. As he tipped the cup, he looked earnestly over the top of it in order to catch a glimpse of Della.

—hostility—frustration—what makes me want to act on these hostility feelings—what makes me do the things that I do—I want her but now it is too late and I didn't help the situation—I am striken and smitten—is that her—no guess she moved from where she was. . .

By now Joe was starting to feel that his head was a small ball that he must balance on his neck and his arms worked in fits and starts when he commanded them to do so. After some minutes, he plunged again into the crowd to renew his search. The crowd parted momentarily as people shifted slightly to left and right. Through the opening he saw something that caused him to gasp.

—Delilah—no Delilah—how can you do this to me—you will ruin me—destroy me—how can you kiss another and here we were thinking that the other was so very stable—oh no I can't look. . .

He pushed closer to where Della was sitting in a dark corner entwined in a deep embrace with the boy with the black hair.

—it isn't true—it is a nightmare and I will waken like I always do—I am hallucinating—she doesn't know what she is doing—he—he has his hand on her leg—I'll stop it—she needs help. . .

Striding forward he pushed the crowd aside and made his way toward the couple. As he came to a halt a few feet away from the unsuspecting pair, he shrugged his shoulders and thrashed his arms in a moment of indecisive helplessness. Then he looked up and saw that the boy was slowly coming to the realization that he was near. They stared at each other with muddled expressions on their faces as Della slowly swung her head around and looked at Joe.

—those beautiful eyes are looking at me once more but not

as they did—oh my God—her expression—she has tears in her eyes—never saw her cry like that before— her face is wet—so wet with tears—she cried last night but not like this—he is hurting her—if he is I will kill him—she is turning her head away and hugging him very tightly—she does not want me—it is true and nothing I can do will make her love me—I've really flubbed things up now. . .

Hanging his head in deep despair, Joe wandered aimlessly away. As he looked at the warped pine wood floor he visualized Della's expression, her contorted, tearful, beautiful expression.

"Hi, Joe," came a cheerful sound directly in his path.

Looking up, he spotted a beautiful, tall red head he knew, facing him.

"You really look terrific tonight. I don't know how many of my girl friends have asked me tonight who the tall handsome fellow with the strong arms is."

—she is trying to build me up—no she is not Della—let's see what is her name—I know her name—she looks like sunshine itself—but it's too late—too late. . .

"Oh, I'm just wandering around having a few beers and thinking," he replied slowly as he looked at her ivory white teeth.

—she must know that I was thrown over and feels sorry for me—but I don't want pity—no—but she is very pretty—why is she wasting her charms on me when she could be entrancing one of those other guys. . .

They stood facing each other as she cheerily kept up both sides of the conversation while Joe pondered his contemptible fate. Then, as the band began to play a slow song, Joe gazed at her blankly and asked, "Would you like to dance?"

She accepted as though she was extremely delighted. They began to move slowly. Joe realized that he was getting very unsteady on his feet. As he stared downward at her flaming hair, she pressed very close to him. A feeling of extreme relaxation fell over Joe; the beer was passing into his blood stream and yet an uneasiness lit his mind as though a cigar were being crushed against his cerebrum.

—when the wine turns red—when the wine turns red—when the wine—what have I done—I have ruined my life for nothing—nothing and now there is only ruins left—red when the wine turns red—when the wine turns red—red—red—red wine—

ruins—nothing but ruins and debris—the wine has turned red—oh God, help me—please help me from my despair to come from the depths. . .

Joe backed off and as the red head looked after him questioningly, he suddenly tumbled away and out the door and into the cold night's sprinkle. Leaning against a parked car, he drew several deep breaths in order to clear his unclear head.

—what has happened—red wine—when the wine turns red—

Superimposed on the back of his memory we the image of Della's tear-stained face staring up at him and then turning away to the shoulder of another.

After steadying himself, he forced his legs to carry him down the street. As he reached the intersection he calculated whether he could risk crossing the path of an oncoming car, but as he started to do so he realized he had guessed wrong; the auto screeched around him, almost traveling over the curb. Making his way through the park, he became slightly amused by the way the lights bounced with every step that he attempted and the way the ground came crashing toward him with each thump of his fence-post legs. He lifted his head and stared at the green statue of Garibaldi as he passed.

"All hail, gallant warrior! How many times have you drawn your sword for a devirginized Miss or a failing Mister?" he mumbled aloud as he stumbled on.

Throwing the door open with a crash, he staggered into his bathroom. Upon emerging from that lighted room a few seconds after, he tore off his pants and fell on the bed.

—I will go to church tomorrow—I will go to church tomorrow. . .

He closed his eyes and immediately his bed rose from the ground and twisted and turned as though trying to throw him out. Opening his eyes, he tried to balance himself focusing on the light from the bathroom; but after he had steadied himself he closed them again and the bed bucked up and down, standing him first on his feet and then on his head. Finally he gave up and, riding with the bouncing bed, he fell into a deep sleep.

After who knew how long, Joe suddenly sat up in bed and, without fully realizing what he was doing, leaped up and dashed into the bathroom. Kneeling before the toilet in the nick of time, he felt his whole body seized by a cramp as if his stomach would come up, but instead, a thick, revolting stream of vomit poured from his mouth.

—I'm puking—puking—ughaaaaa. . .

He belched gas a few time and the taste of the acidy residue caused his mouth to feel rotten and putrid; then, with another overpowering burp, more rivers of the foul tasting mixture shot up from his ulcerated depths.

—I will never drink again—Oh God, help me—I will go to church tomorrow and I will never drink again. . .

After staring glumly at the cloudy potion in the bowl, he finally regained his feet and found his bed again; he immediately fell into a deep stupor.

"Wake up, Joe. Wake up!" called Joe's roommate, shaking him.

Mumbling mournfully under his breath, Joe turned over in his bed and saw Butler Baker staring down at him.

"You know that you want to get some studying done, don't you? It's almost three o'clock," said Butler as he set his suitcase down and walked into the bathroom.

After sitting up in bed, Joe looked around the room and then slowly remembered what had happened the night before. He pulled on the pants that he had left sprawled on the floor and felt his way to the refrigerator as Baker stepped from the bathroom.

"Well, how was your weekend?" asked Baker as he threw his suitcase on his bed and began to dispose of its contents in a nearby drawer.

"Ugh." replied Joe as he reached for some tomato juice and splashed it into a glass.

"It was that bad?" Butler inquired as he folded a shirt and tossed it into the drawer.

"It was more than that bad! It was one big nightmare and I just woke up from it," Joe said, tipping the glass and sitting in one of the chairs at the table.

"What happened? Did you have a fight with Della or something?" Butler asked in a comforting tone.

"We didn't fight, but we did break up. It's a long story. I don't want to bother you with it."

"You can tell me if you want to. You know yourself that talking it over sometimes does some good."

—guess it would be better if I got it off my chest—forgot to go to church—it's about three and no church holds services this late. . .

"Well, my little tale goes like this; two nights ago. . ."

Joe explained in some detail how he had told Della that he had not made it into graduate school and then went on to say that last night he had made a fool of himself and Della had left him.

"Maybe it isn't over then," said Butler. "She might not be shunning you because you can't become a doctor or even because her father doesn't think you have the right ethnic qualifications."

"No, it's true that she doesn't love me. You didn't see her facial expressions and the way she acted. She was downright cold to me and I don't think it will change. In fact I'm sure it won't."

"What are you going to do then?" inquired Butler.

"I guess trying to repair the loss would only do more damage to my ego; I guess I will have to start building again from the ruins and 'kick cold turkey.' If I tried to see her again it would ruin me I am sure. She doesn't care anything about me and she has proven that it," Joe explained, hanging his head.

"You're not going to see her again then?" inquired Butler.

"I'm afraid it's too late. You know, you and Della would make a tremendous couple. Her father would surely approve of you and you have some money and a good future. And here you love a devout Methodist. You're on the wrong side of the fence."

"What fence? You know that it has been rough on me forgetting that a fence separates Chris and me, but it does seem to be working out well for both of us. One thing I have always wondered is which farmer built the fence in the first place, but I haven't come up with the correct answer yet," pondered Butler, slamming his suitcase shut and putting it under his bed.

"Well, I guess you can just chalk that up as one of the kicks in the ass that life gives a person," Joe exclaimed, setting the empty glass down on the table.

—my stomach feels foul—wonder if I really have an ulcer—my whole intestinal tract feels as if it has all decomposed into one flowing mass. . .

For the remainder of the day, Joe sat at his desk fighting to make the best of the time remaining before finals, but it was still no use. His mind wandered to the ski slopes of the winter and the hikes of the summer, and he battled with each fantasy to have himself accompanied by some other female than Della but it was no use. He could not picture himself made for anybody except her.

—wish I had some terrible disease to take my mind off of this torment—this is worse than puking every hour of the day—how can I escape myself when sirens are calling. . .

"Please tie me to the mast!" exclaimed Joe suddenly, breaking Butler's stream of thought. He was engrossed in the text, resting on his stomach as he reclined on his bed.

"What did you say?" he asked, looking over at Joe.

"If the sirens call, please tie me to the mast and don't let me go and talk to Della," Joe pleaded with Butler.

"Well, I'll try!" Butler exclaimed astonished.

Joe tried to make the best of the day but he got little from it.

After a sleepless night, Joe arose early and walked across town to his classes. He returned late that afternoon feeling slightly uplifted by his brisk walk home. Upon entering his room, he sat right down at his desk, took out his diary and made an entry: "Monday, April 12

Hello again! Broke up with you know who and am pretty broken up about it. Life has lost its lustre. Now I must find new meaning. Something to cling to. Want to make a tremendous comeback at the school work but that doesn't seem to be working. Grind, Grind, Grind,—why is it that I can't seem to force myself to study? I must, but seem to be procrastinating all of the time.

Rock Sullivan and Sally something or other are making a movie in front of the main building. People lined the Square to see them. Sullivan's a ham. He is playing an escapee from a mental institution and a cop comes up to him and tries to arrest him and walk-ins from all over the park run up to see what is going on and get mad at the cop for hurting the poor guy and then Sullivan escapes in the riot.

Bought a new pipe. Spent too much. When my money runs out, I will really be scared. What's the matter with me? It is med school I should be scared about but that's all over now. Maybe I should become a pimp.

If I must study—why am I not?
Calm down—the world hasn't ended
make ends me
read words
know ideas
Oh, for the neurotic days of yesteryear when I did so well.
Work, work
What was I just thinking?
What? *What!*
My mind is a blank
blank is my mind
is my mind blank
blank my mind is
mind my blank—is. . .

Oh, what will become of me? While I am being tormented I am losing precious time.

My head's spinning—the paper seems to come closer. It's coming closer—a few inches from my nose and my head hasn't moved. My hands are not my own. I can hardly move them right—write—they seem too big—so foreign. Snap out of this daze!

What makes me feel like this?

Question, sir—what makes my hand so big and foreign?

There, it is better now—no the daze is returning—What is happening? I need a smoke to calm down.

Where is my new pipe? Ah hey—what an awful life. I seem to have lost all vigor.

They say extreme stress causes ego defense mechanism—which one is this?

Fantasy? Could be!

Repression? Definitely!

Rationalization? Why not!

Withdrawal? That's it!

I'm afraid that I can't do it deep down inside so I am relaxing and therefore if I flunk it won't be because I tried.

I better write an *'Ode to Ego'* and pep it up:

"Oh Ego, please come too.
Oh Ego, I mean you.
Oh Ego, you make me blue.
Can't you see the mess you're putting me through?
Get motivated!"

Feeling a little better, he picked up a novel that he had been assigned for his English course and began to read. The book was *A Portrait Of the Artist* by Joyce. After reading several pages, he looked up and realized that he had gotten something out of it.

—let's see—he's saying that at first an author has to work at a book and its characters but after he becomes engrossed in it the story begins to pick up itself and go on without the author and the writer can sit back from the stage and enjoy the happenings that are in front of him paring his fingernails or something like that—I have done fairly well at keepng her from overcoming my consciousness but now all of a sudden I feel desperate like I can't live without her—I knew that it would hit me sometime—oh what can I do to alleviate this pain—they call it heart-ache and my heart really does feel like it is going to collapse or something if I don't do something—wish Butler were back from classes so I could talk to him—I will work this energy off even though I don't feel up to it. . .

Rising from his chair, he walked over to his barbells that were standing in the corner of the room and with a swoop picked up a one-hundred pound weight and slowly began to curl it.

—I should have warmed up—I will hurt my back—somehow I should care if I slipped a disc—nobody seems to care anyway my knee seems to be kicking up again—what a mess I am. . .

Vigorously, he went through French curls and then pullovers. After that he went back to front curls.

—I'm getting tired—I will stop—but I haven't really done much—haven't even worked up a good sweat and I want to quit—what's the matter with me am I getting soft—I'm turning into a baby and who knows maybe I will start babbling in a minute—come on get three more out—one twooooooooo—I must quit my arms are too tired—I really am getting chicken—one more threeee—eeeeeeeeee. . .

With a jerk of his back, he finally got the bar to his chin; then he quickly let it down on the floor and stood for several moments, leaning forward with his arms hanging down in a limp position.

—whew—that really made me pooped—I sure have been babying myself for the past few months. . .

After exercising, showering and nibbling at a small serving of tasteless food, Joe forced himself to sit at his desk and stare at the pages of his text, hoping some of the knowledge would assimilate into his buzzing head.

The next evening he was sitting at his desk in a deep revery when the telephone rang. Looking over his shoulder, he watched as Butler slid out of bed and strode over to his desk to pick up the receiver.

"Hello," answered Butler.

Butler stood with a blank expression, but then all at once his eyes widened as he started with a surprised expression at Joe. Still holding his ear to the receiver, he waved his arm toward Joe and moved his lips for Joe to read. Mournfully, Joe shook his head and then sadly burried his face in his crossed arms on the desk.

"Yes, how are you?" Butler continued.

"I'm sorry, he isn't in right now and I don't know when he will be back," Butler continued after a pause.

After a few more aloof words, Butler hung up the telephone and said, "That was Delilah's roommate. She wanted to speak to you. You should have talked to her. It couldn't have done any harm, could it?"

Joe's breath came hard and fast as he said with a spinning head, "You don't know how I feel. I can hardly understand it myself, but I only know that I could not bear to see Della again."

"Well, it's up to you!" exclaimed Butler, shrugging his shoulders and returning to his soft perch.

—why would she want to call me —I know that Della would never have the guts to call me—no I am getting delusions of grandeur to think that her roommate would intercede for her—maybe her roommate wants to level what Della left merely ruined. . .

For the next two hours, Joe pondered deeply on the possible significance of the telephone call. Finally he snatched up the phone to call the number that he knew so well, but it was as if this time he would make a mistake in the dialing. It was almost as if he wanted to. As his finger found the last digit, his breathing became deep and the lump in his throat seemed to be choking him. He was afraid he wouldn't be able to force any sound from his lips if someone answered. Quickly he placed the receiver in the cradle and tried to calm himself. The disconcerting shakiness was causing him to vibrate.

—I can't make a fool of myself—I must live with myself so I better do what is right—but how can I be sure what is right— why have I lost all confidence in myself and everybody—what would Manuel have done in a case like this—I wish he were here to help me instead of dead—will call tomorrow—it is too late at night now anyhow—wonder if Della really wants me— she must be fickle—but no—that isn't like her—wish I could remove these trees so that I could see the woods. . .

Joe finally questioned his roommate about every detail of the short telephone conversation until Butler seemed slightly annoyed at this microscopic examination. Finally Joe went to bed, but he spent a feverish night of indecision.

The next day, Thursday, April 14, Joe, still undecided, sat in a large crowded lecture room waiting for his English professor to enter. Professor Pharoah was one teacher whose class he enjoyed very much.

—if I call her she may feel that she really didn't want me back and at my expense—but maybe—here he comes—he is rather short but so stately looking with that mustache—all eyes are on him—what tremendous effort and capabilities it must have taken to reach his academic stature—the way he stands before the class and quiets them with a look. . .

"As you well know," the professor began, "we are attempting to understand the distinguished works of James Joyce and I hope you have thought about the *Portrait* and pondered over *Ulysses*. In the near future we will attempt to wonder about the dreamland of *Finnigans Wake*. Are there any questions from my previous lectures about the *Portrait* before we begin discussion of the next book?"

"Sir," came a voice from the back of the room. "I wonder if

you could explain the significance of the name of its main character, Stephen Dedalus."

"I can see that you missed an important lecture," Pharoah said with force. "I would strongly suggest that you obtain the notes for that period; however I will say this about it: the name Dedalus alludes to a character from Greek mythology who was said to have constructed a pair of wings from wax and feathers and escaped from the restrictions of a prison tower in which King Minos of Crete was holding him. In this first flight of man, Dedalus escaped to Italy and freedom, and Joyce was showing in his book how he escaped the restricted atmosphere of his environment and found freedom in free and unrestrained arts."

—shall I give him my evaluation—will he be impressed— maybe it won't come out of my mouth correctly—wish I could talk with his force and conviction—I will. . .

Joe raised his hand and felt his metabolism rise sharply as the professor and then the class turned his way.

"Sir," he said in a shaky voice. "I agree perfectly with what you have stated in your previous lectures about the name, but I feel that Joyce meant the name to even go so far as to give in two words—Stephen and Dedalus—the whole structure of this work. I feel that they outline the intense conflict that Joyce felt between two opposing poles of his personality."

Joe listened to his voice as he spoke and realized how raspy and rough it sounded when he was nervous. Was this his voice?

"The one pole that Joyce shows in his *Portrait*," he continued quickly, "is the Dedalus pole, and I feel that this goes far deeper than just man's first flight. I believe that this last name depicts a sexual, sensual, artistic, and secular half of Joyce's personality, because, looking into the mythological story of Dedalus, we find that Dedalus was placed in prison because of his artistic inventive abilities, which had culminated in the creation of an object which looked like a cow; and that the queen of Minos had hidden in this cow in order to have sexual intercourse with a bull. This, according to mythology, results in the birth of the Minotaur."

—they are listening to me—the whole class is hearing what I have to say—maybe what I am saying is worthwhile. . .
"homeland by his own people and the church, setting free the name 'Stephen' refers to Saint Stephen, the first Christian

martyr; and this part of Joyce is the pious, religiously oriented pole of Joyce. Joyce seems to be symbolizing a dichotomy in his own personality, or conflict between religious and artistic values, he felt he could not be an unrestricted and complete artist unless he were outside the prison of the church. And so the story ends with our main actor leaving his homeland and seeking freedom in a far land away, freedom from the restrictions that living in Ireland had put on him. Therefore Joyce felt that the Stephen part of his personality was stoned in his homeland by his own people and the church, setting free the Dedalus in him."

—is he impressed—wish I could have had more time to explain fully what I meant—I didn't explain myself quite correctly—he doesn't seem to be making any comment on it—he is pointing to another person in the class—that person is asking an irrelevant question that doesn't have to do with what I said—what did that small silence mean after I had finished—what did that expression mean—it looked as if he was impressed by what I said—what if he approached me sometime and asked me if I would care to go to graduate school in the English department and then I became his assistant—stop dreaming it will never be true—a poor idiot. . .

For the remainder of the period, Joe continued to sit sprawled in his chair, looking up in awe and admiration at his professor. He felt a slight tinge of satisfaction; he had gotten some recognition, if only for a few seconds.

Finally the class came to an end and Joe folded his notebook and ambled into the hall and into the elevator. Just as the elevator doors was closing he glanced up and saw Della standing in the hall, turning her head as if she were looking for someone. Joe's heart leaped from his chest and began to beat double as he pressed forward in the elevator in an attempt to get out of the crowded car.

—what is she doing here—she is supposed to be going to her French class now—is she looking for me—yes she must be looking for me—she misses me—oh no—the elevator isn't going to stop—I must have walked right past her and she didn't see me.

"Fourth floor please," Joe called excitedly to the elevator operator.

"Odd floors only!" exclaimed the short, round headed elevator operator.

"O.K., three then," Joe said, irritated.

As the doors opened, Joe sprang forward and leaped up the stairs, making his way up the several flights to where he had seen Della. Many people were slowly ascending the narrow stairs, others were zipping down at a fast clip. This confusion slowed Joe's climb.

—wish these people would step to one side—can't they see that I am in a hurry— when I skip steps it hurts my knee—hope this stair climbing isn't going to hurt me—come on—come on—people can't you see I'm in a hurry. . .

Finally he burst through the stairwell doors out onto the floor he had just left, but the halls were crowded and Della had vanished. Straining his neck and zigzagging his way hurriedly through the crowd, he made a path to the room where Della had her French class, he waited until the class was almost half over, but she didn't seem to be in it. He stood in the hall, listening to the complicated pronunciations of the teacher as she wrote on the blackboard, expecting Della to step up at any second. His mind buzzed with thoughts of her and of the many good times that they had had together. Then the flash came to him.

—what if she weren't looking for me—she was talking to one guy at the beer blast and I think he is in my class—maybe she was waiting for him wanting to punish and torment me more—it wasn't like her to meet me at my classes. . .

Suddenly he felt out of place standing by the door of this class room. It was as if he were naked in the hall and somebody might come by and see him there. Quickly he slipped away, and hanging his head, he found his way to the street and directed his feet eastward.

—I'm a little early but guess I will go now—it will keep my mind off of this feeling—walk fast and forget about how you are—this strange sensation makes me feel as if I am going to die—as if my whole rib cage would fall from me. . .

Walking briskly, at times sprinting ahead through the sharp city air, Joe finally made his way up town. After walking for some time, he found himself standing before a large, stately looking hospital that was tucked away among other buildings. Before entering, he glanced around and cringed as he saw the MD license plates that lined the street. Watching his feet, he ducked into the swinging doors and made his way down a single hall to another portal, Just then two women came by talking fast to each other, and he also heard the speaker paging a doctor. After slipping into a small chamber, he found his starched gray jacket, and taking off his coat, he forced his arms into the stiff sleeves.

—I love this atmosphere—wish that it didn't haunt me now with the remembrance of my failure. . .

Proudly throwing his shoulder back, he signed his name on a page headed Volunteers and then walked to the elevator. As he emerged from the elevator on the pediatrics floor he could hear several children yelling.

"Looks like you really have a mess of noisy ones today," he remarked to the nurse.

"We sure do," the nurse remarked in a distressed voice. "Are you Joe?" she inquired.

"Yes, I am. How did you know?"

"I have heard about you and the way you can handle the children."

"Well, I am notorious then," Joe remarked.

"Nicely notorious," she exclaimed with a smile. "Want to try and tame that tribe of Indians that we have today? They won't listen to any of the nurses and we have been having a terrible time with them all day."

"I'll give it a try," Joe answered as he turned down the hall toward the noise.

—overestimated—always overestimated—I'm not really good with children—people tend to see the good things I do and brush over my failures and then when the critical analysis of what counts comes—I don't know if I can take those noisy brats today—I just want to be left alone without the nurses telling me where to go and what to do. . .

Joe gazed longingly at the small babies, who were rolling around in their cribs, as he passed. Upon reaching a room full of young boys, he surveyed the situation to see what could be done.

"What is your name?" he asked a small boy who came running past him whooping.

The boy went right on past without even noticing. Advancing resolutely and taking a deep breath, Joe addressed a few words to a group of four boys who were in a huddle: "How would you guys like to play cars?"

"Cars?" exclaimed the leader of the group, walking toward him.

"Yes, we can play race cars," Joe exclaimed, trying to sound enthusiastic. Walking over to a cabinet, Joe removed several toy automobiles that were on the shelf and passed them out to seven of the boys who had followed him.

"This is the way we do it," he explained, kneeling. "We start back of this." He made an imaginary line on the floor. "Then push the cars as hard as you can and the car that goes the farthest wins. Would you like to play?" he asked, motioning to two boys who were quietly watching what he was doing.

"Are you a doctor?" one boy asked.

Joe felt his face flush deeply.

Now the ward was quiet except for the crying of one baby and the low cheering of the boys as they pushed their cars ahead, each trying to win.

—for a few minutes I have them diverted but soon they will go back to their old ways of annoying the nurses and really sick patients and I can't think of any other games.

Joe's fears were confirmed. After ten minutes, the children were off again, yelling and screaming through the ward.

—don't feel like I want to keep up with them today—I just want to have quiet and do as I want without being told what to do. . .

With this thought Joe made his way back to the cribs at the head of the hall. Looking in the door, he saw several babies standing in their beds pleading to him with their eyes to hold them.

—I love them because all they demand of me is a little loving and they are quiet—they don't have to be amused all they want is to be held. . .

Trying to be impartial he walked to the first crib and bent over to see a tiny baby staring up him with a big smile.

"Goo, goo, you're a very pretty baby," he exclaimed in baby talk as he lifted the soft wriggling form. "Yes, you're a pretty baby with those big blue eyes. The painter, Keane, would be surprised to see that eyes do come as large as yours."

—what is this horrible feeling that I have—I am afraid that I will drop this beautiful bundle of life—how can I have such

112

a feeling—am I a monster—wait let me look closer at this emotion. . .

Joe walked to a nearby chair and sat down, still smiling and making faces at the delighted infant in his arms.

—no—I am really having dark feelings that I can't understand—it's not that I am afraid of accidentally dropping this precious thing but that I am afraid that I will act out this compulsion to dash the baby on the floor—how disconcerting. . .

A cold shudder raced through Joe's body as he sat pondering this unacceptable impulse while the lamb-like child looked up at him contentedly, soft and satisfied gurgling noises floating from her mouth.

—she is so trusting and yet. . .

Joe thought about the human race and what the consequences would be if everyone acted on all of his irrational impulses or even if another person simply realized the feelings that a stranger was having.

—the child's mother would rush in here and snatch her child from my arms if she realized that I had this feeling but it is the sane man who is not ruled by his impulses but by his reason. . .

Joe saw that the baby was holding her arms out to him, so he pulled her to his shoulder. As she groped at his lapel with her chubby fingers, he patted her on the back and strolled around inspecting the other infants.

—I should make an ode to a baby—all they want is a little hugging and they are contented—guess if I were a mother I would not feel quite that way—they all want me to hold them—wish I had time to amuse them all—it's so quiet and peaceful in here—I could stay here and take care of them forever—here comes a student nurse. . .

"Hi!" Joe exclaimed as the nurse entered. "You must be new on this floor. I haven't seen you before."

"Yes," she exclaimed as she walked up to him. "The students change floors every now and then to get experience on every floor."

"Don't you love this floor?" Joe inquired.

"This is by far my favorite. I love to take care of the children, but today has really been hectic, trying to get the older children at the end of the hall under control. I hear there is one boy, a volunteer, who comes here every week. They say he can handle those brats when they won't listen to the nurses. Mrs. Soloman was telling me that he was also playing with a baby a few weeks ago and when it came time for him to leave, the baby toddled after him crying for all it was worth. She said it followed him all of the way to the elevator leaving a long puddle of tears behind it and the nurses were surprised to see that the child could walk more than a few feet."

Joe nodded as he heard these words and opened his mouth to make a comment when the student nurse again interrupted.

"That is a beautiful baby you have there. Just look at those blue eyes," she exclaimed, moving closer and shaking its hand.

"Would you like her?" Joe asked, holding the baby up to her.

"They are such delicate things that I feel as if I might drop it," she exclaimed receiving the child.

After an examining, startled look, Joe walked away to a crib in the corner and picked up a dark-skinned infant that was standing in its crib watching his every move. The baby rested its face against Joe's chest as its curly hair brushed against his neck.

—you are a beautiful child—you are patient while many of the other children cry and scream to be held but you wait in silence—guess we better go and find out what the mob out there is doing and see if we can calm the nurse's nerves—if only people wouldn't overestimate me all of the time—what if I were to fail with this tribe of youngsters and the nurses saw—I would lose my notoriety. . .

Holding the clinging child with his left arm, Joe walked into the room where the older children were busy yelling and climbing over beds.

—what could these kids be diagnosed—they look healthier than I am. . .

"How would you like to play an exciting game?" Joe asked as the children stopped momentarily to gaze at him.

"What game do you have?" asked one child in a thick Puerto Rican accent.

"You all go quietly into the playroom and I will show you the game," Joe said, trying to sound enthusiastic again.

The children ran whooping down the hall past the nurses' station while the nurses cringed before the coming onslaught. As Joe walked into the playroom he saw all faces were turned to him, hoping that he would have a great exciting game for them. Glancing around the room Joe said, "The name of the game is Find the Dolly." He walked over to a table that had a small plastic doll on it. "Someone hides the doll while the rest of us stay outside, and when the person who hid the doll says 'ready,' we all come in the room and try to find the doll. The one who finds the doll first can then hide it and let the others do the looking."

Not acting overly excited, the children began to play the game as Joe, still holding the quiet, grateful infant, directed the proceedings. After some time had passed and two fights had nearly broken out between two of the larger youngsters, Joe ran out of games and patience, and began to feel like he wanted to be left alone to do as pleased. Seeing that the children had lost interest, he threw up his hands and left them to their own devices. Walking into the babies' room again, he quietly amused the infants for the remainder of the time.

After some minutes, he glanced at his watch.

—five o'clock already—I better get going—have a lot of studying tonight—it has worked fairly well—I have diverted my mind from disconcerting thoughts about her but now it is all coming back to me—why do I feel that this sensation is like a disease. . .

"Well, little one, it's time for me to go. Here, I must put you back into your bed and get home so I can finish out the semester. There, you can sleep and have a good time thinking of your mommy and other things that little ones think of. Your face tells me that you're going to cry. Please don't cry. You have been such a good and brave little baby. I imagine that you get much less attention than many of the other children, but you acted so bravely before. Yes, don't cry. I will hold you for a while longer. There, there, now stop your whimpering. Sure, you're just as human as the rest of the children, even though some people might not think you are as beautiful as any of the others."

Just then a cart stacked with food trays was pushed into the room by a short plump woman.

"Are you going to help us feed the young ones? We sure could use the help," she said in a high, cheerful voice.

"That one you have is really a hard one to feed. He hasn't

eaten for two days," she exclaimed, thrusting a tray at him.

"I guess I can put off my homework for a while and see if I can help him," Joe answered, taking the tray which held different colored substances.

—maybe all he needs is a little loving and understanding—the poor fellow—he might be fighting off Turner's Syndrome. . .

"Here we go," Joe exclaimed brightly as he held a spoonful of green matter to the child's mouth. "Come on, try it. It's good."

Finally he forced the food onto the child's tongue and, smacking his lips the infant obediently swallowed it.

"See, it wasn't so bad. All you need is a little time and care," he whispered as he watched the woman forcing another child to eat as quickly as possible. "You must understand that she must feed all of these children herself and can't stop to study your psychology like she should. What she needs is more people to volunteer help. Here, try some of this. It looks like sirloin steak."

After the baby had emptied the contents of the plate, Joe wiped his mouth and put him in his crib; he realized that he must get back to his apartment and do some work if he was not to waste the whole day. Hurrying quickly out so he would not know whether he was missed or not, he finally reached the sidewalk and made his way along the streets toward home.

—oh Della you have finally come to haunt me again—why can't you leave me alone and let me forget about you before I go out of my mind—the night is beautiful and so invigorating—feel much better knowing that I have done a little to help better the human race—there are so many people who are out to destroy all the others who are unlike themselves—that bum looks like he is going to stagger into me—wonder what it would be like to be a bum and wander about the streets with nothing to do—really has an ugly face. . .

Upon reaching his apartment, Joe force fed himself and then immediately sat down to work. He managed to forget about Della for a while, and concentrate on his studies.

The next afternoon Joe hurried out of his last lecture for the day and ran west to the church near Sheridan Square. As he entered the dimly lit fortress, he made his way to the last seat in the side aisle and said a quick prayer, for the service had already started. Looking up, he stared intently at the minister who was already in the pulpit.

"Matthew 27:38: '. . . then were there two thieves crucified with him, one on the right hand and another on the left. And they that passed by reviled him wagging their heads and saying, "Thou that destroyest the temple and buildest it in three days, save thyself. If thou be the Son of God, come from the cross:" Likewise also the chief priests mocking him, with the scribes and elders said, "He saved others; himself he cannot save. If he be the King of Israel, let him now come down from the cross, and we will believe him. He trusted in God; let him deliver him now, if he will have him; for he said, 'I am the Son of God.'"'
'The thieves also, which were crucified with him, cast the same in his teeth. . .'

"We are gathered here together to celebrate the darkest day in all Christendom; Palm Sunday, the eve of Christ's crucifixion. Any yet, my beloved, it is in fact one of the brightest day this world has ever known because it preceded Easter day which is the day for which we thank the Lord

"How many times have we heard the phrase, 'Christ died for your sins'; or 'believe and ye shall be saved through the blood of Jesus Christ your Savior; or how many many hundreds of times have we heard the words 'Savior,' 'blood,' 'lamb,' 'crucifixion,' 'salvation,' 'cross' and similar terms? Yet, how many of us actually realize what these terms mean to us? How many of us actually realize what Christ went through on that dark day? Try to imagine right now, my people, just what he did for us. First, add all of the sins that the whole human race can have committed through all of the untold ages and put them on the person of one being—Christ. Then imagine him being mocked, spit at, beaten and crowned with a crown of thorns. Then imagine his loneliness after all his friends had forsaken him, imagine his physical exhaustion after having had no sleep all night, and weight him with a cross, carried over several miles. Are you getting the picture? But that isn't all, my people; now nail that flesh to the cross. Picture yourself with nails being driven through your hands and feet. It would hurt, wouldn't it? Yes, it may seem painful, just having your hands and feet pierced with sharp nails, but now stand the person up and imagine him hanging only by his hands and feet. Yes, ouch is simply an understatement. Now leave him hanging there in

117

the sun for hours with no one to offer him sympathy, and many to jeer and mock him, and then hear how a man who is sharing a similar ordeal tells him to save himself.

"Yes, my people, it must be a terrible thing to suffer such torment and yet have it in one's power to be able to save oneself with a word. You may think that it would be easier to suffer such torment if a person had it in his power to stop it whenever he wanted to, but think about it. What would it be like if you had resigned yourself to go through torture, yet you knew you had it in your power to say to your torturer 'stop' whenever you wanted? Think about the situation and I am sure you will realize that this power would not help you to endure the torment, that on the contrary, it would make it harder for you.

"Yes, fellow believers, whether we can imagine it or not, whether we realize it or not, Christ did much for us. We should not blame any scapegoat, or condemn anyone for our misery but ourselves. Too often we are so willing to blame our troubles on others when it was ourselves who caused them.

"What did Christ our Lord do in such adversity, my people? He suffered in silence and did not even attempt to get even with his tormenters, because he realized his suffering was for the ultimate good of the human race. In fact, he did not want revenge, but even asked forgiveness, saying, 'Forgive them, Lord, for they know not what they do.'

"Yes, my brethren, he died so that he could obtain the ultimate victory which was that the whole world should be saved. Yes, too often this great message goes in one ear and out the other because the church-goer hears it so often, but we must realize what Christ went through to know just how much love he did have for us. He suffered in silence so that we might be snatched from the eager fingers of the evil one. But we must believe in him. That is all he asks of us. He says, 'Believe and ye shall be saved.'

"This is a glorious gospel, for it is not a funeral which we are celebrating today, but a resurrection. Not death, but life, and life within the reach of anyone who wants to follow; so finally we will come to know Christ and his abundant grace. Out of death comes life. What a glorious and original way to show the world how misguided it is. Of course, this does not mean that we should sit and waste away until death overtakes us. On the contrary, this new forward look should give us new life to go on and do the things which Christ would have us do; and therefore this death of Christ leaves it up to us, and it can mean a new and vigorous life ahead. Of course, we will run into stone walls and fall, but just as Jesus suffered in silence, so must we, feeling happy that some day we will win, just as he procured victory, for it says in Luke. . ."

CHAPTER III

—seems as if I am always hurrying—there it is on the opposite hill—can't be late my first day at work—hope I will like it there—feels so good to be out of school and the pressure off—at least I passed all of my courses and now I am free—yes free as a bird and all I have to contend with now is making some money and resting—relax and try to forget—and to think I told her to try to remember the bad experience she had and now I am trying to forget—must learn to cultivate a taste for other girls and get rid of this feeling of isolation that haunts me—better go faster or I will really be late—that would not look good on my first day—I have a diploma and it is all mine and no one can take it away—hope the army takes their time to draft me—maybe later I will feel like trying to go into graduate school—I would make a good dentist or biologist but now I know that it would not work—maybe the army will be good for me and help me find myself—red light ahead—why is it that I always get red lights when in a hurry—just when I get a little forward motion the light changes—hope this one doesn't take long—ouch this leg is really bad—maybe I should have taken another Percaden pill. If I go in limping, they won't let me work—I will have to try and walk as straight as I can—wonder what it will be like to work at this mental hospital—hope I will be placed on an admissions ward so I may try a hand at helping some of them—hurry up light change I am late—there it goes—get moving—car stalled—let the clutch out too fast—never can seem to get used to this car—there moving again—I know that it will be great to be able to try and help rehabilitate those poor patients—I will get a feeling of satisfaction that I won't get at a higher paying job—wish that guy in front of me would go a little faster—frustration—the whole world is frustrating—am really anxious to see what Bethlehem is really like—it can't be as bad as those books that I have read—the people who write books that tell of the horrors of mental institutions are only telling the bad parts and magnifying them, but I imagine they all could use some help and lots more money—probably Bethlehem is no exception and it could probably use more funds and more doctors—wish I could have been one of the psychiatrists too—squirrel running across the road—did I miss him—yes—wonder why my heart always jumps like that when some insignificant little animal runs in front of me—let's see which fork do I take—oh yes there's a sign—Bethlehem Hospital —Authorized Personnel Only—really hazy on this side of the valley. . .

Joe guided his auto through the gray morning fog up the long winding driveway. The sun gave a phosphorescent glow to the heavens. Joe scrutinized the large rambling structures that covered the green summer hillside. Faded red bricks jutted out of the earth forming wings to taller structures. The bare red brick, interrupted only by tall windows, each capped with one granite keystone, gave Joe a blank eerie feeling of evil curiosity which might only be satisfied by a look behind those walls. It was as if a collection of eyes behind all of those dark windows, was watching this lonely car as it sped up the driveway, and the spirits in those dark chambers would come to life when Joe entered. As he steered around the building, he thought he heard a high pitched cackling voice; the noise made him start. Slowing the auto, he turned his head and caught a glimpse of someone pressing against the wire grate over the window, his hands stretched in a V position over his head.

—poor fellow—probably is afraid of himself and doesn't like being locked up—if they had more doctors in the world they could turn out more patients and those poor bits of humanity would at least have the pleasure of living outside of one of their cages—seven o'clock—I am a little late—seems that no matter how hard I try to be on time I manage to be late. . .

Turning the car, Joe parked it in the parking lot he was directed to and then got out. He made his way to a side door where he was also directed. Ringing the bell, he stood peering through the glass in the door and waited.

—I have to walk as straight as possible or they will send me home—yes I should have taken another pill to kill the pain better—if I work for awhile my leg will get better like it did before and if I take care of it better it will stop hurting—someone's coming. . .

121

The thick wooden portal opened slowly to reveal a slightly bent elderly man who was unshaven and wearing a faded tweed suit.

"You must be Joe Mephibosheth?" he asked in a friendly but subdued voice.

"That's right," Joe replied in a cheerful voice. "I was instructed to come to this door."

"Yes, of course. Follow me, please."

Joe followed the man down a long dim corridor at the end of which another door was locked and unlocked. Then they entered a small office.

"This is Mr. Mephibosheth," the man said, speaking to someone out of the line of Joe's vision.

"Come in, Mr. Mephibosheth," called a woman's voice as Joe stepped over the threshold. Before him at a large desk sat a middle aged woman with a serious countenance and a voice to match. "You're late," she said softly as she pushed a bobby pin through her hair to fasten her nurse's cap more securely.

"Yes, I am sorry," Joe said, hanging his head momentarily and cutting his sentence short of an explanation.

"Please sit down," she said, motioning him to a chair. "My name is Mrs. Machir. I will be your supervisor for as long as you work on these wards. Have you studied the literature and rules that were given you by the front office?"

"Yes, I have."

"Are there any questions about it?"

Her lips moved and Joe thought about his leg and how it was paining him. He hoped that she would not notice it. After a short interview, she removed a ring of keys from a drawer and held them up for Joe to see.

"These will be your keys from now on. You will be held directly responsible if they are stolen or lost because the locks to this hospital have not been changed for many years—due to the lack of money; therefore losing your keys is a serious offense. This key unlocks all of the male wards. If you see an M in front of the ward number you will know that it is a male ward and that you can open the door; however, your key will not open the female ward doors which are marked F. This key goes to the window guards and this one to the shower. This is the key for the attendant's toilet and the rest you can find out later as you work on the wards. Come and I will show you where you will work."

Following her quickly out of the office, he soon found himself approaching a large pair of double doors at the end of the corridor. A pungent aroma of stale tobacco came to Joe's nostrils as they entered a large chamber. The room was dimly lit because there was exposure only on one side. Joe could see about seventy men scattered about the expansive concrete floor. The patients were dressed in street clothes and most of them were sitting in wooden chairs; others were walking slowly about. Joe could see that a few were watching his movements and he experienced a sensation of power and excitement as he looked steadily ahead and wondered what this environment would hold in store for him. He was agog with the possibilities. Soon he found himself being led down a hallway lined with wooden doors; each had a small window covered with thick wire screening. These portals, Joe could see, opened to cells. As they strode past, Joe saw a boyish looking figure who called to him from behind one of the apertures, "Come here! Could I talk to you a minute! Hey you! you, you, you, could I talk to you a minute!"

—wonder what that guy did to be put in. . .

"Is there something wrong with your leg?" the nurse asked, startling Joe.

"Why do you ask?" Joe inquired quickly, feeling very self-conscious.

"You seem to have a limp, If you have a bad leg you shouldn't be working here because you will be on your feet all day."

—will she send me home—my leg will get better. . .

"Oh, well!" he exclaimed, trying to act as if he had just noticed it. "As a matter of fact, it has been hurting me a little the past few days, but I doubt if it is anything serious. If I weren't able to work, I wouldn't have come today." Joe gritted his teeth and bent his knee a litle more to walk correctly.

Mrs. Machir opened two more double doors and they proceeded up another door-lined corridor to a similar auditorium filled with men.

"OK, if you're sure that it doesn't hurt you. It's better to say if you are having physical problems because there could be dire consequences."

—wonder what she means by dire consequences—these men

123

don't look much different than anyone else—it's rather quiet in here and everybody seems to be minding his own business—this leg—wish I could cut it off—wonder if it looks as I'm limping now. . .

Looking ahead, Mrs. Machir then questioned, "What does a boy with your education want to work as an attendant for?"

"I just want a rest from school and to kill time until I decide what I want to do or until I get called into the service. Anyway, maybe I'll decide to be a social worker or something, and this is good experience," he explained, looking at still another pair of doors that they were coming upon.

"Then you won't be with us long?"

"It's hard to say. I may be drafted in a couple of months or I may never be, but one thing is for sure and that is, I would rather be working at a job in which I felt I was doing a little good for humanity than one where I was making more money but despised the work."

She did not answer as she inserted her key into the door with an M38 painted on it. The barrier swung open and they stepped inside. Suddenly Joe's head swam with impressions quite different from those which he has just accustomed himself to as they had passed through the other wards.

—this ward is noisier—that smell—it stinks here—smells like human excrement—that ugly spiny man huddled in the corner by the cell door—the patients down the hall are dressed differently—wearing ragged blue jeans—that man is almost naked—air is stifling—so smelly and the sunlight shining through the window reflects the dust in the air—makes the room look hazy and thick—what is this godforsaken place. . .

Joe stood dazed, peering down a similar dim hall lined with cells; but in the auditorium at the end, he saw heavy, thick, wire-screen windows and many creatures who were sitting listlessly on benches or walking through the tunnels of sunlight. The physical structure of the ward didn't seem much different to Joe, but it was definitely different. It had a dangerous, forbidding atmosphere, and the people that Joe saw looked very different. Most of them were shaven nearly bald and showed angular faces with protruding ears. These creatures had a motley, menacing appearance which made Joe feel as if he were in another world, one of unreality, colored with browns and grays.

After recovering from this thick momentary impression, Joe

noticed that Mrs. Machir had turned to one side and gone into the cell directly to the right. The open door revealed a large cubicle with a wire window; in one corner was a cloth mattress strewn with pieces of shredded cloth. A clean looking Negro wearing a white shirt and black tie was directing a wrinkled, barefoot patient as he picked up the torn particles. Joe could hear this attendant tell the nurse that one of the patients had gotten one of the attendants around the neck. Finally, after exchanging a few more words which Joe couldn't make out, they came out and faced Joe.

"Mr. Angus, this is Mr. Mephibosheth. He will be assigned to your supervision. Mr. Mephibosheth, you stay here and Angus will show you what to do. He is in charge on this ward."

"Pleased to meet you," Angus said, shaking hands.

"The pleasure is all mine, Mr. Angus," Joe returned, feeling ill at ease.

"Well, I must go now so. . . Oh yes, while I am thinking of it," Mrs. Machir said in her low monotone, "send that patient's report to the front office as soon as possible."

"Yes, I will get to it right away, Mrs. Machir," Angus answered politely as he took his key from his belt and let her back out through the door from which she had entered.

"We have to take the patients downstairs to eat breakfast," Angus said as he closed the door again. They started to walk down the hall past the skinny man who was huddled against the wall.

"How many patients do you have on this ward?" Joe inquired; he was trying to keep alert so as to be ready if any of the patients they were approaching attacked him.

"The census today is ninety-two, but it varies from time to time," he answered turning his head as if looking for someone.

"Goodman!" Angus yelled, "Come on over here. I'd like you to meet our new man. The front office finally hired us some help."

Angus was looking at a man who was on the other side of the ward holding a pair of old shoes. Joe estimated this distinguished looking attendant to be in his fifties; the man had a brush cut and deep folds marked the sides of his mouth, extending to the corners of his nostrils.

"Well, it's about time we had some help around here!" he exclaimed in a slightly hoarse, authoritative voice. Just then he dropped the shoes into the lap of a seated patient and yelled,

125

"Put them on!" The man cringed and quickly obeyed.

Having reacted rather nervously to Goodman's actions, Joe tried to cover it by initiating the introduction and offering his hand as the attendant approached.

"My name is Mephibosheth, Joe Mephibosheth."

"Everybody calls me Goodman, so that's what you can call me, Mep. . ."

"Mephibosheth," Joe corrected.

"Well, I've got work to do," said Angus as he opened the door to a cell that was an office.

"If you can get used to the smell of the piss and shit you can get used to this ward," Goodman exclaimed, slapping a small man on the back who was curiously edging closer and making Joe nervous with his approach.

"We're running off schedule," Angus called from the office, cutting the conversation short.

"Thirty eight, let's go!" Goodman yelled in a commanding voice.

Just then the room began to swarm with a multitude of faces and contours. The motionless suddenly became mobile and this throng made Joe realize how full the room really was. Tall, short, fat and small patients gained their feet and began to shuffle, walk and grope toward Joe who was standing at the opening of the corridor. Taking several steps to the side, Joe stood and eyed the motley parade. Some were dressed in wrinkled street clothes, but most were wearing baggy coveralls and blue shirts. Many had torn and dirty clothes. As he stood to the side, Joe watched their faces turning his way; their heads bobbed as they came by and went down the hall toward an open door. Some were clinging to their baggy coveralls, others were making gestures, and many bent their shaven heads toward the floor.

—what make these people seem so unreal and evil—what is the difference from the other two wards—most of these are dressed in blue work clothes—maybe it's their faces or the smell here. . .

Standing by incredulously, he examined this ghastly parade. Some of the patients gazed his way, others seemed to make crude gestures toward him. One tall man hobbled along, dragging one leg behind, and as he passed Joe noticed that his eye was on him. The other eye of this man was glassy and dead, and his left arm was shriveled. Trying not to notice that he being watched, Joe concentrated on this thin straight creature, and all at once noticed he had brought his right arm from his side and, with a peculiar twist of his wrist and a clicking sound from his mouth, was addressing a hoarse, almost inaudible hello to him.

"How are ya?" Joe returned quickly with a short smile.

"I'm fine, how are you?" the man said, making that clicking noise with his mouth between hoarse blasts and simultaneously giving the rising gesture again with his good arm.

"All right," Joe replied almost inaudibly, glancing away not knowing what to expect.

The man stood for a second and then began to be jostled in the crowd. Pushing one of the patients who had bumped into him, the man hobbled slowly away, still making that sucking noise in his cheek.

"Come on over here and give me a hand with these stragglers," Goodman called to Joe as he roughly pulled a seated patient to his feet by the shirt. The patients slouched past Joe as he made his way toward the attendant.

"Here, shove Benjin over to the door," Goodman commanded, pointing to a bald Negro man who was making gestures in the air and who seemed completely preoccupied.

"Come on, Benjin. Let's go eat breakfast," Joe pleaded pleasantly.

"Are you Mamma? I'm Papa! I'm Mamma and you're Papa. That the wall. Bench! Bench!" The man jabbered away as he pounded the flat of his palm on the dark wooden bench and then put his hands in the front of his loose overalls.

"That's not the way to do it!" Goodman exclaimed as he yanked Benjin to his feet and shoved him forward, "He's like a wheelbarrow. He usually doesn't move unless he's pushed. Gowann, Benjin!" Goodman shouted at the standing man who was busy pointing his fingers around and naming the different objects that he saw.

Realizing that this man was probably predictable, Joe pushed him gently down the hall.

"Charlie, are you Charlie? See what I got," he said, reaching into his pocket of his faded jeans and pulling out a dirty sock. "Sock, sock," he said, emphasizing these words in his deep, clear bass voice.

"Yea, sock, now come on!" Joe repeated, pressing him gently toward the open door.

"It's good to chew on, see!" Benjin stuck the dirty end into his mouth.

Shocked, Joe quickly yanked the cloth from his mouth and exclaimed in surprise, "No, you'll get sick chewing on that." He then pushed the man slowly to the top of the steps and the patient began slowly to descend.

Just then Joe noticed that the old man who had been leaning against the wall of the corridor was still huddled there. He went over to awaken him and suddenly noticed that this man also had one eye. The other socket bore a mixture of reds and grays in its irregular interior. As if with the spring of youth, the man leaped to his feet and started quickly toward the open door.

Looking around, Joe saw Goodman herding the last straggler. All at once Joe saw Goodman's face change and his eyes and mouth widen as if in alarm.

"Look out!" he yelled at Joe. Swinging around Joe felt a slashing pain in his bad leg and saw that the old man was recoiling to give him another kick. Stunned from the pain, Joe tried to elude the blow as Goodman leaped down the hall and knocked the old man off balance.

"Who gave the dummy shoes?" Goodman called into the air as he shoved the man against the wall and forced him to the floor. Then he pulled at both of the dummy's legs and yanked off his shoes. Standing back, Goodman then watched as the man quickly slinked down the stairs.

"The dummy's got quite a kick for an old man," he said turning around and addressing Joe. "Are you all right?"

"I guess so," Joe gasped under intense pain. "You go . . . go on. I'll be down in a minute."

"Are you sure you're all right? We can get an X-ray taken to be sure because they are pretty strict about reporting accidents."

"Yes, I'm sure I'm OK. Thank you for stopping him from kicking me again," Joe said in a breathy voice, still feeling the intense pain shooting from his knee joint.

"Think nothing of it," Goodman exclaimed in his good natured, dogmatic voice. "Lock the door at the bottom of the stairs when you come down," he added as he stepped around the corner at the first landing of the dark stairwell.

Taking a deep breath, Joe glanced toward the office to be sure Angus wasn't watching and then, gritting his teeth and listening to his heaving breath, went forward. He lowered himself step by step, half a step at a time, and every movement of his leg made him writhe with pain.

—what are the consequences—will I be fired—must force myself to walk. . .

Each movement made him feel as though he was dipping himself in ice water, and he could feel his face become hot as he reached the bottom of the gray stairs.

—purgatory—if only I could trade this in for a wooden leg until it heals. . .

Glancing down, Joe saw a pile of human excrement to one side of the steel door in front of him. He eyed it again, but it was as if he experienced the sight of human feces lying before him every day. The pain preoccupied and controlled his mind and only a peripheral awareness of the brown matter reached him; surprise and disgust were far from him as he advanced into the cellar and locked the door behind him with his keys.

Clamping his insensitive fingers around his keys, he then walked toward a bright screened-in area where the patients were seated. He had a vague awareness of pipes that ran above his head along the long passage way, and he noticed that the smell of concrete and moistness in the air cooled his nostrils; he felt his eyes constrict with each agonizing step and felt his blood being drained to the sensitive, swelling limb.

As he stood immobile before the portal of the brightly lit dining room, a greater awareness of his environment returned to him.

The patients were all seated on heavy steel benches and bending over long, shiny, metal tables. The clatter of spoons, their only eating utensil, and low muttering, interspersed with the loud demands of the attendants, played a strange symphony in the air.

Goodman was walking around telling the patients to stay seated. Another pleasant looking Negro attendant was spooning oatmeal into an old man's mouth. This patient would unwillingly take the food into his cheeks, but then let it seep from between his lips and down his chin into the spoon that the attendant had poised there. The spoon was then shoveled into the patient's mouth again and the second time, he swallowed.

129

Another attendant was leaning against the wall watching out for troublemakers.

"They've got good table manners, don't they?" Goodman exclaimed as he walked toward Joe. "See that one," he said, pointing to a man who was bent over his oatmeal: "At every meal, he drinks his coffee and then pisses in his cup. Keep an eye on that one over there because he steals the patients' food, and don't hit that one because he is really mean. Getting him riled will turn him on for hours. He's like a rattlesnake. If you leave him be, he's all right, but watch out if you stir him up. That real big one there looks mean, but he's one of the meekest ones here. He's friendly and does what he is told and even saved me from getting killed once. A patient hit me with a bench leg once and knocked me cold, but they told me that Jud Icarus caught him before he could hit me again. Jud held him down until help came. They say that he killed his brother, but I find that hard to believe and anyway, if I was ever in a fight, I'd like to have him along."

Goodman surveyed the room as he talked and then yelled, "Sit down, Romanoff!"

Joe knew that these sights and sounds would horrify and depress him if he were to pay strict attention, but as it was, his senses were dulled and his mind distracted by the pain and worry over his leg.

One shirtless creature was consuming the whites of hard-boiled eggs and then rolling each yolk across the table onto the floor. Another, who sat very straight, poured all of his food into one heaping bowl and then licked his dishes clean and stacked them neatly into a pile after having wiped each one carefully with his shirt tail. When he had finished, this patient reached across the table and collecting the other empty plates, began to wash them in the same way. The attendant who had been leaning against the wall, walked up behind him and with one strong hand on each shoulder, forced him back down on the bench; then he stood over him as he ate the concoction of fruit, cereal and eggs that was in the bowl in front of him.

—is this mental illness—it can't be—the orientation book said that they aren't much different from us—maybe this is a very regressed ward or maybe mental institutions are snake pits. . .

Joe knew that he was also supposed to be keeping order, but he stood immobile and watched as the patients ate with their

130

fingers, lapped with their mouths or shoveled with their spoons. As he surveyed this faceless group, he saw one man whom he had already encountered. The dummy who had kicked him had gotten up from his bench and walked to the edge of the wall where he stayed squatting the same way he had done upstairs. That reminded Joe that there was another patient with one eye and he looked around for him. Sure enough, he found that eye staring directly at him as this crippled creature shelled an egg with his good hand and bit off the end. Just then Joe's attention was attracted by a quick moving gesture beside the man with the egg. This shaven, muscular-looking being grabbed an egg from another patient and popped it, shell and all, into his mouth. Joe could see the semblance of a smile on the man's face as he chewed the egg and swallowed. Joe's attention was then caught by a man who was consuming every third spoonful of cereal and dumping the other spoonfuls on the table.

Most of the patients had eaten very rapidly and were now becoming preoccupied by other things. Some were making peculiar gestures and others were eating their neighbors' leftovers, but most were sitting quietly.

The three attendants were attempting to keep all of the patients seated. One young boy was pacing the floor with his hands over his head and reciting over and over in a forced, high-pitched monotone: "What does a boy do? What does a man do? What does a boy. . ."

"Sit down, Alvin!" Goodman yelled in an annoyed voice. The patient cringed and ran hastily to his seat as Goodman rapidly approached him. As soon as he was no longer being noticed, Alvin resumed his previous pacing and verbalizations.

Joe noticed a middle-aged man standing in front of one of the tall concrete pillars directly ahead. This milky-skinned patient was staring at Joe and he could see that both of his blue eyes expressed a deep and violent hatred.

Just then another attendant entered the room. He quickly introduced himself as Barron and began looking around the cafeteria and calling different names. At his call, several patients got up and followed him upstairs.

After this new attendant was gone, Goodman yelled, "Thirty eight," and the whole hall became mobile. The attendants crowded the patients into a disorderly group in front of a thick wire gate that led to a tunnel underneath the hospital.

The gate was opened slightly and Goodman counted each patient as he passed through. Then he went to the front of the line and took the lead as Joe and the Negro attendant, who was called Ephraim, followed.

As they proceeded down the long concrete and stone basement, the group elongated and Ephraim and Joe nudged the stragglers along. Ephraim guided Benjin in front of him as he pleasantly mimicked the patients' constant chatter; Joe realized that Ephraim resembled Benjin inasmuch as they were both rather short and bald and both had benign, contented expressions. As they journeyed deeper along these dark, winding pas-- sages, Joe found it necessary to bend, for the hanging pipes made the overhead clearance become less and less. This put undue pressure on his pain-riddled leg. Following mechanically behind, Joe found he was indifferent to his present task, as he was aware of little beside the pain. Each step made him writhe, and his mouth became dry as the sweat beaded on his forehead.

Joe watched the concrete floor unwind beneath him as he limped along, stooping forward to miss the pipes. Looking up and straining his eyes, he peered at Ephraim, walking straight ahead and wondered why the latter didn't say something about his limp and the difficulty he was having in keeping up with the procession.

Mixed with Joe's anguish was a feeling of self-recrimination an anger over his pitiful state. This added fury animated him to such an extent that he began effectively to ignore his affliction, and with several lumbering steps, he caught up with Ephraim and began helping him urge the patients onward.

"Where we going?" Joe inquired with a sandy mouth, nudging Benjin and another patient forward, one with each hand.

"To the barber shop," Ephraim replied with an understanding glance. "Every week we take the patients for a haircut and twice a week for a shave."

"Oh!" Joe answered, not knowing what else to say.

—this experience would be weird if I didn't have this knee —oh for the day when I could walk and run—this will probably be my first and last day on this job—wish I could feel more than pain and see more than red—it would be an experience to be able to perceive this clearly—I will forget about this leg—it will finally go away—what—am I yellow that I can't stand a little pain. . .

As he walked, Joe did his best to help Ephraim, but he could not easily forget his nauseating affliction. He looked at Benjin and then at his leg and saw how this man, even though mad, lifted his legs, bent his knees and came off his toes as he walked. Envy flowed from Joe as he saw that Benjin was not tormented with physical pain.

After many more agonizing minutes, Goodman finally halted the group at the front and began to count the patients off through an open, brightly lit portal.

As Joe finally stepped inside the new room, he found some patients lying on the floor and others getting into chairs that lined the far wall. At one end of the room there were half a dozen barber chairs. Joe was considering the extended agony of having to patrol these patients until all had haircuts, when Ephraim turned to him.

"We need somebody to guard the door to make sure none of the patients sneak out," he said, pointing with an outstretched arm to an armchair that stood by the door near the corner of the room.

Rocking with a sigh of relief and glancing into Ephraim's brown eyes, Joe saw unspoken understanding.

"Thank you," Joe replied, slightly embarassed at this unforeseen hospitality.

Joe carefully lowered himself into the chair and stretched his bad leg in a straight line. Soon he began to feel settled and felt the blood gush upward toward his emptied cerebrum and his temples pounding at the pleasure of being still.

As the pain gradually receded, his mind began to react to his environment and he commenced to study the spectacle before him. He saw round brown spots on the wall behind each of the chairs where patients before had rested their dirty, oily heads. Glancing to one side, he spied a man urinating against one of the brick pillars.

"Stop that, Watchung!" Goodman's voice rang out across the room. The startled patient quickly obeyed as Goodman approached.

"Get a mop!" Goodman commanded. The patient quickly disappeared to return with a new-looking mop and hastily begin wiping the puddle of water around.

"Now, put it away and go sit down!" Goodman ordered, pointing directly at Joe. The patient disappeared again and then came toward Joe and sat on the floor against the wall directly to the left of Joe's chair. As soon as the man was seated, Goodman strode toward Joe, calling as he came, "Alvin, come here!" After he had repeated this several times in progressively more authoritarian tones, a young boy appeared. This was the boy whom Joe had seen in the cafeteria. He was the one who had been walking around with his hands over his head. The patient approached cautiously with his lips moving as if he were repeating something to himself. Goodman stood straight and watched Alvin approach. Then he pointed to the corner of the room to the right of Joe's chair. Alvin took this place and sat crosslegged, watching Goodman's every step.

Surveying the room, Goodman's eyes came to rest on the dummy who had kicked Joe. This old man was lying on the floor beside a row of lockers. Quietly, Goodman walked over to the dummy and nudged him with his foot. Startled, the old man sat up and pulled his knees toward his chest. His eyes traveled back and forth between Goodman's feet as though in apprehension of an impending blow. Immediately Goodman lowered his right hand and, grasping the dummy, brought his arm up and pointed it in Joe's direction. The old man, gaining his feet and circumnavigating Goodman, slinked toward Joe and sat to the left of the younger man, the one whom Goodman had compelled to use the mop. Goodman then strode over to Joe.

"Keep these fellows sitting where they are. This one," he added pointing to young Alvin who was mumbling to himself, "shits all over the place, sticks his hand up his ass, and bothers the other patients with his songs."

Goodman then pointed to the man at Joe's left and said, "Watchung must be watched because he stuffs things down the toilets and clogs them up. You know about the dummy's tactics. The dummy can't hear so you must get his attention to give him an order. Oh yes, don't touch Alvin, he always has shit on himself."

As Goodman went back to patrolling, Joe examined his three charges. Alvin sat crosslegged, rocking back and forth; his black hair was streaked with dirt as was his entire face. He had a broken nose which was pushed to one side. Even though the boy looked in his late teens, he was sucking his thumb while he held his other hand in the back of his overalls. Suddenly Joe realized that this was not dirt on his face and hair, but excrement.

Watchung was sitting in a forward position and spitting on the floor between his legs. He would wipe the spittle around with his index finger. This young looking man, like Alvin and the dummy, didn't have a shaven head like most of the other patients. His handsomely constructed features and robust frame contrasted strongly with the deeply lined face and slight body of the pale old man beside him.

—young, middle aged and old—it takes its toll on all and respects few—Watchung looks as if he could don a business suit and brief case and run with the race but he wallows in his own saliva and exposes himself to degradation—Alvin would be able to fit into high school class and wear a college sweat shirt if he would wash his face, but his gestures and verbalizations would betray him—the old man shows the ravages of time and a tormented face but he too could fit into a soft rocker and recite wise verse and talk of better days—wonder how old the old man is—he walks as if he were a boy and gains his feet rapidly—wonder if he knows arthritis— he doesn't seem to—that man—he gets from the barber chair bows and lowers himself to one knee—does he think he is in church. . .

"Who is that man over there? The one who just got out of the barber chair?" Joe inquired when he noticed that Goodman had wandered near.

"Him?" Goodman asked, pointing.

"Yes."

"He was studying to be a priest until he went looney."

"Does he still go to church?" Joe inquired.

"You can't be serious? He doesn't even know what a Bible is." Goodman replied with a hearty laugh.

"Well, it's hard to tell from their looks," Joe said defensively.

Joe sat for an undefined period of time studying the patients and trying to decipher and catalogue their actions. After a time he found that his two younger charges had become very restless and he had a difficult time persuading them to remain. Joe even raised his voice and found they listened somewhat but felt remorse at having had to talk to anybody in such a tone. Finally, Goodman came over and stoned them with threats, and they became still again.

Twice one patient tried to sneak through the door, but Joe ordered him back. Once the dummy got up quickly and kicked a passing patient with his bare foot. This patient walked on as if not noticing and the dummy quickly looked at Joe as he sat again against the wall.

It startled Joe once to look up and see the man who had been staring at him with such hostility in the cafeteria. This man just stood straight and stared directly at Joe with an expression of hatred in his piercing blue eyes. Then Goodman came behind this man and with the flat of his hand, delivered a hearty slap to the back of his neck. The man did not jump, but just kept staring at Joe.

"Hi'ya, cutie. How are ya today?" Goodman asked the man in joking tone. "You see this fellow here?" Goodman said to Joe, "He has two holes in his head where they took parts of his brain out."

"You mean a lobotomy?" Joe inquired.

"Yeh, that's what they call it," Goodman said, pulling the man over to Joe and making him bend over so Joe could see the top of his skull.

On each side of his cranium, just above the man's forehead, were two concave places, the size of half dollars, where the bone had been cut away, leaving only the skin. A shudder ran down Joe's back as he put his arm on the man's shoulder to pull him down further and get a better view. It was then that Joe realized this man was not as placid as his calm exterior would indicate; he could feel with his hand how his whole body was shaking with a tremor. The patient reminded Joe of a dormant volcano which was imperceptibly rumbling in its deep interior while outwardly calm.

As both men released him from their grasp, the patient made a right face, military fashion, and walked over to stop abruptly before a row of lockers. He then leaned forward rigidly and placed the palms of his hand and his forehead against a locker door; after which he quickly walked off on a tangent. Goodman had disappeared and Joe's attention was distracted by a loud rasping voice which rang above the rumble of the crowd. Joe noticed that the sound was coming from a man who seemed to be in his early thirties, with a twisted, pale and yet youthful

136

countenance. The man wore the usual attire, but his black work shoes were several sizes too large for his slight stature.

"I'm going to kill you," he yelled loudly, but there was no one he seemed to be addressing. "If you don't get out of here, I'm going to kill you." He screamed the sentence forcefully and then stopped as if listening to someone. "No, I'm not going to go out with her. She's ugly! Moxey, you tell him who I am and that I mean it!" the man continued, pausing every time he finished as though to listen. This man continued to converse with his imaginary assailants and was still at it every time Joe happened to refer back to him.

Finally the dreaded time arrived when Joe had to walk again. Goodman came over to him and said, "Well, we got to go back now. You lead the line. Go down the passage about a hundred feet and hold the patients as I count them out. Take the priest with you. Hold the back of his head down like this so that he doesn't bump his head on the pipes. He bumped his head a good one when we were coming up."

Joe had gotten up and taken the man by the arm and the back of the head, as Goodman had shown him, when the shock hit him. The dull, nagging pain in his knee exploded into a raw, screaming sensation. Instantly, all of Joe's muscles contracted and he could feel redness covering his entire face and neck. Knowing he was under Goodman's scrutiny, he finally forced himself on beside the priest as the initial shock subsided slightly.

—wonder if he is dangerous—he keeps his head down nicely— it's going to be rough trying to keep my head bent and his also and still try to walk—I'll put more weight on him—he doesn't seem to mind my pulling his arm down—we must lead the line— under the eyes of all—I'll have to walk fast—my back will be turned to them. . .

Each successive step made his body cry out for rest and jammed his brain processes, but he lumbered forward, hoping that numbness and insensibility would overtake him. He waited until the motley crew had finally gathered itself within the limited space of that narrow subterranean artery. Goodman yelled above their heads for him to lead on.

Gritting his teeth, tensing and forcing his charge's head down, Joe turned his back, bent over and with a splashing breath, staggered onward. He did not care about his haggard flock or if the priest hit his head, nor did he care that his job was in jeopardy. His only concern was to be able to end the day in good conscience and his only wish was for an end to the torture.

As he groped along, Joe could hear the dragging sound of shoes and rubbing cloth. He considered how preoccupied he was with his own infirmities. It was as if it were a funeral march and he was the appointed leader who had no choice but to lead onward down the ever continuing way. The pounding feet, low moans, inaudible verbalizations, plus his own uneven breath, played a funeral dirge to the rhythm of his resounding knee pain. It was as if he were leading from Warsaw to the gas chambers, his own body constantly betraying and humiliating him, to arrive at the end and find total destruction and disgrace.

blindness—blindness—blindness—we make ourselves blind by our own desires—the appetite gets stronger and the human will overcomes and then myopia overtakes—anomalous trichromacy leads to dichromacy leads to monochromacy leads to the ankle and the foot bone—ouch ouch. . .

Finally the dim passage way became higher so that he and his companion could walk erect without hitting the pipes. Looking back, he saw that the very tall ones in the crowd still had to stoop slightly. By now Joe's leg was getting numb, and he could feel a stiffness creeping into it with every pulse beat as it swelled, filling his pant leg with bloated flesh.

Forcing himself painfully up the stairs, Joe stood in the corridor again and watched the patients ascend from the dim depths.

—I have power over them—they are locked in like mad dogs and only I have the power to leave—they can't escape. . .

This new feeling of omnipotence gave Joe an exalted and confident feeling. The contact with humanity in such a debased condition gave him a feeling of superiority and increased potency.

Goodman came up the stairs and closed the door after the last patient; then Joe followed behind as he strode down the hall and seated himself against the wall beside the office door. Angus was still seated in the office, leaning over the desk.

A few feet away from Goodman, Joe stood watching the patients as they became settled. Some forced others from their favorite spots on the benches.

Feeling weary from the exertion, Joe ambled over to a bench

138

in one corner of the room which contained a harmless looking creature who was seated on the far end. Carefully, Joe lowered himself onto this thick wooden bench. A roar of laughter rang loudly through the air. Glancing, he saw that it was Goodman.

"What are you doing? Are you out of your mind?" Goodman gasped, trying to get his breath. "Don't sit on the benches! They have piss and shit all over them! Come here." The attendant motioned toward a chair beside him.

Embarassed, and gasping a few words of surprise, Joe got up and sat down beside Goodman.

"What kind of ward is this?" Joe inquired in astonishment as he watched urine splash onto the floor from the seat of a bench that was facing the television set, which was directly on the other side of the room. Joe stared at the back of the head of the guilty patient.

"On this ward we have the incontinent and unclean ones. Occasionally a doctor sends a patient here to punish him. Gore, get a mop and clean up that piss," Goodman commanded as he lit a cigarette.

"Do they all urinate in their pants like that?" Joe asked.

"Not all of them. Some are working patients who are here to do work on the ward and others are house broken."

"Are any of them dangerous?"

"Yes, some. See that Negro over there? He's strong as an ox. He picked up one of those benches once and threw it. It broke a patient's arm. If you're careful with some of these patients, you won't have any trouble. See that bushy headed one over there, the one with the flattened nose?"

"Yes," Joe answered.

"He thought that he was tough when he first came on the ward, a few years ago. One day when he tried to jump an attendant, we took him in the seclusion room and knocked the shit out of him. He hasn't acted up since."

Joe looked at Goodman quickly to see the expression on his face. The older attendant's countenance revealed a tough looking ruddy complexion, and the expression was forceful and unyielding.

—doesn't he realize what he is telling—it can't be this bad—the paper I read said that striking a patient is punished by expulsion—he seems like a nice guy. . .

Joe watched Goodman from the corner of his eye as this

attendant took his lighted cigarette from his lips and flicked it across the room. It landed on the floor near a fresh puddle of urine and two patients scrambled to recover the prize. Joe sat sour-mouthed and dumbfounded as the priest crossed the room to lower himself on one knee before the TV. Another patient tore the last shred of his blue shirt from his back, and still another, a skinny man, walked around the room bending over and touching the floor as if he were picking up imaginary objects.

"Come over here, Alvin!" Goodman ordered, as the dark-headed figure moved cautiously toward them.

"He's putting his hand up his ass again," Goodman said, pulling his chair away from Joe's and pointing to the floor between them. "Sit down," he commanded.

Holding his arms defensively in front of him, the boy squirmed his way onto the floor.

"Sit against the wall," Goodman yelled, raising his fist high.

Reaching his smelly hand upward to stave off the impending blow, Alvin slid himself against the wall and sat with his back to it.

—is Goodman all caricature—he saved me from that old man and he seems like a nice guy but he is so cruel—is this whole institution like this—it's supposed to be the best public institution in the state—I'd hate to see the worst. . .

"Always keep an eye on Watchung," Goodman said. "He collects all kinds of crap and stuffs it into the toilet. If you see him get up, order him back to the bench where he is right now."

Goodman then got up and Joe began to rise.

"Oh, sit there," the attendant said understandingly. "There isn't much to do right now. Just keep an eye on Alvin."

Joe nodded, embarrassed at the little he had done.

Goodman leaned over and said in a low voice, "Make sure you get up and look busy if the Supervisor comes through."

A flush surged to Joe's face as he looked away and Goodman walked into the office.

—he's talking with Smith—wish I could hear what they're saying—are they talking about me—maybe they'll send me home. . .

As he gazed over the room, Joe realized that the newness was wearing off and he was accustoming himself to this world of ragged derelicts. Each glance brought new information and abominable sights; but as time passed, Joe began to be slightly less alarmed and more habituated to his environment. Still quite numb, he began to examine the individual patient's faces. They were still a rather uniform group because Joe had not yet had time to study the features of each.

—that man is urinating on the radiator—should I stop him— no—excrement—excrement—this place is wallowing in stench and mustiness—how can human beings be so slovenly and vulgar—maybe I am not seeing them right—maybe it is a per- formance for me but most don't even seem to recognize my pre- sence—wonder what they think about and if. . .

"Ahhh!" Joe shrieked as his arm jerked back reflexively from an unknown stimulus.

It was Alvin.

"Don't touch me!" Joe exclaimed with a raised voice as he watched the filthy creature draw back.

"I wanna urinate! I wanna urinate! I wannnnna urinnnnnaaate. I. . ." Alvin wailed in a high pitched nasal voice.

"Now you stay there," Angus ordered in a mimicking tone, as he and Goodman darted from the office.

"So how do you like it here?" Angus inquired, sitting down on a stool to Joe's left.

"All right, but some of these patients seem awfully regressed."

"Woooh! Dig that word, regressed! Where did we ever learn such a big word as that?" Angus said in a humorous non- offending voice as he widened his dark eyes to reveal clear and dazzling whites.

"You know, many of them are really messy," Joe said.

"Yes, I know. I'm only kidding," Angus said with a deep throaty laugh.

Feeling less strained and wanting to be polite, Joe chimed in with a few chuckles.

"Yes, they are very untidy, but I love every one of their dear little hearts," Angus said, gasping as if every word were uproarious.

"Yes, it will get on your nerves for a while but if you watch where you're going and don't slip on any shit, you'll be all right. This room is like a cow pasture in that way," Angus continued, starting to calm down.

"I believe it," Joe answered, wondering why Angus didn't laugh at this genuine joke.

"Gore! Get a dust pan and clean up that shit over there and

141

wipe up that piss!" Smith commanded.

The small, wrinkled man who had cleaned the seclusion room before started walking to the bathroom.

"That's funny!" Joe said in wonderment. "I didn't see that shit there a few minutes ago."

"These guys will surprise you. Some are faster than a hired gunman from the old west. They can pull down their pants and take a shit before a person could get his gun out of the holster. One thing we don't have much trouble with on this ward is regularity."

"Yeh," Joe said.

"I wanna urinate. I wanna. . ." came a whine from the floor. Joe looked at Angus.

"Be quiet, Alvin!" Angus said. "He knows you are new, Mephibosheth, and he's trying to take advantage of you."

"Really?"

"Yes, you have to establish your authority or the patients won't listen to you and may get out of hand."

"Yeh, I guess you're right," Joe said, trying to anticipate the future.

"I wanna urinate. . ."

"No!" Joe said taking the initiative.

Joe talked with Angus for several minutes and then Angus disappeared again into the office. As Joe sat there, he realized that he was the only attendant, at that moment, who was in view of the patients. Several had been watching him, and three members of the scraggly crew came hesitantly up to him and asked for a cigarette.

"I don't have any," Joe answered above Alvin's constant whine.

"Light? Have a light?" asked another as he nervously held a hand rolled cigarette before his mouth.

"Here," Joe said, lighting a match.

Joe had become so engrossed with what was going on that he didn't even notice when Alvin ceased his pleading. Looking down, he found Alvin urinating on the floor and the water spreading over the floor and under his shoes.

Quickly, painfully, Joe got up and away from the flood. Finding a mop in the bathroom, he wiped up the mess. After he had finished, he found that Alvin was running around the room. This touched off a chain of events that sent Joe into a waking coma; he found himself trying to tidy the patients under Angus's direction, and changing extremely soiled overalls. All morning he worked with Goodman and the other attendants, changing patients' clothes and directing patients on clean up chores. In the late morning, Goodman accompanied him upstairs with about a dozen patients to direct them in scrubbing the floors and making beds in the room where most of the patients slept at night. Joe was very cautious, and noticed little because of his pain. He longed for the day to end.

In the afternoon there was another messy meal and then Joe took half an hour off of his own lunch. He could not eat and by now longed to ask the supervisor to be sent home. The minutes ticked by slowly and by quitting time, he found his leg almost unbendable and himself aching with agony.

After driving home, he walked into his barren two and a half room apartment, threw himself on the bed and lay there in mute despair. Reaching to the bedside table, he turned on the radio in an attempt to distract himself from the throbbing in his leg and the sound of his deep panting, but it only intensified his anguish to realize that the world knew nothing of his torture. After a time, he forced himself feverishly to his tiny refrigerator and limped back with a six pack of beer. Hastily, he gulped the first can and at a more moderate pace consumed the rest.

The taste of the brew unfolded images of his last days with Della. There was something magical in each sip of the liquid that carried details of those fateful days which Joe thought he had forgotten. With each sip, however, the vividness of this deep-seated hurt subsided as well as his present physical pain.

Finally, relaxation began to soothe him with a gentle hand as he lay quietly on his back, gazing at the crack in the ceiling.

—hope it's nothing serious—why does the taste of beer remind me of you—if you could see me now—a babbling crying idiot wallowing in self pity and self recrimination—if you could see me now you would look with a hardened face and walk away—reality creeps in as the scorching sun burns away the haze of self deception and reveals disillusionment—but actuality is too harsh and illusion too easy—am I really a coward—would someone else with the same affliction endure this with less cowardice—oh to be whole—I could lie here for days and no one would know or care if I lived or died.

He lay there for some time until finally the intensity of his thoughts began to wane as sleep overtook him and enshrouded him with oblivion. It was dark when he suddenly awoke to a stab of pain in his leg. He realized that he had shifted his feverish torso in his sleep, disturbing his inflated knee joint.

—*Ouch*—the beer has worn off—maybe I have a fever—it's stifling in here—had a horrible nightmare—maybe if I remember it this queer feeling will go away—I was upstairs in the sleeping quarters of the ward and was sitting on a high bed against the wall—the patients were in their beds all around—as I got down and started to walk around the room the patients got up and followed me—or were they after me—we walked around and around—the big fat one was right behind me and he was mumbling to himself as we marched along—a man in a gray suit came in then and then I woke up—wonder what it means—why was I in a bed higher than the others—was I one of them—maybe I have a fear of becoming—no that can't be it. . .

Joe pondered deeply as to the meaning of this dream as he stared into the hazy blackness of his room. The darkness stood dully over him and the dimly perceived objects scattered about the room receded and advanced to Joe's vision in varying textures of light and shadow as his heavy eyeballs turned here and there. Suddenly a muffled noise came to Joe's ears and a tenseness shot through his body, causing his eyes to widen. He strained to see in the darkness.

—there's somebody in the room—no—that's impossible— why am I so scared—I must have a high fever and my senses are playing with me. . .

Concentrating intently, he attempted to discern sounds in the deathly stillness. A new feeling boiled inside of him, one which he could not name. It was similar to the feelings he used to get when he was a child and was afraid that a raving maniac had broken into the house and was going to kill him with a knife. Yet this present feeling was new because Joe had seen that the mental patients were not raving maniacs. He knew that his room was empty and therefore he was more deeply troubled. He knew he could chase off an intruder but this fear was irrational and denied his understanding. The sweat rolled from his face as he pulled the dampened sheet to his chin and attempted to regain his previous unconscious state.

The birds were singing and the light was beginning to give color back to the pile of books in the middle of the floor, and the disorderly array of furniture and clothes scattered about the room. A breath of fresher air gave ease to Joe's heart as he welcomed the day with euphoric relief. His body pounded with new vibrancy as he drank in the rich deep green of the tree outside his window and watched a squirrel jumping on the limbs and fanning up a cool breeze. But he became more sober as he began to remember the realities of his invalid state. Sitting up, he threw the sheet off his leg and examined the soft puffy flesh.

—well kid—you must find a doctor—you put if off long enough—where will I get the money—how long until I can work again—where's the telephone book. . .

As the morning wore on, he managed to fix some breakfast by leaning on a shortened broomstick handle that he had found, and by early afternoon he was just able to hobble into the doctor's office. The osteopath took X-rays and told Joe that he might need an operation on his leg. By late afternoon Joe had been fitted with a brace and gone to a drugstore where he felt shame as a woman held the door for him to leave. Deep down, however, he knew that he experienced a certain tinge of satisfaction each time someone threw a pitying glance his way.

As he returned home, he reclined anew on his bed.

—maybe I love any kind of attention from others—maybe I would make a good invalid and be great at feeling sorry for myself and punishing myself by moving this knee—maybe I am a masochist—now I have freedom from the rat race—maybe that is what gives me this feeling of partial satisfaction—I can read and take a forced vacation that I direly need—I'm not even going to worry about running out of money. . .

Picking up a book, Joe read into the evening and finally turned off the light and went to sleep.

In the middle of the night, he found himself suddenly awakened as if someone had touched him with an electrically charged hand. Again, the sweat deluged his whole frame as he wracked his brain to find the meaning of this sudden sensation.

—what's the matter with me—am I going crazy—I have that feeling again that there is somebody in the room—I must disprove this—I must show myself that this feeling is ridiculous. . .

Raising his head and being careful not to disturb his throbbing knee, Joe examined the shadows of the chamber to prove that this terror was pure fantasy. He shot a glance at the chair at the foot of his bed and at that same moment, his whole body turned into a cold pile of sweaty clay. As the perspiration now flowed, it felt as though long thin fingers were coldly caressing his flesh.

oh my God—there is someone sitting in the chair—*oh my God oh my God*—I am hallucinating—it's a skinny Negro and his face is horrible—oh God help me—I must keep my composure—I must prove to myself that this is not true—the light. . .

Slowly and carefully, he fumbled for the lamp. With very deliberate movements, he flicked the switch on. The radiance momentarily blinded his eyes. As the yellow brilliance and strain of forced light adaption faded, he slowly turned his head to the chair.

—It's empty—*yes yes* it's empty—my clothes are strewn over the back and that makes it look like a body and shoulders of the man—a menacing frightful looking man—but wait—the head of the man—what form did I mistake for his head—there is nothing on the far wall that could have come forward as a head—am I going mad—is my mind trying to prove to me that I'm crazy—was that really a hallucination. . .

The aftereffects of this frightening ordeal overtook Joe and he could feel himself starting to quiver as nervousness and chill made inroads on his limbs. Feebly extending his arms, he hastily pushed the chair over and the clothes fell onto the floor.

—is this a split personality in myself being projected outside of me or was this caused by a need to punish myself—I wonder if mental patients are all terrified with their hallucinations or whether they find them pleasurable—I thought that a fantasy world was built because of overstress and that it was usually pleasurable—some of the patients who seemed to be hallucinating appeared to be terrified—maybe I am going mad—my whole being is yelling at me now at get up and run —to get out of this cell but I will ruin my leg for sure and where would I go at this time of night—Imust stay here and fight it. . .

After extensive dialogue with himself and analyzing, Joe started to feel more relaxed and finally decided it was best to continue his slumber. Still feeling somewhat agitated and troubled by this experience, he finally forced himself to turn off the light and go back to sleep. After recovering from the startling click of his bed lamp and the realization that the light had fled, he squinted his eyes and drew the sheet completely over his body. He listened to his senses which were again telling him that he was not alone. After a time he realized that morning had come quickly and the shades had fled.

For the next three days, Joe convalesced in his room, devouring the books that he had longed to read during the past school year. Many times he marveled at his ability to concentrate so thoroughly in this new cell, whereas he had been totally unable to do so on that dark street in Greenwich Village.

In hopes of a rapid recovery and great apprehension that an operation might be necessary, Joe reclined in bed and rarely saw the sun except through his window. Periodically, day and night, he would sleep; and each night he would experience a similar terror to that of the previous night, until he finally persuaded himself to keep a light burning in an adjacent room. The third evening, Joe was lying before his lamp with the illumination from the next chamber seeping across the floor from the partially open door. Upon glancing up from his book, he examined the room, which was painted in various shades of gray. As he examined one black corner, he felt the sweat of panic sweep over him. He was imagining someone fitted into that dim shadow. This phantom was as tall as the ceiling and its eyes were staring directly at him.

—oh no—I am having another waking dream—before it only happened when the lights were off but now they are invading the light. . .

Attempting to fight, Joe looked away. But as his eyes moved, the shade stepped toward him so as to tower over his bed. Recoiling, Joe hurled his attention back and the intruder simultaneously fled to his previously occupied space. Repeating to himself that this experience was not real, Joe looked away again and again, but each time the blurry figure leaped forward only to recede as Joe frantically brought it in focus again.

—are these experienced from God or from the devil—is this what they mean by saying that one is possessed—ghost stories— ghost stories. . .

Taking action, Joe turned the lamp toward the wall and watched the intruder melt into oblivion. He reviewed the different ghost stories he had read.

147

—why do ghost stories have so much flavor for people—before these stories meant little to me and didn't scare me—now—yes now—they would probably have their desired effect—are these beings I fear what people call ghosts—yes it must be—these visions are ghosts and they are substanceless like those proverbial beings and I fear them like most men in the stories—wonder what causes it—maybe fear of my father—it's possible but I never knew him well—maybe I have paranoid tendencies—wonder why I know they aren't real—but wait—my big fear is that I should see them in detail—oh my God—what is the matter with my brain—what have I done to warrant this type of punishment. . .

Scanning the room, Joe realized that it had become more alive than he had ever before experienced it. This being, or the many beings, were everywhere; behind chairs, under the table, in corners. They fled as Joe glanced in their direction, but attacked as he looked away. Again terrified, Joe forced himself to turn off his reading light and then, squinting his eyes tightly, he wrapped himself entirely in his sheet so that none of these beings could touch his skin. Finally he fell into a deep slumber from nervous exhaustion and mental fatigue.

Three weeks passed and it was the first week of July when Joe traded his crutches for a cane. The pain had subsided greatly and the amount of fluid and swelling had been reduced around his knee; but his leg had decreased in over-all thickness and tone as compared with his other one, from atrophy. His nocturnal awareness had waxed and waned, but they still terrified him. Generally, the sense of not being alone and the fear of perceiving the unreal had become so strong that it had even followed him into the day and was a constant obsession. He often found himself having to prove to himself the lack of substance of a shadow or the nothingness of a darkened object. A deep need grew inside of him to constantly test reality in his attempt to fight his unknown foe, and often he felt the compulsion to attack a silhouette to prove to his satisfaction that it was mere fantasy. If the phantom should step from the shadows and reveal himself in the full color and substance of broad daylight, Joe knew this would verify his insanity and make him lose all outward composure.

Another week passed and Joe found he could locomote again,

without aid and with greatly reduced amount of pain. Anxious to discover the source of his fears, he decided to continue employment at the institution. He felt that by exposing himself to this environment again, he could dissolve all the myths and fears that he had conjured up during his weeks of absence.

After making arrangements, he found himself walking onto ward 38M early on a hot morning. He found the patients as he had expected, and the same poignant smell and the same revolted feelings renewed themselves without the benefit of distraction. Moving around the ward very carefully, Joe found that the charge attendant was Barron and that Goodman was on pass. Angus was on vacation.

Barron was a heavy set man in his forties, with two eyes that looked in different directions. Besides these crossed eyes and a slight cynical upward turn at the corners of the mouth, Barron gave a first impression of being kind, but his features conveyed a seeming melancholy.

With Barron and the other attendants, Joe proceeded to distribute shoes and socks around the room and saw to it that they were not discarded by the patients.

As Joe was bending over a small, fearful patient, encouraging him to put his feet into a pair of oversized and mismatched shoes, he looked down and saw something on the floor.

—a drop—another—is it dirty water—no it's scarlet—blood—yes it's blood—Barron must see this. . .

"Barron!" Joe called, "could you come here a minute."

"What do you want?" Barron asked, sounding slight irritated.

"I want you to see something," Joe answered, slightly repelled by this change in Barron's attitude.

"Well, what is this guessing game? Out with it! We don't have any secrets here," he said impatiently.

"I see something on the floor," Joe stammered.

"What?" the attendant's voice demanded.

"Blood!" Joe exclaimed, regaining his composure.

"Blood?"

"Yes, blood!"

"Well, all we need this morning it to have to get somebody sewed up, because of the laziness of the night crew. Well, don't just stand there! Find out whose blood it is."

Glancing around, Joe noticed other drops nearby. He followed them to a secluded corner of the large chamber where he found an old, wrinkled man standing in a small red puddle with his hands forced into the back of his coveralls.

"Here he is!" Joe exclaimed as he realized that Barron had come up beside him.

In the next few moments they took the struggling man into a seclusion room and examined him.

"Take your pants off," Barron ordered. As the man removed his bloody coveralls and exposed his back side, Joe drew back in horror. Protruding about six inches from the patient's anus, was a scarlet colored fleshy bulb. Joe could not understand whether this was foreign matter or part of the man.

"What is that? Is it hemorrhoids?" Joe asked bewildered.

"Quick, grab his arms," Barron demanded. "No! Don't touch his hands, they have shit all over them. Don't let him touch his ass!"

Together, they forced the frightened patient to lay on his chest on the bed and Barron instructed Joe to hold his arms and keep him still. Then Barron stood up and looked at Joe. "Hemorrhoids?" he laughed in a raspy voice. "That's a good one! Hemorrhoids! No, this is not hemorrhoids. He has pulled out his ass."

Joe didn't want to show any more naïveté so he kept silent and again peered in wonderment at the protruding mass.

"They get their hands up their asses so far that they pull their bowels out," Barron added. "I'm going to give you some practical experience," Barron continued as he left the room. As Joe struggled to keep the man still, he could hear Barron telephoning the doctor and the patients shuffling past on their way to breakfast.

Soon Barron returned.

"Here is some saline solution, gauze and tape. I'll let you clean up this mess."

As Barron restrained the man, Joe cleansed and dressed the wound as best he could in preparation for the surgeon's visit.

"Do you get many cases like this?" Joe asked, trying to forget his churning stomach.

"This case is nothing compared to some. You know the patient, Watchung? The one who stuffs things in the toilet.

"He did a nice job on himself a couple of years ago. He

pulled his guts inside out much farther than this."

"I could see that from Alvin, but I haven't seen Watchung play with that area," Joe said.

"Even these idiots learn. They have to go through complicated surgery and usually are tied down for months so they won't try it again," Barron said. "Alvin is still young, but sooner or later his time will come. That's one of the reasons we must keep an eye on him."

—funny how Barron talks as if he and I were the only ones in this room—this patient hasn't made a noise but I wonder if he can understand what we are saying—he is like a poor struggling rabbit with a broken leg—he wants to be left alone. . .

Joe then held the patient and soon the surgeon came and with rubber gloves on his hands forced the moist red protrusion back into the man's rectum and then left. A stretcher was then prepared and the man was bound tightly to it and taken off the ward by two patients and an accompanying attendant. Barron walked into the office as Joe was sterilizing his hands.

"Have you ever taken the patients upstairs to make beds?" Barron inquired.

"Yes," Joe said reluctantly.

"OK, then that's your next job." Barron then proceeded to call the names of different patients and they gathered quickly before the door which led upstairs. Walking into the middle of them, Joe counted twelve of them as they went upstairs. They waited near the top of the stairs for Joe to open the door to the dormitory and as he made his way past their silent visages, he realized that he was alone with them. Trying not to think about it, and being very slow and deliberate in his steps because of his leg, Joe unlocked the door and smelled the musty interior of the upper room. The patients went automatically to work, folding the sheets, doubling the mattress back on the bed, and sweeping the floor. Several of the workers stopped their work and lounged around and Joe realized even more that he was at the mercy of some of the larger ones because of his bad leg. Looking around he examined the man whom he had been told had thrown the bench across the room and another who had nearly killed an attendant with a pitcher on the violent ward. Two of these husky ones could overcome him and take his keys and escape. As he continued to scrutinize the different faces, Joe's eyes came to rest on the tall one

151

whom Goodman had said had saved his life. This patient was bending over one of the beds and wiping the urine from it with a sheet. Being careful not to walk through any puddles on the floor, Joe went across the room toward him.

"What's your name?" Joe inquired with a kind voice.

"Me?" the patient asked in surprise as if he had not seen the attendant approach.

"Yes, my name is Joe Mephibosheth. What's your name?" Joe asked, recognizing the extreme shyness of this seemingly stalwart individual.

"Jud. Jud Icarus," the patient said taking an awkward pose and holding his arms stiffly at his sides.

"Please to meet you, Jud," Joe said.

Jud stood with his head hanging; then, fidgeting his arms behind him, he clasped them together near the small of his back.

"How long have you been here, Jud?" Joe asked in a confident voice, realizing that he was now the master of this personality.

"I don't know. About five years, I guess," Jud answered, shifting his weight from foot to foot a few times and snatching quick glances at Joe's face.

"Do you like it here, Jud?" Joe asked in a fatherly voice.

"No," Jud said, after some hesitation.

"I understand you're a good worker," Joe continued as he studied Jud's rough visage. "You want to come with me while I get the mops and soap."

"OK," Jud said in a happier tone as if he now had a purpose.

Joe unlocked a nearby closet which he had been shown on his first day, and Jud carried an armload of mops and handed them to several lazy patients who were seated on the beds.

Joe took the ammonia and antazone into the bathroom and dumped it into a large push pail that another patient had filled with hot water.

As the morning wore on, Joe supervised and even joined in the mopping and other tasks to be done, being very careful not to over exert his weak leg. Finally they descended the dark stairs again in time for the noon meal. While in the cafeteria, Joe thought he had finally become accustomed to the plethora of peculiar sight and sounds until he saw one of the teenage patients sneak over to where a man had pissed in his cup.

"Drink it!" the boy commanded in an authoritative voice.

The seated patient hastily seized his cup and consumed the contents.

"Get back to your seat!" Joe yelled and immediately balked at the sound of his own voice.

With a defiant smile, the boy calmly walked back to his bench.

Feeling himself under observation, Joe turned around and saw the patient with the lobotomy standing before the pillar and staring his way in evident hatred. Defiantly, Joe made his way over to this man and ordered him several times to be seated. The man only blinked his eyes rapidly and retained upright posture.

"Sit down, Reuben," came the voice of one of the other attendants. Reuben obeyed.

After lunch, the crowd was herded upstairs. The heat of the day was increasing and the stench of the room and its occupants also rose until Joe felt as if his stomach would heave. When Barron released him for lunch, he quickly made his exit, found a large shade tree, and gingerly picked at a lunch that he had prepared.

When he returned to the ward half and hour later, it was almost empty except for three workers mopping the floor. The patients were all gathered on a large railed in porch, adjacent to the auditorium.

"I didn't realize that you could trust them outside. Aren't you afraid they will run away?" Joe asked as he approached Barron, who was seated before the porch on a bench with two other attendants.

"We will let you chase them, Mephibosheth, if one does start running," Barron exclaimed, smiling as he looked at the attendant beside him for recognition.

"Oh, I see!" Joe said, deeply offended by this.

—doesn't he like me—maybe he holds my college education against me—maybe I am too lazy—will work harder at the next job that he gives me. . .

By the end of the day, Joe was painfully foot sore and afraid that he had strained his leg too much; but as the days passed, his limb started to get stronger and his nocturnal awareness also decreased. However, they were still strongly engrained in his consciousness.

A week passed and Joe's stomach began to feel stronger; the

extraordinary was starting to become commonplace to him. One day after work, Joe came home to his stifling apartment and searched for his long neglected diary.

"July 20

Deer Diarrhea,

Long time no see. I am now in a sphere. The job at the hospital is interesting but I do believe I have caught a slight bug call schizophrenia. Of what variety I cannot ascertain. My night visitations are regular but the terror has dulled. I have built a habit for this awareness and now I am easily startled in the dark. When I returned home at night I feel compelled to scare the demons from the closet and from dim corners with a light. When I sit in my auto, I must make sure no one is accompanying me on the trip. I wish the Good Lord would see fit to take this feeling of being haunted away and cure me of this thorn in my knee. Also I wish He would help me to find a new goal for which I might strive.

I cannot understand what these weird dreams and awarenesses mean or what causes them, but I definitely wish I could conquer them."

Joe had taken off July 21 and 22 as his pass days. Upon returning to the ward after this time, he was greeted by Barron. "You're late!" Barron said, facing Joe.

Joe could not tell which eye Barron was looking at him with. "I'm sorry, I overslept," Joe said apologetically, but he was seething inside with hostility.

"Never mind that. We got a new patient while you were gone. I want you to help me dress him," Barron said with a sadistic look on his fleshy face.

Joe felt hatred for Barron. But as he looked at the attendant's face, he could tell that the new arrival would undoubtedly spell excitement and he sensed an unacceptable longing inside that made him eager to assist Barron, even though it might mean another injury to his leg. The charge attendant then moved to the seclusion room door, turned on the light and swung open the thick wooden portal. Looking over Barron's shoulder, Joe saw excrement smeared on the floor of the small cubicle. In one corner lay a black plastic covered mattress with a thick quilt on it. A large form lay under the quilt and two large, ebony feet stuck out from its bottom.

"White! It's time to get up. White! I guess he must be in a deep sleep," Barron said, as he went over and pulled the quilt off the naked figure of a young man.

"Wha' goin on, man? Wha' goin on?" White asked, chewing his words through his thick lips and forcing them out the corner of his mouth.

"Time to get up, White," Barron said, motioning to Joe to move closer to be ready to grab him.

"I wanna sleep, I wanna. . .!" White felt his feet for the quilt.

"He's very nearsighted," Barron said, as he moved around to the back of the figure who was still groping for the blanket.

"How well can he see?" Joe inquired, looking at the lad's distorted visage and the peculiar deep furrows imbedded into the back of the patient's round, closely shaven skull.

"He can see your form, so don't stand in front of him. He clobbered the sense out of one of the patients yesterday."

"What his diagnosis?" Joe asked as he watched White start to get to his feet.

"He's mean and mentally retarded. Quick, grab his arm!"

Just then the patient started to swing his arms in a wild arc; he connected with Joe's shoulder, knocking him against the nearby wall.

Recoiling, Joe lunged for the moving arm and after grabbing his wrist, as Barron had done with White's other hand, together they placed their free hands side by side on the patient's back below the neck.

"I goin' to kill ya, I goin' to kill ya!" White screamed as he struggled violently.

"Pull his arm back and twist the wrist in," Barron yelled as Joe struggled with the flopping arm.

"Like this?" Joe asked, pulling the arm back so that the angered form was in a position similar to a swimmer when he starts a race.

"Harder, harder! Twist harder! Break his arm!" Barron yelled, struggling to keep his feet as White wriggled around to face them.

"I kill ya, I kill. . ." White yelled even louder.

155

"Will you twist harder!" Barron shouted angrily.

"But I will break his arm!" Joe barked.

"Break it!" Barron screamed above the threatening shrieks of the patient.

"All right!" Joe said through his gritted teeth as he applied greater pressure. Joe felt a snap in the prisoner's shoulder socket and knew that any more would tear the cartilage.

"Sonabitch, sonabitch, sonab. . .!" came the cry as the struggling subsided somewhat and the boy was forced to his knees.

"Will you be good?" Barron asked as he lifted the extended arm higher, making the boy lean his head to the floor.

"I be good boy. I be goo. . ." the patient repeated as he ceased struggling.

"Give me that arm," Barron commanded as he freed Joe. "Now go and open the clothes closet door."

"Sonabitch, sonabitch. I kill you," the boy said, starting to regain his feet again.

"No, you won't, you bastard!" Barron forced his knee into White's back and shoved him prostrate to the floor.

"Will you do as I say?" Barron screamed at Joe who was standing ready to help.

"Yes, sir!" Joe left the room and crossed the auditorium as fast as he could, being careful of his aching leg. After opening the clothes room door, he hurried back and walked beside Barron who was shoving the screeching figure down the hall.

Upon arriving at the clothes room, Barron applied more painful pressure and forced White to the floor again.

"Will you be good now? If you're good and get dressed I will let you go," Barron said.

"I will be good boy!"

"Promise?" Barron said again.

"I be good boy," White said, ceasing his struggling.

Barron let go, and White got up, straining his eyes at the blurry figures around him.

"Gotta wash my hands, man!" White said as he tried to go to the door.

"Put on your clothes and then you can wash your hands," Joe reasoned, holding a pair of overalls to White.

"I don't want no clothes, wanna wash my hands," White repeated hurling the pants across the room and swinging his strong arms wildly.

"OK, you're asking for it," Barron said, tackling White and throwing him on the floor.

"Jud, come here," Barron yelled.

Soon Jud Icarus entered the room as Barron and Joe held the boy firmly to the floor.

"Put those pants and that shirt on him!" Barron commanded as the tall figure stood awkwardly over them.

Finally the patient was dressed and let loose on the ward. Shaking from the excitement, Joe followed White as instructed, to make sure he didn't hurt anyone. White stumbled heavily around the ward, tearing off his shirt; then he went into the bathroom and turned on the water and stood for five minutes rubbing his hands together under the water. Looking at his own hands, Joe saw that they were very dirty and greasy from White's smelly body. By this time, the patients were in the basement eating; Joe took one of the trays that was sent upstairs and put it on a table. Then he cautiously directed White to a chair in front of the food and watched him finger the hard boiled eggs and hot cereal, and put bread into his mouth and swallow without chewing.

Soon the pleasant Negro attendant, Ephraim, stepped to the top of the basement stairs and the patients started to stream onto the ward again. As they were getting settled, Joe followed White until he finally seated himself at the corner of one of the benches. Looking around, he saw Goodman directing one of the working patients who was cleaning out the seclusion room from which White had emerged. Ephraim was going about the ward buttoning shirts and handing out discarded shoes.

Walking into the office, Joe watched Barron as he took colored pills from the medicine cabinet and put them into different cups. Coming closer, he read some of the labels on the bottles: Mellaril, Stelazine, Cogentin, Elavil, Maxibolin, Taractan, Trilifon liquid. As Joe watched, he noticed that Barron was taking most of the pills from different containers marked Thorazine.

"What does Thorazine do?" Joe inquired as he watched the attendant.

Barron looked at Joe with a questioning eye. "What do you think it does?"

"I don't know. Does it act as a tranquilizer?" Joe asked in a meek voice, trying to be friendly.

"What did you go to college for? They sure must not teach you much there. Sometimes I think colleges turn out nothing but arrogant imbeciles."

"Maybe you're right," Joe said in a calm voice, but he was burning inside as he turned to go.

"Now you wait a minute!" Barron said in a demanding voice.

"What?" Joe exclaimed in a strained voice as he realized that the attendant was talking to him as if he were one of the patients. As he turned, Joe saw clearly that Barron's left eye was steadily fixed on him. Taking a wide stance and clenching his fists at his sides, Joe peered angrily at the attendant.

"What do you want?" Joe asked belligerently.

"You asked me a question and then walked away. Is that what they teach you to do in college? You guys are all alike—cocky as hell. When you work on this ward, you're going to listen to your superior and your superior is me. Do you understand that?" Barron asked with a smirk on his face.

Joe's face began to burn as he stood silent.

"No, I'm going to tell you what Thorazine does and you better listen and learn. Do you hear?"

Still remaining silent, Joe felt his mouth curl into a snarl, his abdomen tighten and his toes dig firmly into the floor.

Barron threw his head back slightly as though sizing Joe up.

"Thorazine makes those mental patients out there become not so over-active. It calms them down. This ward would be even more dangerous than it is if we didn't have this calmer downer. Do you understand?" He looked at Joe, but did not appear to be satisfied with his silent response.

—calmer downer—his use of language is really lousy—it's about as organized as his face—calmer downer—what an ignorant bastard. . .

Joe stood with squinted eyes, staring heedlessly back at the attendant who was facing him.

"All right, unless there are any more questions, you may go." Barron said in what now sounded like a cheerful voice.

Not to be dismissed so lightly, Joe said, "Yes, I have a question."

"What do you want to know?" Barron exclaimed as he started sorting the pills again.

"I see on those cards: B.I.D., T.I.D. and Q.I.D. First of all I would. . ."

158

"First of all, do you know what those letters mean?" Barron interrupted.

"Of course," Joe asserted, raising his voice, "B.I.D. means twice a day. T.I.D. means three times a day and Q.I.D., four times a day."

"Very good, now what do you want to know?" the attendant asked happily.

"What I want to know is why you are giving the patient that belongs to this card a hundred milligrams of Thorazine when the cards says fifty milligrams T.I.D., and why are you giving this patient here a fifty milligram Mellaril pill when it explicitly says here twenty-five T.I.D.?"

"How stupid can you get!" Barron exclaimed, still sounding confident. "What is two times twenty five?"

"Fifty," Joe answered quickly.

"And two times fifty?"

"A hundred," Joe said again.

"OK, then, what's the big spiel?" Barron said smiling.

"The big spiel is that you are giving the patients twice the dose for their morning requirement."

"That's true, but it all averages out, because we don't give it out in the afternoon. Do you see now?" Barron explained, completely satisfied.

"I see. But do you realize that is unethical and illegal. If the doctor tells you to give it out twice on your shift, then that's what you should do." Joe explained, feeling more satisfied now because he was getting revenge.

"Don't look at me. It was Angus who started it. If I started giving it out twice a day now, it would screw up the patients' systems. Talk to Angus when he comes back. I'm just following orders."

Barron continued to justify his position for several minutes, but his smirk was now gone. Joe felt better because he had Barron at bay.

Finally Barron stopped for a moment and surprised Joe by saying, "Now get out of his office, I'm busy. I have patients to care for whether you care about them or not. Don't come in here until you've cooled off."

Steaming, Joe stormed from the office and walked over to Goodman who was standing at the head of the floor smoking a cigarette.

159

"Did you hear that?" Joe said excitedly.

"No, did you have a scrape with the walking lip?"

"I sure did, that guy is. . ."

"Crazy?" Goodman interjected.

"Yes, and mentally retarded too!" Joe exclaimed excitedly and then went on to explain what had happened.

"Take it easy, pal. Don't let that phony get to you. You're too sensitive. Don't be so sensitive or this ward will affect you. Take everything with a grain of salt and don't let that wind bag blow you over. He gets a little power now that Angus is gone and tries to shove everybody around," Goodman explained, flicking his lit cigarette across the room.

They conversed for several minutes and Joe found himself coming to like Goodman. He began to look at Goodman's name as being more appropriate to him than he had thought before, and consequently he tended more to overlook Goodman's faults.

Finally Barron emerged from the office with a tea wagon full of pills and yelled the names of the different patients. A patient was kept busy filling three cups as the attendant directed the patients to the tea wagon and made sure each put his pill in his mouth and then drank from one of the containers. Then Goodman seated himself in one of the attendant's chairs while Ephraim wandered around tidying the patients.

"Goodman, have you ever seen something—well you know, had the feeling that there is something there when it really isn't?" Joe asked hesitantly.

"What do you mean? Do you want to know if I have ever had a hallucination?"

"Something like that, but I didn't want to put it that strongly," Joe answered.

"Well, once I sat down to the table and looked at the soup I was going to eat and saw Alvin there. It scared the hell out of me," Goodman confessed openly. "Is that what you mean?" he continued.

"Yes, something like that. Every night I seem to get these weird feelings that someone. . ."

As Goodman listened he was watching the room; suddenly Joe saw his expression change as he leaped to his feet.

Glancing quickly around, Joe noticed that one of the patients was lying on the floor and another sturdy-looking one was walking around waving his arms in the air and touching everything and everybody nearby.

"Barron," Goodman yelled as he made his way quickly to the patient who was writhing on the floor. Ephraim was soon beside him as they lay the patient on his back and pulled his clenched hands away from his face.

"Oh no!" Ephraim exclaimed in horror as he looked at the blood seeping from the man's crushed left eye.

"What happened?" Joe asked.

"It's Polotski. He hits people in the eye with his fist and tires to put their eyes out," Goodman said quickly as he left the bleeding patient to Ephraim and Barron, and searched the room for the stocky, red-faced man who was moving quickly in all directions touching the faces of oblivious patients who seemed to tally unaware of their potentially dangerous situations.

Joe quickly followed Goodman to the smiling man who was now dancing around in circles. As Goodman overtook the patient, he landed a bludgening blow to his shoulder at the base of his neck. With the same smile still painted on his face, the patient staggered forward. Then, before Joe could think how to help, Goodman had grabbed the man by the arm and flung him several feet up the hall.

"Open the seclusion room door!" Goodman yelled at Joe as he dragged the flopping body. The man's face still bore the same euphoric expression.

"Help me get these clothes off him," Goodman said. They quickly disrobed the man. The patient seemed oblivious to what was going on. He leaped into two more circles as Goodman grabbed his arm and brought his foot up implanting it so deeply in the man's stomach that his feet momentarily lifted from the floor. Then, with a mighty fling, Goodman threw the man onto the floor of the cell and slammed the door. Peering through the wire screen, they watched the patient as he regained his feet and renewed his wild dance.

"You've seen the two patients on the ward that have only one eye?" Goodman asked.

"Yes."

"Well, that's a sample of this bastard's work. He's put other eyes out, too."

As the injured man was being put on the stretcher and hurried off the ward, Joe tried not to think. He repressed all pangs of

161

conscience and kept his mind solely occupied with the job at hand. First he found a chair where he could sit and rest his aching leg. Across the floor, he could see Alvin sleeping contentedly on the table, his thumb in his mouth and his other hand in his pants. Near Alvin was a man who was smoking a cigarette. This patient stood straight with a faint smile on his dark face. He would lift the cigarette to his lips, inhale deeply and then placidly open his mouth and let the fumes float out and up the front of his face, savoring each puff with deep satisfaction.

Soon Barron came from the office and walked into the bathroom. Upon emerging, he threw a rancorous look at Joe and said, "Why weren't you watching Watchung? He clogged two of the toilets and they have flooded the floor."

Joe looked around and saw Watchung seated defensively in his usual spot.

"If you can't keep an eye on him, put him in seclusion," Barron continued. "Jud! Gore! Get some mops and clean up the bathroom floor." Then Barron turned to Joe and said, "Well! I said throw Watchung into seclusion."

Joe walked over to the patient.

"Watchung," Joe said, "You have to go into the room."

Without a word, and as if without regret, the patient followed Joe who closed him in the cell next to Polotski. As Joe walked back up the hall he marveled how few words he ever heard from the patients. He had never heard Watchung utter a sound and Polotski never talked either. Joe wondered if some of these people were mute from birth or whether they didn't find it advantageous to communicate.

Later Goodman, who had returned from taking the wounded patient to intensive care, came over to Joe and said, "The food truck is in for lunch downstairs. There's chicken today. I'll give you a paper plate and you run down and get some chicken legs for Barron, myself and you."

Looking up, Goodman called to the other attendant, "Are you sure you don't want any chicken, Ephraim?"

Ephraim shook his head.

"OK, that's legs for three of us," Goodman confirmed.

After he had gone downstairs, Joe found several large pans of chicken parts; he selected three chicken legs.

—I shouldn't do this—why didn't I say no—it's not right to

take the patients' food but still I didn't have time to pack a lunch and I am broke—it won't hurt to take some just once—but there doesn't seem to be much for all of the patients—I really am very hungry. . .

"Three legs!" Goodman exclaimed as Joe returned. "I said legs for three, not three legs. Barron alone can cram down four. Here I'll go get it then."

Joe declined the offer and came back with the plate heaped with meat.

"That's better," Goodman said as he started to eat one. "Hey, aren't you having any? Here is a big one and I'll pour you a glass of milk."

Joe looked at the others enviously and then accepted the offering of meat and milk; his conscience began to throb in rhythm with his leg. After they had finished their free banquet, the attendant who was supervising the basement called on the extension telephone, and the patients were sent downstairs. On his way down, Joe walked over to where Watchung was and opened the door. "Go and eat, but come back here when you come upstairs again." Also Joe took one of the trays of food, put some on a paper plate and then placed in on the floor in the seclusion room where Polotski was. After he withdrew, Joe watched for a few seconds as this patient grabbed the potatoes, chicken and beans in his hands and danced around the room while sloppily consuming the food.

Standing again at the top of the stairs and watching as the patients came from the basement, Joe realized that his words carried authority when he saw Watchung go straight to his cell and close the seclusion room door behind him. This event gave Joe a heady sensation of authority and yet it brought also, in its wake, a longing for even more recognition, a longing that Joe knew could easily become insatiable; he also felt anxiety about the fact that he was not really being constructive in his thought and duties.

After the patients were settled, Barron told Joe he could take a break. Going out on the lawn, Joe found a shady spot on the lawn and lay there in the grass for a short nap.

—the sun is really bright—wish I could lay here all day and not have to go back—just lay here and let the ants play on my feet and the birds fly happily overhead and let the squirrels hop happily over me—think I will go. . .

163

"What ward do you work on?" came a voice nearby.

Opening his eyes and bracing himself on his elbow, Joe saw a skinny attendant sitting on a bench nearby, eating his lunch.

"Thirty-eight M," Joe said feeling somewhat sorry he had been interrupted from his revery.

"Really? Thirty-eight M, huh! How do you like it?" the skinny man said, taking a large bite out of his sandwich.

"Can't say that I do," Joe answered.

"I don't blame you a bit. That ward is sure a mess. You wouldn't catch me dead working there. Those attendants there, Barron and Goodman and the others, what I've seen of how they work, they're worse than the patients. At least they could be kind to those poor smelly bastards."

"It's a hard ward to work on and those attendants there have a rough time, but I agree that they are cruel," Joe said, wanting to end the conversation so he could relax again.

"These guys should have been fired long ago, but you know how civil service says that no one can be fired," the man went on, swallowing a mouthful of coffee.

"Maybe you're right," Joe said, laying back down.

Upon returning to the ward, Joe found the contrast between the fresh air outside and the stuffy atmosphere inside striking. He found it hard to breathe and it was an effort to accustom himself to the stagnation and stench of the ward. The room was quiet except for a few random noises. White was sleeping on a bench next to the wall, his head snuggled against a fat man who was chewing a mouthful of rationed smoking tobacco. Joe sat silently in a chair beside Barron who was watching the patients. Joe scanned the room in an attempt to occupy his mind so that quitting time would come faster.

—I should try and be nice to Barron—should try to understand him—wonder how any person can keep his sanity having to take care of these patients for several years—I will not let it make me hard—I must keep my sensitivity and try to be kind. . .

"Sit down," Barron yelled suddenly at a patient who was wandering aimlessly in front of them.

"Why do you always make the patients sit down?" Joe inquired gingerly, having made up his mind to say something innocuous.

"If they're seated then they can't get in trouble and bother the other patients," Barron answered, not sounding annoyed.

"Aren't there games and things that they can keep occupied with?" Joe asked.

"We sometimes get puzzles and games and some of the patients go to occupational therapy, but most of these patients would rather sit and hallucinate," Barron said civilly.

—hallucinate—hallucinate—that story about the man who went from the U.S. to England in a small boat—when he was on the water from many days he started to have auditory and visual hallucinations—those experiments I read showed that people who go without sensory stimulation for a long time have strong tendencies to hallucinate—maybe that's my problem—I was cooped up in that room for all of those days—maybe that's it— my imagination became too strong because of lack of outside stimulation—whew—it makes me feel better—hey that gives me an idea—maybe hallucinations are simply an aftereffect of schizophrenia—many of these patients have withdrawn from the world and sit all day—maybe their withdrawal came first and then hallucinations followed because of sensory deprivation—maybe I have made a new discovery—but why haven't those nocturnal sensations gone away because I must surely be getting enough stimulation now—maybe I have built up a tendency or habit— I only do have this when I am alone though. . .

While Joe had been thinking, he had been vacantly watching the moving form of Ephraim, who had just returned from his lunch. This attendant was wandering around tending the needs of the patients when he stopped before one, helped him to his feet, and walked with the young man towards Barron,

"Look at this man's ear," Ephraim said as Barron stood up.

The patient's ear was frightfully swollen; loose skin and pus oozed from every pore of the irritated knob.

"How did it happen?" Barron asked, examining it.

"I. . . I washed it with hot water," the patient explained fearfully after some hesitation.

"Take some alcohol and clean it off and we will have the doctor look at it," Barron said to Ephraim.

Just then a commotion caught Joe's eye and looking up, he saw that the fat man had pushed White off the bench and was now wandering around like a wounded moose.

Catching the patient, Joe saw that his fleshy cheek had deep teeth marks where White had bitten him.

"Oh no, everything's happening all at once," Barron said after inspecting the man's wound.

Soon after this, the doctor came and examined the patients.

An hour after the doctor had left, Goodman returned; Joe smelled liquor on his breath as he related to him what White had done.

"That's nothing," Goodman said with a pleasant smile. "I was told that not long ago when White was still home, he bit the family collie dog and the mutt ran away and never returned."

"You're kidding," Joe said.

"No, I'm not. It's in the record," Goodman replied as they both roared with laughter.

Soon the patients were herded onto the large back porch. White, who didn't want to move, finally got to his feet in a fury, and taking the outside door with both hands, threw it back against the projecting door frame, cracking the door in half where the frame hit it. After a strenuous struggle, Watchung was evacuated from the seclusion room and White was thrown screaming into it.

"I don't know how they ever kept that big ape at home all of this time. They must have kept him in chains," Goodman said, puffing.

Again everything settled down and Barron, Goodman and Joe sat on benches on the lawn, in front of the porch, while Ephraim busied himself with tidying the seated patients as he sang "Rock of Ages" in a low voice.

Having found a place out of the scorching sun under a big oak, Joe sat meditating deeply.

—Ephraim is a good man and I hear him always humming hymns and he doesn't bother anybody and just does his job— here I eat the patients' food and sit all of the time—no wonder God has seen fit to give me a bum knee and makes me spooky. . . that patient is standing on the bench and taking his clothes off—Ephraim's stopping him—this sun is sure hot—this view seems like an eternal paradox—those souls in the deepest degradation and yet the sun shines on them and illuminates them so you can see every minute detail—it seems a contradiction— they should be sitting in the shadows hidden from the scrutinizing eye just as a funeral should be held only on dark rainy days—wonder if any of them will. . .

"Joe, did you hear the new joke?" came Goodman's voice, breaking into his thoughts as he came over and sat beside Joe on the bench.

"No, what?" Joe said, cringing inside knowing that it would probably be another dirty joke.

"There was a baseball game one day and the attendant sat the patients in the bleachers. He would say 'stand, nuts' and the nuts would stand, 'sit, nuts' and the nuts would sit; but things really got messed up when a man came along yelling peanuts."

Joe wanted to object, but he pretended to laugh, feeling a pang of conscience while Goodman gazed momentarily at his face. Not knowing what to say, Joe verbalized the first thing that came into his mind.

"Hot day, isn't it," he said as he watched a stream of urine flow from the edge of the porch to the ground.

"It sure is. Did you know the meat wagon carted five people away to the morgue yesterday because of the heat?"

"How many people usually die per day on the average?"

"Oh, I'd say about one or two," Goodman replied.

Joe talked with Goodman for quite a while.

CHAPTER IV

The days passed slowly and Joe came on the ward one morning feeling pretty cheerful. He was determined to make the world go his way and let nothing spoil his enthusiasm.

"Well, well, don't we look chipper today?" Goodman said jokingly with a side glance.

"Feel pretty good. You don't look half bad yourself," Joe joshed. "Your wife been feeding you vitamins lately?"

"You wouldn't catch me dead taking those things," Goodman said, lighting a cigarette. "As a matter of fact," the attendant whispered, so Angus, who was in the office, couldn't hear, "I had a couple of shots of pickmeup this morning."

"Oh! Snake oil!" Joe answered in a low tone.

"Yep," Goodman said, acting drunk momentarily.

"I hope this turns out to be a quiet day. We're due for one." Joe said in a conversational tone.

"Well, we didn't have anybody to sew together yet," Goodman exclaimed. "Say, would you like to do the honors of waking White up and getting him dressed since I did it yesterday when you weren't here."

"I wouldn't really," Joe exclaimed, hoping Goodman might offer to help him. They would be able to do it more quickly and effectively if they worked together.

"OK, I'll tell you what. How about if I give you a hand?"

"All right, if you want to, but you don't have to. I can do it." Joe noticed the mischievous gleam in Goodman's eye and knew a practical joke was probably coming.

Flicking his cigarette onto the floor, Goodman started toward the seclusion room as he gasped half laughing, "I'll get him up and you dress him."

"Oh, so that's the catch," Joe answered jesting. "Never mind then. I'll do it myself."

"Nope, you wanted help so I'll help you."

"Come on, never mind," Joe replied, becoming serious now.

"Nope, I'll get him up," Goodman insisted as he unlocked the cell door and disappeared inside. Soon he came out dragging a mattress with White half on it. Joe made his way down the hall as fast as he could as White got to his feet, swinging his arms and yelling,

"I'll kill you, sonabitch. I'll kill yo. . . "

"OK, he's all yours," Goodman laughed as he stood back.

"Thanks!" Joe gasped sarcastically as he tried to dodge the blows. Finally out-maneuvering White, he leaped at the patient's back, got an arm lock on his right arm, and grasped the other wrist tightly. "Come on, time to get dressed, White," Joe said, trying to sound calm and forcing the patient towards the clothes room.

"Do you want any help?" Goodman said seriously now, but still laughing.

"No, I've got him now."

"I must say you are quick when you want to be. Jud!" Goodman yelled, "Get some clothes for White."

Joe forced the violent man into the clothes room and pushed him against a row of lockers, pressing his arm up hard to make him submit.

"Will you get dressed?"

"Sonabitch, I kill you. Sona. . ."

"Will you get dressed?" Joe pressed harder as he stared at the deep furrows in the back of White's head. The muscles in his arm strained as he pushed. His side started to hurt sharply and looking down, he saw that White was pinching him with the arm that was extending backward. Quickly, Joe jerked White away from the lockers and threw him on to the floor so he would release his painful grip on him. Joe could see that White was unfeeling this morning and therefore he instructed Jud to put clothes on his violently struggling body.

As they were putting a blue shirt on him, White's arm got loose and struck Jud a vehement blow in the cheek. Shaking it off, Jud continued with his task as if nothing had happened. The salty, pungent odor of White's unwashed skin filled Joe's nostrils with disgust. Finally, after White was dressed, Joe took him into the bathroom and stood him before the sink. The patient then turned in the water and washed his hands for several minutes, as he very frequently did. Meanwhile, Joe

169

walked into the office and, taking a bar of soap, washed his own bare arms thoroughly.

—wish I could calm down as quickly as White does by simply putting my hands under water—White is quiet by now and I still shake from the exertion—why don't I quit this lousy job— I could get better money elsewhere. . .

Joe laughed at himself as he thought of how he had sat before the supervisor and naïvely asked to be put on an admissions ward because he wanted to do good for humanity.

The morning dragged on slowly; finally Joe went to lunch. Upon returning, he entered the ward by way of the screen door that led from the porch to the ward. After much conversing with Goodman and attempting to keep the patients still, he saw Angus come in from the office and walk about the ward.

"Who left this door open?" Angus's voice rang clearly through the air as the attendants looked at the open screen door that the charge was standing by. "Who was the last one through this door?" Angus demanded again.

"I made sure the door was locked when I came through," Joe said.

"You left it open!" Angus exclaimed.

"I did not!" Joe said defensively.

"Well, who did then? The man in the moon?" Angus demanded.

"The lock is kind of tricky. I've done the same thing before," Goodman explained, trying to smooth over the situation.

"Never mind, count the patients," Angus sighed.

Benches were moved to the middle of the room, dividing the floor in two; then all of the patients were herded to one side and Goodman counted each across.

"I get eighty seven," Goodman declared.

"That's what I was afraid of. There's supposed to be eighty eight," Angus declared.

"Let's see who's missing," Goodman said, examining the multitude.

After running down the list of names, they found that a patient named George Probity was gone.

"You go outside and see if you can find him while I call the police," Angus told Joe.

With renewed enthusiasm, Joe made his exit and headed straight for the woods where he thought the patient might have fled.

The dew that the sun had still not burned away, made Joe's feet wet as he strode through the tall grass. The sun made the vegetation look faded and washed out, but deeper in the woods the shaded areas gave the leaves a rich brilliance as if they would bleed green if squeezed. Straining his eyes and being carefull with his tired hurting leg, Joe made his way through a thicket of deep vines that lay in an opening in the trees.

— better find him or my name will be mud around this place— feel so free out here—wish I could tramp through the woods all day. . .

As he walked along, he thought about the stories he had read about raving maniacs running loose from mental institutions, and about how very few of this type of patient there really were. He thought about such a patient's hiding behind a tree and pouncing on him savagely as he neared, and about having to defend himself as Samson had against the Philistines. But by no stretch of the imagination could such an attack become a reality, for George Probity was a small, meek man who was easily frightened and very sluggish.

Joe returned an hour later, tired and empty handed.

It was late afternoon of one long tiring day and Joe was seated in his usual place watching Alvin. This young patient was overactive and the whole day he had been singing the phrase "I went to London to see the Queen," over and over. Now he was sitting beside Joe's chair.

"I wanna shower," Alvin whined.

"You already had one," Joe said in a tired voice.

"I wanna shower. I'm full of shit! I'm full of shit!"

"Shut up, Alvin!" Joe snapped, raising his fist as if to hit the boy.

"I went to London. . ." Alvin sang again as Joe tried to ignore him.

This song went on continuously for fifteen minutes.

"I wanna shower," Alvin pleaded again.

"Shut up, you shit-eater and keep your hands out of your ass," Barron yelled as he kicked Alvin in the calf. The patient had been trying to get up.

For several days Alvin had been very overactive and his body bore many bruises because of it.

Joe's nerves were ready to burst and he was sure that he would make this his last day.

171

"I wanna shower!"

"Let me see!" Joe said, looking into the back of the shirtless boy's coveralls. "You aren't going to get a shower, so shut up."

Alvin became silent again. Joe was deep in a fantasy about going swimming after work, when he felt something land in his lap. Glancing quickly downward, he saw Alvin's hand withdrawing; a large mound of excrement lay in Joe's lap.

"Ahhhhh!" Joe shrieked in horror as he leaped to his feet and watched part of the pile plop to the floor while the rest clung to his pants. In an unthinking rage, Joe turned on Alvin and, with a mighty thrust, planted his foot into the cringing boy's side.

"Hold still," Goodman ordered, striding up with a mop in one hand and a ruler in the other. Running the edge of the ruler down the front of Joe's white pants, Goodman flicked the clinging feces onto the floor. Quickly, Joe went to the clothes room and changed into a pair of blue hospital pants. As he emerged from the clothes room, he saw Gore walk away with a dust pan full of excrement. Goodman was wiping the dirty area with the mop. Without noticing, Goodman swung the mop into the face of the smiling Alvin; then he watched as Alvin licked his face with his tongue.

"Yum Yum, you like that, don't you?" Goodman said mimicking Alvin's ludicrous smile.

It was Sunday morning as Joe came into the ward.

—Vico—Vico—Joe Mephibosheth you are caught in a sphere—around and around you go—always predictable—very cyclical—the key still turns hard in this lock—when are they going to call in and get it fixed—ward smells as bad as ever—guess I'll never get used to it—it's as if everything had stopped where it was when I left and just came into motion again when I put my key in the door—hope Angus is here today and not on pass—can't stand the days that Barron rules—oh no Barron's in charge—better prepare myself for an unpleasant day—why is it that my mind is so active and rational in the morning but as the day rolls on it becomes very dull and dreamy—as if I am in a world of unreality but one where my thought are subterranean and I must make an effort to really know what I'm thinking—it must be boredom and disgust that makes me flee from reality—why is it that I only see and remember the unusual and exciting while the menial slips by unnoticed—church today—the supervisor better let me go to church or I will have a good excuse to quit—what is it about this lousy smelly job that makes me stay—I should have quit long ago and gotten a job where I could make some money—maybe I enjoy this because it has shown me that being a psychiatrist is to work in an area that is mentally dangerous and relatively unknown. . .

Joe was given his usual task of dressing White. After much cajoling and even more arm twisting, the boy was clothed and released on the ward. As he emerged from the clothes room, Barron called from one of the cells.

"Mephibosheth, come here."

Joe made his way to the room where Barron was bending over a patient lying on the bed who was wearing undershorts.

"What's the matter, Barron?"

"I found Jacobs lying in the bathroom and he wouldn't get up. He must have slipped and pulled a tendon or a muscle. You stay here and watch him while I call the doctor."

Joe examined the tall, mute man. His left leg lay extended in an awkward position with the outside of his foot lying flat, twisted to the left side. Just below the hip the leg was swollen but not discolored. The man's acne-pitted face quivered as he lay quietly; Joe thought he read an expression of extreme pain written on the man's drawn lips and glassy blue eyes.

"The doctor said to take him to X-ray," Barron said as he finally reentered the room.

"I don't think this man should be moved. He looks like he has a broken leg," Joe said anxiously.

"Nonsense, you guys are all the same. Any idiot can tell that it isn't broken. Now watch and learn. Wiggle your toes, Jacobs."

The man moved his long dirty toes.

"There see," Barron said, turning his face to Joe and staring at him with an intent eye.

"What does that prove?" Joe asked cynically.

"What does that prove! What does that prove!" Barron repeated in a high nasal voice, mimicking Joe.

Joe felt his face burn as he tightened his arm in an attempt to keep from hitting Barron. He felt his body still quivering from the effort of having to struggle with White every morning; he knew that his blood stream was charged with adrenalin from his previous activity, and it would be awhile before he could become calm again.

"Yes, what does that prove?" Joe repeated through his teeth. "I have been known to be wrong, but I really do think this man has a broken leg."

"You really are an idiot," Barron snapped. "And you were going to be a doctor. You wouldn't even make a good dunce. Here I have only an eight grade education and I'm smarter than you! You go to college and come thinking you're God Almighty himself. Well let me tell you right now, buster, one of these days someone is going to knock you down a peg." Barron was furious.

"Now watch!" Barron continued.

The attendant leaned over the patient and started to lift his knee so that his foot slid back to his buttock.

"Don't!" Joe gasped automatically, as if it were he who was being manipulated. Catching himself, he waited for a barrage of cynical remarks, but noticed no change of expression on the patient's convulsed face.

"Straighten your leg, Jacobs."

At this command, the man extended his leg to a lying position with still no change of expression.

Barron then turned his sinister face to Joe's chafing countenance. Joe could read a faint expression of triumph in the attendant's contorted smile.

"If this man's leg were really broken, he wouldn't have been able to move it."

Joe stood in silence that admitted defeat, but he was still somewhat skeptical.

"Go get a stretcher," Barron commanded.

The patients were returning from breakfast when Joe returned, pushing a stretcher.

"Jud, Gore, Saul—Come here!" Joe called as he stopped the stretcher before the door.

The three patients came into the room.

Joe was instructing them how to lift the patient onto the stretcher without disturbing him by using the blankets when Barron came in steaming.

"Get out of this room, God Almighty, and take your disciples with you," Barron said furiously as he swung Jacob's feet onto the floor and helped him limp to the stretcher. Joe strapped the man down.

174

"Now, can you follow orders? Take Saul and push this man down to X-Ray. They've called the technician and he will be be there in a few minutes."

"Do you mind if I take Jud instead?" Joe asked gingerly, with a churning stomach.

"You never give up, do you! Next thing, you'll want to give White a parole card," Barron said, throwing his hands into the air.

Without a word, Joe instructed Jud to push as he opened the doors ahead of them to proceed through the labyrinthine wards and corridors. Finally they seated themselves before the X-ray office in the dim deserted basement, and waited for the technician to arrive.

"I can't stand that ward. How have you stood it all these years, Jud?"

"Oh, I don't know," Jud said, rubbing his huge hands slowly together as he rested his elbows on his knees.

"Do you like it here?"

"No, I guess I don't. My brother and I used to have a great time together. I wish he could come and get me so we could, have more great times."

"Where is your brother now?" Joe asked, looking at Jud.

"He died a long time ago."

"Oh!" Joe said suddenly realizing that this might be the brother that Jud was alleged to have killed. Realizing the potential danger, but extremely curious, Joe pried further.

"How did he die?" Joe asked in a kind voice.

"Wolves—wolves killed him when we were hunting. Yes, that's how it happened. They blamed it on me, but it was wolves," the patient said, wringing his hands slowly and bobbing his head nervously toward the floor.

"Did you kill him?"

"I guess so, but it was an accident. We were hunting and a wolf was sneaking up from behind. I shot and hit Jesse. Jess and I used to go everywhere; he was so good to me, why would I want to kill him?"

"Does it bother you to think about it now?"

"No, just sometimes I have nightmares about it."

"Oh, what kind of nightmares?" Joe asked, becoming very interested to realize that Jud could talk rather intelligently.

175

"They are all mixed up, but mostly they are about animals."

"Animals? What kind of animals?" Joe asked.

"All kinds—tigers, dogs."

"Do they catch you?" Joe inquired, thoroughly engrossed in the conversation.

"No, but I can't understand why they don't."

"Why?"

"Because I can't move very fast."

"What do you mean?" Joe asked.

"Well, I just mean that I run hard, but can't get away very fast."

"Do you mean you can't move like you're under water, or like a weight's tied to you, or do you mean like slow motion?"

"Yeah, something like that," Jud said, shifting his position on the seat.

Just then the technician stepped up and opened the X-ray room. Pictures were taken and after they were developed Joe studied them.

"That's quite a break," the technician said. "See here in the hip socket how the bone is broken clean in two?"

"It is broken then?" Joe asked triumphantly and immediately felt remorseful that triumph had been bought at the price of pain for the patient.

"It sure is. It is worse than most I have seen because it's hard to set. They'll probably have to operate on it to set it, and maybe even put a metal ball in the socket."

The technician made a telephone call and then instructed Joe to take the patient to get an EKG. After the patient's heart was tested, Joe delivered him to the intensive care ward.

Upon returning to his own ward, Joe saw Saul and some others dressed up in shabby ties and outdated dress jackets. Goodman had gathered them together and was counting them.

"What's up?" Joe asked Goodman.

"Church time."

"Wasn't I supposed to take the men to church?" Joe asked.

"We didn't know when you would be back. Would you like to take them?"

"Do you mind?"

"Not at all," Goodman said. "I wouldn't know what to do with religion if I had it. I'm destined for the other place anyway."

Goodman got Barron's consent to let Joe take the patients and gave Joe the list of patients on the other wards who were to accompany them.

"Can't I go with you?" Jud beseeched in an unusually boyish sounding voice.

"Your name isn't on the list," Joe said, "but I'll ask Barron."

"You must be out of your mind," Barron exclaimed at Joe's request.

Joe stood fast by his argument, feeling secretly that a human soul was at stake.

"You don't know these patients like I do," Barron said, visibly annoyed. "You sure do know how to get under a person's skin. Get out of here and take Jud with you, and I hope you won't be sorry."

Relieved, Joe instructed Jud to quickly put on a dress suit. With a childish enthusiasm which Joe had never seen in Jud before, he scampered into the clothes room and soon returned, dressed in a rough brown tweed coat that was very short at the sleeves, and a pair of wrinkled dress pants.

With Jud walking proudly at his side, Joe and the elect marched to three other wards to gather the other patients on the list.

After counting thirteen patients through the outside door into the pleasant morning sun, Joe and Jud led the procession across the street to the chapel.

Walking quietly into the church, Joe saw a collection plate on a table next to the door. Feeling into his pocket, he realized that he had no coins for the offering. Turning around, he counted the patients again: there were still thirteen. He then found two row in the back and they all sat down; Jud sat next to Joe who sat on the aisle.

Knowing that Jud was watching his every move, Joe bowed his head and tried to say a prayer; he felt awkward because he had not talked with God very much in the seven weeks since he had been working at the hospital.

"Dear Heavenly Father,
I thank thee for all of the blessings you have given me and for helping my knee to improve. Also I thank thee for my sanity and please help me keep a healthy mental out-look. I really can't think of much more to say except, please

help those poor mental patients to really see you and believe in you and please help me not to fall into mental
degradation.

This I ask in Jesus' name.

Amen."

Somehow Joe felt that this prayer still left him empty. Sitting
back, he watched the other attendants bring their charges into
the church and stand proudly by in their white coats, while
overseeing them into the seats. Suddenly Joe realized something.

—I didn't bring my white coat—the attendants are supposed
to bring their white coats to church—I'm the only one—lucky
I'm sitting in the back of the room—hope Mrs. Machir doesn't
come in and see me without it. . .

The service began. They sang, read from the prayer book,
stood up and sat down. Joe sat sternly in his seat and followed
the service, very conscious that Jud was watching his every
move. This close attention gave Joe a secret pride.

The sermon came next and Joe noticed that Jud was not
watching him any more. His head was hanging and he was
fidgeting in his seat. By the time the sermon had almost ended,
Jud had become extremely restless and was muttering lowly to
himself as he clenched a hymn book close to his face.

Suddenly Joe realized that there was something very wrong
were becoming louder and louder until Joe could make out
some of what he was saying.

"I'm a killer, murderer. The wolves will get me. The roaches
eat me. Eat me. Eat me. Eat. . ."

The muttering became quite loud as Jud rocked back and
forth, kissing the hymn book now. Joe put his arm on Jud's
shoulder to try to quiet him. Very soon Jud's words were imperceptibly run together but the muttering reached a shouting
volume as Jud stood up and began waving his arms. The minister
continued as if nothing were happening, but the attendants in
white coats began to come up the aisle as Joe stood up to try
and calm Jud.

"Quick get him outside!" one attendant said as many white
arms reached over and pulled Jud to the aisle and out the
church door.

Stunned, Joe could only follow the men in the white coats as they went down the front steps and stopped in a circle on the front lawn. Squeezing through the attendants Joe saw Jud's huge, terrified body huddled in a ball on the grass. The shadows of the surrounding figures danced around in the shaded center.

"Don't let them take me back. Take me with you. Please don't let them take me back, Please. . . Please. . ." Jud sobbed in convulsions.

"Take it easy, Jud. Take it easy," Joe exclaimed, not knowing what else to say.

As Joe stood before this sobbing hunk, he felt something nameless welling inside of him, something that terrified him horribly. It was as if he, Joe, were the center of attention, as if the attendants' hands were poised to grasp him. Yes, the two of them were the same; but no, this was unacceptable. No, it was more than unacceptable, it was horrifying! Their minds were one. They felt the same, knew the same, panicked the same. No, this must not be. Joe stood back, panic-stricken. He wanted to break this feeling, to sever it. He wanted Jud to fight. This would prove they were not the same.

Suddenly Jud's face changed. No tears were present as he started to get to his feet and his voice changed from a high strain to a loud thunder.

"I can think on my own. You're not going to take me back!" Jud yelled as the white coats closed in with Jud and Joe in the middle. Pile after pile was formed and wave after wave of assaults moved in and back as white coats got dirty, rolling on the dirt and grass, trying to subdue this huge, struggling form. Joe held tightly to Jud's leg and then to his head as they all lost and regained their grips on him. Finally, the full force of all the attendants came heavily down on the patient to pin him to the ground. Joe finally backed off, tearing the last remnants of his own shirt, which partly shrouded his head, to tatters.

Jud quit struggling and Joe persuaded the attendants to take him back to 38M. Eight attendants carried Jud, while the rest went back to take the patients out of church.

Shirtless, Joe unlocked the door to 38M and ran, bruised and bleeding slightly from fingernail marks, to open the seclusion room door. Quietly sobbing, Jud took the remnant of his Sunday clothes off and walked quietly into the seclusion room as

179

Barron strode up to the attendants for an explanation.

Jud sat mutely in the corner of the seclusion room as Joe sorrowfully filled out accident reports. He was wearing one of the blue shirts reserved for patients which he had found in the clothes room.

Joe could not bring himself to go to the seclusion room door. Barron oozed the smelly substance of ultimate victory while Goodman stood by looking deeply troubled.

Under Goodman's auspices, the attendants fought all day to try and keep Jud from being sent to the maximum security ward. They finally succeeded.

Joe was in deep despair for the rest of the day. He told the supervisor that he could not take it any longer and must quit.

It was two o'clock and there was only an hour to go in this shocking day. Joe kept his mind from wandering by directing the bed making crew as they unfolded the mattresses and placed the sheets over them. There were all of the familiar faces, but one was missing. One tall, lanky form bent low over each bed and worked laboriously until his task was completed. One dedicated soul worked religiously and obediently followed directions. One hard-looking, silent monolith stood awkwardly by when bidden. A large lump formed in Joe's throat as he thought about Jud, huddled in that isolated shadowy corner, alone and unwanted. As he looked at the side of the dormitory where Jud usually started making beds, Joe could almost see his towering figure swiftly flattening the plastic mattresses and unfolding the sheets. The work crew seemed lonely, and vacant to him without the presence of Jud.

"Saul, where does Jud Icarus usually sleep?" Joe asked one of the patients.

"There," Saul answered with a partial smile and then continuing his work.

"Here?" Joe asked in wonderment as he stood by a rusty, springless bed near the aisle.

"Yes," Saul answered, lifting his head and smiling momentarily as if interrupted.

—this bed—this is always the first bed that Jud makes but it's always wet—every morning he wipes it off with a sheet— Jud doesn't wet his pants but—he must have enuresis—hope they won't be too hard on him—it's probably because he is

180

so big that people are afraid of him—they'll probably just give him more Thorazine—poor fellow. . .

Walking over to the window, Joe gazed through the shit caked window guard, where he had often seen Jud standing. Looking out, Joe saw the woods and grass beckoning in the gentle afternoon breeze. Lonely clouds were gliding across the heavens and darting sparrows made solitary silhouettes against the blue. Joe could feel his eyes swell damply as a single tear collected in each. Squinting and hardening his face, he quickly turned from the window.

"Gore, get up, there's a bed over here to be made," Joe commanded, trying to sound authoritative. But his voice was cracking.

When the beds were all made, Joe led the patients downstairs. The sun had gone behind a cloud and the interior of the ward was dark as Joe walked around looking at the individual faces. Gazing down a row of benches at the many silhouettes, Joe realized that he was seeing these faces now from a different angle. The ears protruded and they seemed pointed at the top. The deathly pallor of the ivory faces seemed to Joe as something dreadful, something from the same mold. These were monstrous features, different and yet the same. These were the faces of devils.

—legions—many are legions—demons have possessed them—they are not their own—no—that is ridiculous—they are simply poor unfortunates. . .

Somehow, this feeling of seeing a room full of night-marish satans struck panic into Joe's heart and he attempted to suppress any further thoughts, refusing to even look again at the seated figures. Instead, he watched the minute hand of the clock. As it slowly came to indicate three o'clock, he fled.

Trying not to think about the painful happenings of the day, Joe drove home where he sat down at his table to hastily devour a few cold morsels of food. The nourishment was tasteless and Joe simply ate because he knew that he usually ate at this time.

—what will I do—don't feel like swimming—it's stifling hot in here—so hot—I must go somewhere. . .

The food forced it was down his throat and landed in thick solid lumps in his stomach. The particles weighed heavily inside him. Joe's eyes darted about the empty room as he thought

181

of all the devils or gods that he had sensed there. This meal was something to get done with. He knew that he could not sit still for long. He must do something. He must get away.

—the walls and floor are wavy—they move back and forth to each beat of my temples—can't remember when I've been so fidgety—feel something like I did just before going on a date with Della—forget this food—I must leave before this room falls on me. . .

Leaving everything as it was, Joe went out the door, got into his car and drove off, still not knowing his destination. The chilled late afternoon air parted and reparted his hair as it grazed the left side of his head.

—yes I know where to go—I will go to my favorite spot on the Thinking Hill—I will look at the world apart from it—I will get my bearings and meaning—I will chain myself to the rock until I have found something to grasp—yes—yes. . .

This new idea struck Joe with a childish delight. He turned his auto in the direction of his destination.

The yellow sun was starting to give a reddish tinge to the lower reaches of the heavens as Joe came to a halt, slammed the car door, and briskly walked into the forest. He could feel his chest expand and contract in a new exuberance as he slipped between large stones and started up a steep grade. Great excitement overtook him; he ran, leaped and jumped, alone in the beckoning woods. Throwing his head limply backward, he slowed down and watched the branches cross his view as they scratched the back of the foamy aqua heavens. He was not being watched. No one was there to observe him except the few uncritical squirrels. With his chin still skyward, he threw his arms out and embraced all of the loveliness and freedom of his surroundings. Hurling this strong unlabeled emotion from him, it whirled around and around and returned to him with a deep breath, filling him with a sensation of well being and supreme solitude.

This was himself that he was expressing and it was not a feeling that he could share with anyone but nature. As he let himself relax, he felt an enthusiasm, a newness, that he had never experienced before. All tenseness and self-dislike fled, giving his a feeling of relaxation that was so strong that he felt as if he would fall into a ball on the ground. Several gurgles of delight flowed from his throat as he raised his head again to get his bearings.

With a leap and a skip, he was off again up the grade, ducking low branches and flying over logs. It was a ballet, a beautiful dance with a performer of one for an audience of fluttering birds and jumping squirrels to the accompaniment of the trees which were waving their many batons to the rhythm of the caressing wind.

A break in a thicket brought Joe to the place that he loved. It was a rocky crag overlooking the synthetic moldings of mankind and yet above and beyond the reach of convention. It was his hideaway where he could dangle his legs over the edge of the cliff and let gravity pull all inhibition out through his feet while he remained strong and unyielding to the call of a leap to distant destruction.

Looking around, Joe caught a glimpse of an invader of his premises. It was an empty beer can sitting upon his favorite seat. Stepping forward, he gingerly picked the enemy up and cast it quickly over the precipice. A feeling of delight filled him as he then climbed on his perch; the last remnant of artificiality had been hurled from his nest.

As the sun set slowly behind him, Joe looked down and watched the world bustle by; he wished he could stay forever. One by one, lights started to come on and the firmament behind him gave a brilliant red glow to the surroundings as the sun went down. It was then that Joe realized that he must return down the mountain and again interact and perform in the world. He had not achieved enlightenment, only relief. He could not flee; Jud was in the seclusion room, his own job as an attendant was behind him and his future was still in a deep fog.

As he gazed around, Joe realized the shadows had deepened and the night had smothered all color. Nothing but shades of black prevailed and the only colors were the distant whites and yellows of the city lights. He must turn his back on these lights to find his car and return. Without hesitation, he stepped back through the thicket into the dark wood. The shadows played tricks with his eyes as he told himself he must be calm and not let himself become alarmed. Just then a shadow leaped across his path making his heart jump. With shaking hands outstretched to keep the branches from his eyes, he walked with trembling steps, trying to convince himself that panic was not the solution. Just then he felt someone treading behind him, as though close enough to peer over his shoulder and rest his chin on Joe's right shoulder blade as they walked. Resolutely, Joe peered straight ahead, fixing his eyes only on his path as movements attempted to distract him. The only sounds that came to his ears were the breaking of debris under his feet and the flow of his quick short breaths. The only sensations he felt were the heaviness of his heart and the looming presence at his shoulder.

Finally Joe reached his car and drove quickly home. After eating again he sat in his easy chair and began to read. After many minutes he realized that his eyes were only following the lines and his hands were mechanically turning the pages. Resting the book on his lap, he listened to his inner thoughts, but he knew that his mind was not moving logically. It was as if a crowd gathered for a heated debate and everyone was trying to get his say at once. The intense roar made everything imperceptible as only words and snatches of phrases could be deciphered above the din as each attempted to express his own viewpoint. In a frustrating attempt to introduce order and harmony to this assembly, Joe tried to send most of the members into the darkness and give only chosen ones the spotlight, but in this futile attempt to sort and cull, Joe still kept hearing several antagonists who screamed from the depths, causing conflict and anxiety.

—what is the purpose of life—what does the future hold in store—you are useless a leech to society—purposeless and insane—the world is lovely and the summer is still blooming— lose yourself in nature—run away—get a well paying job and make money—lots of it and settle down—wander—wander—find yourself—what is the use of living for as you grow older you go against your ingrained beliefs and permanent scars form—scars that will collect and someday destroy you—love and be loved— there is love—go and find it—capture and cherish it—make it unconditional love and set no bounds for it—the world is nothing but hostility and man's basic nature is hostile—it's just that most people don't notice it but it destroys them in the end— there is love—yes I know there is true love and brotherhood—it comes with maturity—what is maturity but a verbal abstraction that everybody talks about but nobody knows what it really means—but there is good and right—there is—there must be

184

somewhere or in somebody—there may be high minded phrases with a myriad of semantic meaning but there is kindness and love—try working on M38 for several years—try being loving and kind—try and be understanding and generous and you will join them—they will preserve a place for you on one end of a dirty smelly bench where you can sit and vegetate your days away— you can meditate and hallucinate and have a nice time wetting your bed—no—love will prevail— true love knows and cares—it is not isolated—is not puffed up—you tried it and found you were no different than the rest—you ate from unpurchased plates and drank from stolen cups—you have shown cruelty and selfishness—you are incapable of your high minded word called love—you have kept only a false sense of morality and slowly ever so slowly that is leaving you—you are nothing but a good for nothing—no no no—yes yes yes—you have no future—what will you do—get a job that you hate—be a nine to fiver and day-dream the whole time—what's the use—give up—quit fighting and go the path of least resistance—I have many alternatives—I will go back to school—yes—I will be a teacher or a social worker —I will learn to love and learn to help—I will try to keep the two greatest commandments—highmindedness again—wait and see —besides you have no money so how can you go to school with-out money. . .

The voices raged hotly on while Joe sat there, drawn into this whirlwind of confusion but with a dawning conviction that he must study again.. He must go back to school. He felt a new hope come over him, something he could cling to. He was de-cided. Tomorrow he would visit State College and try to enroll for the fall semester. After much deliberation, he decided that English would be his major and he would not worry about the money. He hoped and prayed that the money would come.

After coming to this decision, he felt better and decided to see if he could sleep. He would arise early the next day, go to the college, and try to find new employment.

With this renewed feeling of strength and purpose, Joe forced himself to turn the lights out. His bed lamp still burned as he stood before his bed thinking.

—I will pray for help—he hasn't let me down before—I will kneel like I did when I was a kid. . .

Getting carefully down and putting most of his weight on his

185

good knee, Joe buried his face in the covers. It was embarrassing. He hadn't kneeled for many years and it felt awkward and embarrassing.

He prayed:

> "Dear God, I don't know what to say except please forgive me all my sins and help me to know and love you better. I have many problems. You know what they are and what I ask is that you might please help me to iron them out.
>
> This I ask in thy Son's name.
>
> Amen."

Then Joe sat on the bed and wondered why he didn't feel physically uplifted after asking God to forgive his sins. Somehow he didn't feel that God had forgiven him his wrongs. He didn't feel spiritually uplifted, but he did feel slightly better.

Turning off the light, Joe lay down in the dark. The old feelings came back to him, but he closed his eyes tightly and felt less afraid of the night.

The next day, Joe hurried to State College and got an application for admission. He worked all day on it and had neared completion when the telephone rang. It was the hospital and they told him that he could not quit work without giving several weeks notice. Joe finally consented to drive to the hospital and talk with the supervisor. After long deliberation and consultation with his supervisors, Joe decided he would return if he could work on the night shift. He had heard that it was easy work and the patients would all be asleep and besides that, he could study at that time.

It was eleven thirty at night and Joe was walking across the hospital ground to where the night supervisor had directed him. As he walked, he felt rather happy and attempted to refrain from scrutinizing the shadows.

—this will really be the test—Goodman said he couldn't stand the night shift because it spooked the daylights out of him—maybe he has feeling similar to mine—this will be a sure test to rid myself of these cobwebs in my brain—the wards look so dark—wonder where the attendants stay—Barron said that all the night shift attendants do is sleep—what's that ahead—something's moving—oh no—whew it's two skunks—they're real—yes they're real. . .

Feeling restored to really have perceived reality, Joe stepped happily along to ward M34. This was the ward he had first entered his first day of work. As he inserted his key in the lock, he looked through the pane in the door and saw the television on; closing the door behind him, he perceived several attendants lounging on the wooden chairs that the patients had earlier vacated to go to bed upstairs. Walking into the office of this ward, he saw a stocky man seated behind the desk.

"Are you Smith?" Joe asked.

"You must be Joe Mephibosheth," Smith answered.

"The supervisor said you would help me out. I used to work days but this is my first day on nights."

"Sit down," Smith said, motioning to an empty chair. "So you worked days. How did you like it?"

"Kind of messy. I can't say that I really enjoyed it."

"Really. Where did you work?" Smith asked.

"Right down the hall here on M38."

"Oh, well, I don't blame you for not liking that ward. I used to work days there and really hated that smelly, filthy pig pen."

"How did you like working days?" Joe asked, starting to take a liking to this soft spoken man.

"Didn't mind it too much. You got a raw deal when you got sent on that ward. Most attendants avoid it like the plague. Did you get any shit thrown at you?" Smith asked with a smile.

At this question, Joe sat toward the edge of his chair and enthusiastically related some of the things he had had to put up with. Smith listened with an interested look on his face and curled the corners of his mouth at some humorous incidents that Joe related.

"But one thing I must say about it is that it was an experience I'll never forget," Joe concluded.

"Yes, the few times I was there I really hated it. Were you on any of the front wards at all?" Smith asked.

"No, only to take patients to intensive care or taking a new admission to wards M1 and M2. I never worked on them."

"They aren't as messy as some of the back wards, but in the daytime you have all those doctors, supervisors and nurses bossing you around all the time."

"How is their therapy?" Joe inquired.

187

"Therapy? What therapy? As far as medical care goes, those horse doctors do all right, but there are so few psychiatrists and psychologists that the best they can do is shell out the Thorazine and send a few to get shock treatment."

"You mean, it's that bad?" Joe asked.

"Well, they do give some psychotherapy, but really to very few patients, and then only go for a short time. They also send the patients to occupational therapy and music therapy which may be helpful, but all in all, there are just too many admissions to handle them all. I also have to laugh when they send those poor scared student nurses on the wards. A lot of those girls are struggling for their own sanity as it is and with little or no experience they are supposed to help the patients. Besides that, there are a lot of Negro admissions and many of the doctors are imported from who-knows-where. These doctors probably have a hard time knowing how the average white thinks, let alone how the frustrated Negro works."

"What's the matter with this place then?" Joe questioned.

"It's spelled M-O-N-E-Y.

"Also I hear the politics of this place is goofed up, but I don't know enough about that to really make a comment about it."

"How many attendants are there on this ward? Those guys out there look like attendants, but are they all on this ward?" Joe asked, trying to fathom Smith's expression, but not wanting to offend him.

"No, they belong in M37 and M35 and the other upstairs wards. As a matter of fact, you have these three downstairs wards to yourself tonight. That's wards M34, M36, and M38," Smith said, lighting a cigarette.

"All three of them?"

"Yes, but that makes only a total of about fifteen patients. You only have those in seclusion and others who are more privileged," Smith said. Then he continued to explain the simple duties that Joe had to perform in the morning.

The two talked for over an hour on different topics.

"Did you hear about that patient that clobbered the attendant months ago?" Smith asked.

"No."

"Where have you been that you didn't hear about that? I was on ward M21 a couple of months ago when I heard a couple of thuds on the ward below, M20. That ward is the teenager

188

ward. The boys and girls are on the same ward and their bedrooms are down the hall from each other. Well anyway, we came downstairs and found the attendant of the boys lying unconscious on the floor with his head bashed in. A boy was standing over him with a baseball bat."

"Did he kill him?" Joe asked.

"No, the guy's skull is all dented and I don't know if he will ever work again, but he wasn't killed. That isn't the whole story. We got the boy and turned on the lights and would you believe that in the far corner of the room, in one of the boy's bed, was a girl. The two of them were just going to town. That ward is like a country club. Those kids there aren't crazy, they're mean and lazy."

"So what did they do with the boy?" Joe asked.

"A bunch of us took him down to the maximum security ward and on the way we really handed it to him. Later, he was sent up state to the prison mental institution and would you believe that he is out walking the streets today?"

"Really?"

"That's right. I saw him myself in the city just strolling around as big as life."

"Do they let the girls and boys go together like that at night on that ward?"

"They aren't supposed to, but those kids are real sneaky. I thought they had cracked down on them, but I heard that just last week a group of boys was caught climbing out the dorm windows at night to sneak into the girl's dorm."

Joe talked with Smith for several minutes more. Finally he noticed that the television was off and the attendants had wandered away.

"Well, I guess I'll get going," Smith said, standing and walking to the door.

"Where are you going?" Joe asked, somewhat alarmed that he would be left alone.

"I'll see you in the morning. If you need anything I'll be in ward M32 right next door."

Smith disappeared and Joe examined the lighted office.

—it's so quiet in here now—I have charge of these three wards —I better check and make sure everything's all right. . .

Walking into the hall, he looked through the darkness toward M38. All of the double doors were wide open through

189

the three wards, but only very dim patches of light guided the way. Knowing that this would be a good exercise in ridding himself of his inhibitions, Joe entered into the darkness. He remembered how he had walked the same path his first day of work, with Mrs. Machir. As he forced his steps forward, the darkness sucked him onward toward a small light that was still burning on M38.

—these wards weren't this dark when I came on—the attendants must have turned the light off. . .

The darkness hung like black silk tapestries moving in a gentle breeze. It attacked and retreated before his eyes. The blackness seemed to move like leaves being churned by a gale. Each advancing step gave Joe renewed confidence that he was conquering an obsession once and for all. The darkness didn't seem so foreign as it had before; in fact, Joe welcomed its nothingness. But still, deep inside, the fear remained. It was not as intense as it had been, but it was there just the same. Step by step, with his arms partly extended like a sleep walker, Joe forced himself onward into the abyss. His destination was the distant light burning on M38.

—yes—I will make it—half way to go—the only movement is the darkness and there is nothing living there—the patients are all asleep and there is nothing to worry about. . .

He walked on with ever renewed confidence. As he groped his way through the open doors of the ward that he knew so well, the usual smell came to his nostrils, but it was not as intense, probably because the patients were not there. Feeling his way to the seclusion room, he flicked on the light. As his eyes adapted, Joe saw White sprawled in his usual place, oblivious to the world because of the great doses of Thorazine he had been given. After switching off the light, he proceeded to the next room and turned on the light. Suddenly Jud's silent image came in view. He was sitting, huddled in the far corner and staring directly at Joe's face through the door. It was as if Jud never slept and his eyes were always on Joe. Startled, Joe instantaneously flicked the light off again and made his way to the beam at the head of the hall. This was the room in which he had spent so many hours. Glancing around, it came to Joe just how predictable many of the patients were. He realized, as he looked at the benches, that many of the patients had set in the same place, day after day. It was almost as if he could see each one of their faces. Gazing to his right, Joe spied the chair where he used to sit. Walking over to his seat, he slowly lowered himself into it. Looking up all of a sudden, he gave a sharp, choking gasp. The ward was filled. All of the faces were there in their proper places, the lights were on, and Alvin was sitting beside his chair, whining. No, this was not a vision like the one he had had when he had seen a man sitting beside his bed. It was less clear. No, it was not less clear, but on a different level. However, Joe was absolutely sure that this impression was momentary and that it would fade; nevertheless, it was alarming. Joe sprang to his feet and started back down the hall. Casting a backward glance, he saw the now empty chairs. Feeling less agitated, he slowed his pace to be sure of his steps. Walking silently through the next ward and straining his eyes to discern his path, a sound came to his ears.

—it's the sound of somebody taking a deep breath but it is close—very close—too close to be from one of the rooms—a patient must be beside me—it can't be—maybe I am having—no—I know it isn't my imagination. . .

Casting his head around but quickening his steps, he could only see the faint glow from the windows around the ward. Walking into the office from which he had set out, he quickly grabbed a flashlight. Soon he was off down the hall again with the light in his hand.

"What's going on?" came a voice from a bench where Joe had heard the noise. "Who's that?" The voice came again as an attendant quickly sat up, shielding the light from his eyes.

"Sorry, I didn't know who was there," Joe exclaimed apologetically, casting the light around the ward and noticing two other attendants wrapped in sheets and blankets and reclining on other benches. After several more apologies, Joe walked away.

—they really do sleep at night—this is supposed to be my ward and there are three attendants on it—wonder if they're afraid to go upstairs to their wards. . .

Returning to the office, Joe sat down in the seat that Smith had vacated and thought about all of the things that Smith had said and the fact that the attendants really did sleep at night. As he thought, however, he couldn't get the picture of Jud, huddled in the corner of the seclusion room, out of his mind.

—if only there were some way I could help Jud—poor fellow —he will rot in here—but maybe—maybe a person could adjust to this life and finally come to expect and accept it—my parakeet used to love to get out of his cage and fly around the house but when I came back after my first year of prep school, he didn't want to come out—he was frightened of the outside—guess it was because nobody else took him out while I was gone—I must make a resolution to do the right thing—I will not sleep and won't eat the patients' food—if I am to be truly moral and godly I must do this and also I will not mistreat the patients—wonder why Jud isn't asleep—they give him enough medication to dope an elephant but it isn't affecting him—wonder when they will take him out of seclusion. . .

After much thought, Joe picked up a novel that lay on the desk and began to read. The night dragged on and every now and then he looked over his shoulder and out the window to see if the blue glow of morning had come yet. As he sat scanning the pages for several hours, he became very relaxed. The whole building was deathly quiet and several times Joe had to stand and walk around the office, taking deep breaths, so he could stay awake. As he was getting deeper and deeper into the pages of his book, the back of his mind continued to retain the deep imprint of Jud's hard-looking and yet sorrowful face as he sat quietly in the seclusion room. This image was static and only came and went as Joe's interest in his book became more or less concentrated. His surface attention was fairly well occupied by the war story he was reading. The novel had nothing to do with Jud or the institution and yet Joe found himself constantly picturing the scenes described by the author in terms of the institution and most of all of Jud. If the soldiers were holed up in a ruined house, this house would appear to Joe as having many of the components of one of the wards. If a tank rolled by a building or tree, it was an object that Joe had seen on the hospital grounds. If the soldiers were huddled in a snowy trench, one of the soldiers would have Jud's features. If the hero was cautiously edging his way up a deserted road, Jud was one of the soldiers ready to give the main character assistance.

—that's it—Jud is the one who was looking over my shoulder on the hill the other day and the one in my room—no that can't be because I had the feeling of having company after my

192

first day of working and I hardly even paid any attention to or knew anything about Jud then—maybe he was just fitted in myself later—that still doesn't explain how or why I got these feelings in the first place.

Joe read on and marveled at how the whole story, battle after battle and incident after incident, was not happening on unknown territory, but right there on the hospital grounds. The whole human drama was unfolding there on the territory that he had come to know. It was uncanny.

After the discovery of what his mind was doing with this fictional panorama, Joe became deeply engrossed with the story. Again, he marveled at how the bullets and bombs were not hurled from unknown doorways and trees, but from portals and shrubbery that he knew and had seen. After an unknown amount of time had elapsed, Joe became aware of a distant noise or noises. The sounds increased until they distracted Joe's attention. Looking up so as to concentrate on his hearing, Joe joyfully realized what the noises meant.

—the birds are singing—it's still dark but—but—yes they are chirping—no—the outside is a little brighter—yes it is morning— a beautiful. . .

Setting his book aside, Joe turned his chair around and stared through the window guard as he felt a newness come over him. It was like the time he had sat at his uncle's bedside all night and watched, waited and prayed that the man's fever would break without taking a beloved life. Just before dawn that morning, the doctor had come in to see his uncle and had said he would live. Yes, this morning gave him that renewed vitality, a sensation of calm and happiness. He had watched and waited, as he had done with his uncle, and the morning had indeed come.

Joe stared dreamily out the window as the sun slowly reclaimed objects and colors from the darkness. First blue, then green and then the myriad gradations of the spectrum appeared, all gradually increasing in intensity. This was one battle won, but alas, there was a contamination to this feeling, as there was with other sensations that he experienced. Rarely did he ever have a pure emotion. The remorse that he felt was for the fact that he had done nothing all night and had not really earned his pay. Even though a small voice did whisper objections, Joe would not and did not let it spoil that moment.

193

As the outside light started to illuminate his steps, Joe made his way systematically to his three wards and wrote in each ward's log book, as Smith had instructed him. Smith also had told him to help the upstairs attendant clean up the dormitory above M38. Curiously, Joe wound his way upstairs to the bedroom that he had helped clean before, in the daytime. The ward was dim and there were only a few scattered lights on in the bathroom and another in the hall. Most of the patients were still sleeping, but Joe could see a few familiar figures wandering around the room and others watching for the sun to rise.

Looking into some of the locked cells, Joe could see figures sprawled under sheets. In one room he saw Alvin lying on dirty, wet sheets as the water puddled around him. The whole ward had a sour stink that Joe knew. As he was wandering around looking at the different sights, an attendant came upstairs and turned on all of the lights. Many bodies began to stir as the two introduced themselves.

"You wanna unlock those doors over there and I'll get these," the attendant said as he walked to the row of cells at one side of the hall.

"All right," Joe answered.

"Come on, get up, you shit eater," the attendant said as he looked through the open cell door.

Soon the doors were all open.

"You get these bastards up and I'll start cleaning up the shit," the attendant said.

With those instructions, Joe went to the still occupied beds and aroused the patients, being careful not to provoke those he knew were potentially dangerous.

"How come you have to clean up here, when the day shift does it later in the morning?" Joe asked.

"If we left all that crap on the floor, the day crew would really gripe so we have to, at least, get the shit up and some of the piss," the attendant said, grabbing a mop. "Wanna get Gore going on picking those wet sheets off the bed," the attendant said, pointing and then wiping the feces from the bare behind of one of the patients with the dirty mop.

Joe did as he was told and soon the work was done. Careful not to be seen by any of the oncoming day crew on M38, he slipped into the next ward, waited for seven o'clock, and left.

It seemed peculiar to be sleeping in the daytime so Joe, after he had gone home, tired to read for a while. However, as he was not getting tired, he got into bed and wrote in his diary.

"Hey Diary,

How are you? Well, this was my first night on nights and wasn't half bad. Am winning the battle.

Hospital census: 2,500 women, 2,351.005 men, 4 police cars, 500 rats, 1 million roaches, 5 corpses, 1 George Washington, 4 Christs, 2 Mohammeds.

Turned over a new leaf and have all kinds of confidence.

Idea! I just got an idea. Yes, it's true, I just thought of most of the clothes I wear. I love white clothes, but they get dirty very easily so I have black shirts and especially pants. Black and white. They are not really only colors to me they represent the dichotomy which I divide the world into. I realized that most of my clothes are one of these two shades. Why not something else? I must buy a blue shirt and a green pair of shorts. But maybe, my vestments should remain B. and W.

I have applied to State College; the only thing I can do now is pray.

My leg is getting better. I thank the Good Lord for that. . ."

After writing a page and a half, Joe felt sleep caressing him and submitted.

Joe looked at the clock. It was four o'clock in the afternoon.

—I've had plenty of sleep—had a dream—it's slipping—must remember—yes—I walked on ward M38—the walls were burned to the ground and were still smoldering in ashes but the patients were still walking and sitting as if there were walls there—if only I could decide this—it seems of significance—maybe it means that even if they had a chance for freedom—they wouldn't take it—no—maybe it means they don't realize what is around them—oh what does it mean. . .

That night, Joe was sent to admission ward 1M. This place consisted of a long corridor with small dormitories and seclusion rooms lining it. He introduced himself to the two attendants who were in the nursing office but forgot their names. They conversed for several minutes and then one of the attendants left the office, giving Joe a greater feeling of being less scrutinized.

"What kind of patients do you get on this ward?" Joe asked the remaining attendant.

"We get new admissions. Usually they are new here, but some are readmissions."

"How do they act here? I've never been on an admission ward. Is there something I should know or watch out for?"

"No," the man chuckled kindly, "as a matter of fact they aren't much different from anybody else. Most are just poor souls who got off on the wrong track."

"I don't want to sound naïve, but I just want to get the feel of the ward," Joe said, slightly embarrassed.

"I understand perfectly. I'm glad you are straightforward in your questions. Some young fellows your age come here and act as if they know everything. I appreciate an open-minded fellow," the man said.

They conversed for a short time and then the attendant showed Joe around the ward. Walking past the other attendant, who had arranged quilts and sheets in a rocking chair to make a comfortable seat, the attendant in charge pointed to a room with an open door.

"In the morning we always check that room to make sure that the patient's bed isn't wet. If his bed is, then we wipe it up and turn the mattress over and put clean sheets on," the attendant whispered so as not to awaken the sleeping patients.

"I see," Joe said, realizing that the attendant was probably meaning for him to perform this task in the morning. "Does that patient always wet the bed?" Joe inquired.

"Usually. He used to be a medical student."

"What's he like now?" Joe asked.

"Well, he's about as stupid and confused as anyone I've ever seen. He's been here for a good many years."

"Is there any help for him?"

"When you see him you'll realize that nothing but a miracle could bring back any semblance of sanity in him."

"Why is he on this ward then?" Joe asked.

"Money and political pull, I guess. His family probably has both."

After being shown around, Joe watched as the attendant obtained a large rocking chair and placed quilts and sheets on it so as to make it comfortable. Then the attendant placed rolled sheets under each rocker so that it remained stationary.

196

Joe proceeded to make up a rocker in a similar fashion. The attendant then obtained another chair from the day room and reclined in it, reading the newspapers by a lamp. Joe also got another chair and settled down to reading a book he had brought. Down the hall Joe could see that the other attendant had dozed off. Every now and then a patient emerged from one of the rooms and walked down the hall to the bathroom.

After a while Joe thought he heard a rapping sound.

"What's that?" he asked the charge attendant beside him.

"That's the guy in seclusion. He's about as confused as they come."

"What did he do to be put in there?"

"Probably acted up on the day shift and was put in there for his own protection and the protection of the other patients."

"Oh," Joe said as he listened to the periodical raps that got louder and louder.

"Come to think of it, he had shock treatment today," the attendant said above the now loud pounding.

"Is shock therapy any good?" Joe asked.

"Seems to work well on depressed patients, but some people it doesn't seem to do any good for. He was noisy all last night."

A young-sounding voice was heard coming from the seclusion room.

"Help, help me out there. Help out there. Help out there. Help out there!" The voice came in louder and louder bursts.

"Oh, no," the attendant said. "I hope we aren't going to have to put up with his racket another night."

Joe did not answer but tried to ignore the sound and attend to his book. It was no use, he could not ignore this call that he had heard many times before.

"Couldn't we just leave him out and let him sleep in one of these dormitories? Or maybe we could leave the door open part way," Joe suggested, feeling a tinge of anxiety come over him as he thought about that terrifying chamber.

"No, it won't work. He would kill somebody for sure and he surely wouldn't shut up. If he keeps it up, I'll call the supervisor to give him a shot."

The disturbance increased, and as many minutes passed, Joe sat and watched while an increasing number of aroused patients sleepily found their way down the dim hall to the bathroom.

After a short time the attendant got up from his chair and

197

walked into the nursing office. Soon he came out again.

"The supervisor is coming with a shot," he informed Joe as he sat down again.

"Help out there. Help out there. They're trying to kill me. Help. . ." The noise continued. After ten to twenty minutes had passed, Mrs. Suso, the Supervisor, unlocked the door and came in. Going into the nursing office, she filled a hypodermic needle as Joe stood by the office door.

"Grab him quick," the charge attendant said as they quickly opened the seclusion room door and finally forced the naked young man to the floor.

"I'll kill ya! I kill ya! You'll be sorry lady. I'll kill ya!" the man screamed as the nurse quickly cleaned a spot on the man's buttocks and injected him.

Joe could see a dry, chalky, white looking substance smeared on the floor of the cell and on the patient's face and head. He could not tell what it was.

"Take it easy, young man. We're trying to help you," the nurse said, removing the needle and withdrawing from the room.

"OK, let him go," the charge attendant said.

Quickly they got out of the room and just as the door latched the patient's full force landed against the heavy steel portal.

"You'll be sorry, lady. I'll kill ya. Just wait, I'll kill ya."

"What's that white stuff that was on that patient?" Joe inquired after the nurse had left.

"It's foam. Once in a while we get one who is so mad that he froths at the mouth like a mad dog," the attendant said above the noise, as they sat back down in rocking chairs.

They talked for a short time, but the conversation slowly peered out and Joe went back to his reading.

It was three o'clock in the morning and the seclusion room was still noisy when the telephone rang. The charge, who was reclining motionless in his chair, rose and went into the nursing office. Upon emerging, he walked up to Joe.

"Ever go on morgue detail?"

"You mean somebody died?" Joe asked.

"Yes," the attendant said.

"No, I never have. What do I do?" Joe inquired, gaining his feet.

"Go out and wait by the outside door. A policeman will pick you up there and take you to one of the pavilions. Besides the policeman you will have another attendant with you. Mrs. Suso said she will bring the morgue key."

Joe then walked toward the end of the hall. The screaming sounds were diminishing but over the past two hours the words had changed somewhat.

"Help me, lady! Call Suso 85752. Help me lady! Call Suso 85752. Help me. . ." the patient shrieked in a loud, hoarse voice.

A breeze carried a chill through the air as Joe stood gazing into the darkness waiting for the hearse. In a few minutes a panel truck drove up with two men inside. The door swung open and a thin elderly attendant pushed himself to the middle of the seat, leaving room for Joe.

They introduced themselves quickly but Joe didn't remember the names.

"What's up?" Joe asked cheerfully as they drove off.

"This your first time on the meat wagon?" the attendant asked in a high pitched nasal voice.

"Yes, do you do this very often?" Joe asked.

"Not very often," the man said.

They exchanged a few words, but before Joe realized it, the truck was pulling up in front of a single story sprawling building.

"Help me get the litter from the back," the attendant said as they got out of the truck. The policeman remained behind the wheel. The attendant opened the back of the truck and they pulled out a long steel frame covered with cloth and with two wheels on one end.

"Doesn't it bother you to take dead people to the morgue? I mean, isn't it kind of depressing?" Joe asked, noticing that the man was quite old himself.

"Naw, I've been working here for years. This is nothing. Remember I was walking to work up the avenue one foggy night and saw two girls on the other side of the street as I was crossing the railroad tracks over yonder. A car came by and hit them both and killed them—threw them both in the gutter," the attendant went on as they rang the door bell of he building.

"What did you do?" Joe gasped in horror.

"Nothing, kept right on walking," he answered, pressing the doorbell again.

"How did you know they were dead?"

"They were dead. They found them in the morning and an autopsy said they were killed instantly. All I needed was to get mixed up in something like that."

A lump formed in Joe's throat as he prepared to launch a verbal attack: he could vividly imagine the whole accident scene.

—how could he do such a thing—how can anyone be so inhuman—what a ghastly story and he tells it with no emotion—no I am no better—I have seen and done many things that I am ashamed of—I am not perfect—how can I rightfully reprimand this man. . .

Just then a nurse came to the door and Joe wheeled the litter through a women's dormitory to a bed at one end. On top of the sheets was a white plastic shroud in the shape of a woman's body. Around the neck of the completely covered figure was a brown tag.

Looking around, Joe saw several old women sitting up in bed looking at the covered body. Many of their faces seemed to be anticipating a similar, impending future.

"Put the litter there, alongside the bed," the attendant said in a low voice so as not to awaken any more women.

"Now get over on the other side and grab the sheet like this and lift her with it onto the stretcher. That's it easy, easy—good! Now we strap these straps and we're ready to go."

After the straps were tightened, Joe lifted one end of the stretcher and pulled the heavy cargo toward the door. After wheeling the body out into the cold night air, they lifted it into the truck and got in themselves. The truck drove off.

—dear God please help the soul of this woman and please aid this attendant beside me—help us to open our eyes to the ways of men and help them to harmonize with your desires—I ask in Thy Son's name. . .

Somehow that short prayer made Joe feel better as he thought about the inevitability of death. The trees waved their leaves in front of street lamps making shadows dash back and forth on the group as the truck drove along. At last they pulled up to a small, isolated brick structure at the edge of the hospital grounds. The attendant unlocked the door after they had lowered the body to the ground, and Joe pushed the litter onto the morgue floor. Looking around, Joe saw a large stainless steel refrigerator with a dozen or more small doors. As he opened one he felt cold air rush out. There was a dead body in this one. He opened another, revealing still another dead body. Another door opened to an empty chamber. The attendant walked over and reaching in this cubicle, pulled out a long steel tray.

"Help me put the body in," the man said.

As Joe lifted one side of the sheet, he realized that the woman's body was not stiff. She was still warm.

—why don't they wait until the body is cold before they put it in there—it's stifling in there—maybe she isn't dead—maybe— she moved—it looked like she moved.

Joe looked closer at the form that was now lying on the cold tray.

"Did you see a movement?" Joe asked.

"A movement?" the attendant asked, picking up the litter.

"Yes, did she move?"

"No, she is dead," the attendant said looking at Joe question- ingly.

Embarrassed, Joe pushed the tray into the refrigerator and closed the door.

—what if she would revive in that cold dark chamber—what if she isn't dead—she would claw at the walls and scream and nobody would save her—she would die with a terrible expres- sion on her face and nobody would know until they pulled out the tray and saw her stiff clawing fingers—what a horrible thought. . .

Joe shook off a shudder and with his chin high, marched out through the door.

Upon arriving back on the quiet dark ward, he made himself comfortable in his rocker beside the dozing charge attendant. Determined not to sleep, he read into the morning.

Daylight finally came and one by one the patients aroused and walked to the bathroom in anticipation of six o'clock when the lights would be turned on and they could get dressed.

Finally, the attendants aroused themselves and began to fold the blankets and sheets they had used on their chairs. After the chairs were put in the dayroom, Joe went to the room where the ex-medical student was sleeping.

Under the sheet, Joe could see a stern looking face surmounted by short clipped hair. The patient's eyes were open, but Joe shook him as if he were asleep. Startling Joe, the naked figure quickly slipped from the wet sheets and walked noisily on his bare heels to the bathroom. Joe quickly found a mop and wiped up the water and after wiping the plastic mattress with the dirty sheet and turning it over, he made the bed. Looking around, he saw that this large patient had come back from the bathroom. With a scowl on his face, the big bellied man stepped forward. Joe watched in amazement as the angry looking patient got back in bed and lay there with clenched fists. Taking the top sheet, Joe covered the man and left the room bewildered.

The hall buzzed with newly aroused patients and many walked unsteadily as they tried to wear off the effects of their strong medications. Their faces were filled with sleep, but their expressions and gestures revealed nothing out of the ordinary to Joe. The white tile and stone hardness of the spacious bathroom echoed with sounds of running water and flushing toilets.

"Hi, what's your name?" came a cheerful sounding voice from behind Joe. Turning around, Joe saw the smiling face of a patient who seemed to be about his own age.

"Hello. My name's Joe," he answered reciprocating with a smile at the tall skinny lad.

"Everybody calls me Slim."

"How long have you been here?" Joe inquired.

"'Bout four weeks. Do you know how long before I can go up before staff?" Slim asked.

"You mean before the doctors to discuss whether they can dismiss you?"

"Yes, I came here voluntarily and I thought I would get some therapy or something, but all they do is send me to occupational therapy and stuff like that."

"You must understand that there isn't an awful lot of money to give everybody extensive analysis," Joe said.

"Yeh, well all I want to do now is to get out of here. I'm sorry I came here now."

"Have they been treating you all right? I mean, have they been kind to you?" Joe asked confidentially.

"Yeh, I guess they've been nice, but I want to get out and

get some money," the boy said, searching Joe's face with his wide eyes.

"What will you do? How far did you go in school?"

"Guess I'll be a cabbie like my ol' man. He drove, up until his death."

"Well, I hope. . ."

"Joe, you wanna go into the locker room. There's a guy in there standing in front of his locker. Wanna help him get dressed?" the charge attendant's voice interrupted.

"Yeh, shure! Will you excuse me, Slim. I'll talk to you a little later," Joe said, smiling, as he walked toward the locker room.

"See you later," the boy said, and disappeared into the bathroom.

Many patients were standing in front of their lockers but Joe spied one good looking man standing motionles in his undershorts.

"What's the matter?" Joe asked, stepping up.

"Can't decide what to do next," the fellow said in a quick low voice.

"You mean you don't know what to put on next?" Joe asked, feeling he could understand the man's dilemma.

"Yes, I can't remember what to put on. Maybe I should wear my yellow or maybe my green," the man said as he stood motionless staring into his closet.

"Just decide on anyone," Joe said after a pause, seeing that the man was talking about which shirt he would put on. "Take the yellow one," he suggested as he realized the man wasn't deciding.

"But I think it's dirty," the patient answered, reaching for it.

"So what, make the decision and stick by it. Put your arms through the sleeves. That's it. Now the other sleeve. Take those pants—Good! Put your right leg in. Now put the left leg in. You're doing fine. Right sock, left sock. Put that shoe on. . ." Joe instructed, realizing that the man could function if he did the thinking for him.

—I could do so much for these fellows—why did they send me back to that crappy back ward—these are nice people—I could learn a lot and get to know how to help—maybe one of the things they need most is to know somebody cares if they improve. . .

203

"You're doing fine. Now put on the other shoe."

Joe found enjoyment, at that early hour, talking with different patients, listening to and laughing with them. All too soon, it was past seven o'clock and time to go home.

"Nov. 12

Dearest Diary,

Ought to be ashamed of myself, haven't scribbled in you for months. Let me fill you in with the latest smut. Did get accepted into State College—just under the wire. Scrounged for money and now I am in the thick of it. It is not as rosy as I dreamed, I love literature but some of the others courses are a pure boring grind. All I can say is that compared with my elaborate fantasies, reality is very sobering because all is not literature and part is simply rolling up one's sleeves and cramming. All in all, I like it, but am behind because I have had to work two jobs to get the cash. Now I am 'laboring' only for the hospital (nights) and trying to catch up. It's funny but deep down I still have that nagging sense of wanting to fail. Maybe I will try to convert this into fingernail biting. Possibly it is not my wanting to fail but fear that success will be a great let-down. You know, the daydream bit. Also, maybe I am saying, 'Why try' and that way I will have an excuse for failure, but if I work I will have none. . .

At night I feel less haunted. Occasionally I sense a visitor, but my eyes are not tricked now.

Yes, it's all very bla bla and usual. Some things at work make me sick. Last night I was working on an intermediate male ward and a young boy came into the office where I was writing in the book. (The boy was sent to this ward from an admission ward the previous day.) Upon asking him what he wanted, he replied: 'Is there some place else I could sleep?' Me: 'Why don't you like sleeping in the up-stairs dormitories?' He: 'Those guys up there are bothering me. They ask me to come into the bathroom with them.'

Me: 'Why did they say that?'

He: 'They said something about a piece of ass.'

Needless to say, I was furious and gave the boy a room

downstairs to sleep, and wrote about it in big red letters in the log book.

This isn't the first time I have come across this. Many of the homosexuals are not mentally ill and even if they are they should not be put on these wards. They should be separated because their cajoling isn't going to help a poor confused boy.

A couple of weeks ago I was working on the intensive care ward. I felt lousy and wanted to be left alone to study. One of the bedridden patients kept moaning and moaning all night and it put me very on edge. I couldn't concentrate on anything. Anyway, the charge attendant became so annoyed that he clobbered the patient several times while I gave silent consent. The man had bemoaned his fate for many days and everybody had lost patience with him.

Talking about that ward, there is a bedridden patient there who was a doctor. Now all he can do is lie there and smile in a senile way. It makes me wonder.

Something funny happened a couple of days ago. One night I was on an admission ward and had a new admission. He had been drinking, but sobered very fast when he realized what he had done.

He said he was a psychology major from a nearby college and had wanted a topic to write on for his term paper. He said his friends had persuaded him to commit himself and to write about that. As we were going through the admission procedure of weighing him etc., he sobered and became so frightened that I thought he would climb the walls. We helped him calm down, but funny thing was, I believed the story he told. He isn't here tonight so it must have been true.

I could sympathize with this fellow somewhat because I locked myself out of the office one morning on the back ward for the mentally retarded. I had to pound on the door to the next ward for nearly an hour before an attendant helped me.

Funny thing though, this experience gave me a great amount of insight into the real situation and actual perceptions of the patients.

Holy Cow! What time is it? I have been writing too long, must study."

"Dec. 10; 1:00 A.M.; at work.

It was a beautiful day but very cold. I just realized that I did not enjoy it.

I must have it out with myself or I will go mad. Lately I have been a stickler for exactness and have extreme pangs of conscience if I don't follow my mind's dictates. Before, I vowed to myself that I would never sleep on the job. Well, I have become so sleepy at times that I couldn't help it. Before this I had been priding myself because I was so 'good' but now I realize that I have been thinking of myself as a god. Yes, it is true. If I didn't do something right, it would tear my divine conception of myself a little and I would try that much harder, many times only to fail.

Lately I have been getting hungry, because I am short of money, that I have been eating some at work. But it seems I have confused atonement with becoming obsessed by minute things, like turning off all of the lights on a ward when it isn't necessary, or making sure I throw nothing, such as scraps of paper, on the floor. It is getting so bad however, that I almost feel that I can't walk on a floor because I will track dirt on it or wear it out. Got a fever the other night by going alone on a drafty ward that regular attendants don't sit on, because it's too dangerous to be alone on.

Well, anyway it is all very confusing and distressing to me. I must slow down, take it easy and above all, quit punishing myself. I have lost twenty pounds and feel I am getting an ulcer.

One night on one of the wards I met a man who is a staunch Christian and he sleeps on the job, eats the food, and sometimes is extremely rough with the patients. It doesn't seem to bother him and yet it bothers me to see him and hear his prejudices."

—ward 40M—maximum security—why did I tell Mrs. Suso that I had worked on that ward before—if I said I had never had charge of 40M she wouldn't have sent me here—oh well—they say it is the easiest ward in the hospital because the patients are all locked in their individual rooms and there is nothing to write in the log except the census and that the ward was quiet—Smith said that the supervisors rarely make rounds on that ward at night—I'll be all alone—a patient hung himself there last month—they sure kept it quiet—wonder which of the night attendants had the ward that night—if I looked in the room and saw a patient had hung himself it would make me puke—these corridors are sure dark—let's see which door is it—yes here's 40M—they sure don't keep the inside of this ward very lighted—it's spooky and chilly down here—wonder why they put the maximum security in the basement—maybe because the wall are strong—the office—let's see where's the light in here—here—now where's the log book here—it says the census is twenty five patients—the shifts write so little—wait the day report has something here. . . (Delina, W.: Homicidal patient became very agitated today and broke a chair against the wall. He took two legs off this chair and struck patient O'Leary on the side of the face and then kicked the ward door and escaped. The police and supervisor were notified and. . .)

—they make it sound so pat and unexciting here in the book —wonder if they got him—yes—here—the evening report. . . (William Delina—patient that escaped at 2:00 P.M. today was brought back at 8:30 P.M. He was very combative. Placed in seclusion room #18 and given 200 milligrams of Thorazine.)— holy cow—that means he's here—let's see where is room number eighteen—oh yes the room way in the back—what if he should break that door down—he must be big and mean to be able to break through the outside door—maybe he could pick the lock to his room open—everything's almost too quiet on this ward— I better check him and see—where's the flashlight—here—why couldn't I have worked on one of the admission wards tonight— I hate being alone. . .

Throwing his shoulders back, Joe stepped cautiously from the office into the long corridor lined with doors. He imagined many violent situations and pictured a patient on the loose about to jump him from a dark corner.

He kept repeating to himself that his fantasy was running away with him and that all the patients were locked in; and besides many of the patients were not really dangerous. They only wanted to be out and free. Nervously, Joe pointed his flashlight at each corner in turn and then methodically shined his flashlight into each seclusion room's little window to check and see if the patients were asleep.

Going from one side of the corridor to the other, he checked all the rooms. At the beginning of the hall, all the patients were asleep in their beds with covers on them. As he made his way deeper into the passages of the ward, he heard grunts and moans that conjured monsters in his mind and hairy giants to attack and eat his flesh at each corner. Forcing himself to proceed to the end of the hall, Joe found the rooms becoming bare and more smelly.

The patients here were not sleeping in beds with covers; but many were lying naked on the floor with only torn blankets to cover them. Gingerly, Joe made his way to a room from which he heard deep muttering and groaning sounds coming forth.

The yellow beam from his flashlight shone into the blackened cave, but Joe could see no one. The sounds resonated off the scraped and cracked cement and the rusty sheet metal that covered the window, but Joe could see no one. The stench made Joe's nose quiver, but he forced himself to search the visible interior of the room for the hiding demon. Just then he saw something move into the light. It was a man, a human being, made of flesh and blood. He was not too hairy and of average height and build. It could have been anybody. There were no abnormal features to the naked form that Joe could see. He only caught a short glimpse of the figure then the man stepped back into the darkness. With the disappearance of this man went all of the fears and grotesque fantasies that Joe had built up about that ward.

"Could I have a cigarette?" came a voice directly in back of Joe. Instinctively, he swung around ready for a fight. He could feel his body mobilizing for an impending struggle.

"You got a cigarette?" the clear, innocuous voice spoke again. Joe quickly realized that a man was talking to him through the small wire screen in the seclusion room door.

As Joe was raising his fleshlight to catch a glimpse of the man's face, he mechanically stopped the beam on the number printed on the door: it was eighteen. This was the room, Joe remembered, where the dangerous patient was kept. The voice sounded like a young man's but this was the last monster.

Not wanting to engage in controversy with the patient, Joe swung around and started walking toward the office, leaving his visage unexamined.

"Do ya have a light? Do ya have a light? Doyahavalight? Doyahavalight? *Doyahavalight?*" The voice came faster and louder as the words started to run together.

Joe did not know why he fled. He only knew that he did without having proved to himself that this man was not a demon. About halfway back up the corridor he could still hear the voice echoing everywhere; then loud cracking noises rang out. Joe realizing the patient was forcing his full weight against the door.

Upon reaching the office, Joe sat down at the desk and listened to the din. It sounded as if any moment the door to the monster's room would fall and he would pursue him. Joe looked at the office door and felt that he should close it. This would slow his pursuer down while he called on the telephone for help. For some reason which Joe couldn't understand, he left the door open and remained immobile, looking at the neglected school books which he had previously strewn on the desk. He pictured a tall, muscular man looming before the office door at any moment, ready to test his strength against the attendant in a life or death struggle. Joe felt his insides burn with a hostile fire as he thought of the battle. They would kick, choke and throw each other savagely against the wall, but he would fight valiantly.

As quickly as it had begun reverberating with sound, the ward became deathly silent and Joe could feel pulses surging through his body. Suddenly his excitement turned into an enraged panic as he pictured the seclusion room now open and the patient mechanically leaping down the hall to the office. Now Joe wanted to close the office door, but he could not. He was frozen. He would have to fight like a cornered bear. With a tremendous amount of internal strain, he finally mastered his emotion and darted into the hall.

"I am a witch doctor," came a long, vibrating voice down the hall, locating the man, still in the locked seclusion room. "The Lord is behind me. By the power that's vested in me, I will knock the shit out of you. If I don't do it, Lord, I hope you strike me dead, Lord."

Joe breathed a sigh of relief to know the man was still locked in the room and felt ashamed and frightened that he might have been foolish enough to try and take him on alone. As he calmed down, Joe's arms became feebly weak and his stomach felt as if someone were poking a cold stake into it.

"If I don't do it, Lord, I hope you strike me dead, Lord. Lord,

209

bless my mother, Lord. Lord, bless my father, Lord. Lord, bless my sisters, Lord. Lord, bless my brothers, Lord. Lord, bless my enemies, Lord. Lord, bless all my queer friends, Lord, and please bless the attendants in this blessed hospital, Lord, in the Lord's name, Lord. Amen, Lord. . .

Joe wandered back into the office and rested his face in his arms on the desk as he listened to the rhythmic speech that was echoing down the hall.

The voice continued stimulating Joe's ears like a trumpet song blown by the wind. It was as if the source of the sound were immaterial and that it was a vibration surging up through the ages. Many voices of the past and future blended together into a mellow tenor, carrying with it an emptiness.

"I believe in John the Baptist, yes, yes, yes.

I believe in Holy Mary, yes, yes, yes.

I believe in the messenger from the Lord, yes, yes yes.

Give me wisdom, Lord,

Give me knowledge, Lord,

I need the Lord,

I need thee, oh I need thee. . ."

The song rang out for several choruses.

"Lord, have the good sense to let me out of here, Lord. Bless me, Lord, so that I may have the good sense to get out of here, Lord. Oh my God. Keep the devil down, Lord. God, God, God, God, God, God. . ." The words kept coming until all associations were used up in Joe's mind. Finally there was silence and then a loud proclamation.

"I am a messenger from God, Lord. Give the attendant a heart attack, Lord. Make the attendant drop down dead, if he doesn't let me out of here, Lord. . ." The voice kept coming strong and clear. Finally, Joe lifted his head and decided he would not work just yet. He knew that the noise would be too distracting. Looking around, he saw a brassy glow filling parts of the high window pane in the office.

Feeling a tinge of delight at this moonlight, he moved a chair near the window and climbed from it to the top of a sturdy medicine cabinet. This lofty perch gave him a clear view of the outside. As he settled himself, he realized he was sitting crosslegged and that if a supervisor should wander in, he would have to do fast talking to explain why he was situated in such an unorthodox nest. He did not care. This was him and if he preferred a dusty medicine cabinet top to a chair, then he would not conform to such minor conventionalities. Squinting his eyes and leaning forward with his hands clasp together and his arms resting on his legs, he slowly raised his eyes, trying to wring every last pleasure from the scene through the window.

First he gazed at the darkened concrete wall and window sill. Then his stare led him from the yellowing window guard to the window, which was laced with sharp patterns on the corners. Through the pane he could see black metal bars that glittered with minute facets of light reflected from snow crystals. Forming an apron around the bottom of the bars was the shifting, fluffy snow that glistened and reflected like ground quartz. The wind suddenly thrust a strong arm, drawing the window pane forward and then back in its socket. Cold air gushed through, invigorating Joe. Taking a deep breath, he looked out at the foaming, swirling sea of white as the wind gathered small particles of snow into its breast and carried them away, leaving others in their place. The tree outside reflected the moon's yellow on one side, looking like a woman's hand in triple exposure, as though she were reaching for freedom before deciding to draw the rest of her body above the earth's womb. The moon's eternal iris watched the earth's drama in still, stoic solitude. The nearly round sphere's gilt coat revealed no special feature but behind it Joe could perceive intense love mixed with despair, an unrequited love that might have become real, although indecision and nearsightedness could only be seen in the love object.

It was now, again, that Joe realized all was not pure, and that the kaleidoscopic vista was beautiful and, yet agonizing. Reality was so diluted and impure. He, Joe, was staring at nature's wonders through obstructing metal and distorting glass. He could not see clearly and purely, and yet he felt he could. It was as if his eyes were perfect and his other senses complemented them. It was as if his environment had swayed to his wishes but—but it hadn't.

—my knee hurts—shouldn't have sat in this position—number eighteen has quieted down some—why doesn't he cry—it would be refreshing—no that is a sadistic thought—I have procrastinated enough—must study. . .

Joe studied.

It was nearly six o'clock when Joe heard the ward door open

211

and close. Looking away from his book to the door, he watched Mrs. Suso come in with her short quick strides.

"Hi," he said quickly as he stood.

"Oh, you're busy studying. Sorry to bother you, but I was wondering if you could . . . but I see you're studying," she said in a high nervous tone.

"No, I'm done. What can I do for you?" he asked quickly, fully realizing how nervous she was.

"No, I guess," she said, cutting herself short.

"What do you want me to do? I'll help."

"Had an accident on ward 39M. Could you help?" she asked as if anxious to get to that ward.

"Let's go," Joe said, following her.

They quickly made their way through the dark wards and finally hurried up the back steps to ward 39M, the dormitory for 38M. All of the lights were on in the dormitory and Joe saw many of the familiar faces he had known the summer before. Jud Icarus's form caught Joe's eyes quickly because this patient was standing near the door by which they had entered, and he was looking ghastly pale and holding his stomach.

"Something the matter? Are you sick?" Joe inquired.

"Nothing," Jud gasped, turning his head away.

The smell of the ward awakened old memories and emotions as Joe walked onto the large, bed-lined floor.

Smith, two other attendants, and Mrs. Suso were gathered around a bed at the end of the room.

"Where did you find him?" the supervisor asked, nervously looking down.

"Under the bed," came the voice of the attendant whom Joe had helped clean up one morning.

Just then Joe stepped up and, looking over Smith's shoulder, he gasped. "Ugh! what happened?" Before him lay a patient wearing only undershorts and lying on a sheetless, black plastic mattress. The man was covered with blood. The red substance covered his hair and thick clots were forming on the pillow as it flowed from a large gash in the back of the man's head. Crimson fluid also trickled from the sides of the man's mouth.

The patient lay conscious with his eyes opened wide as Mrs. Suso gingerly looked at the bruises and abrasions that covered the man's body. An injury on the man's side made all of the pores, in that area ooze blood.

"Get a stretcher, while I call the doctor," Mrs. Suso said excitedly to the charge attendant of the ward. "What's his name?" Mrs. Suso then asked, stopping and turning to Joe.

"Let's see, his name is Onan. I forgot his first name," Joe said, still staring in horror at the mangled form. "What do you think could have caused it?" Joe asked, looking at Smith.

"I don't know. He must have fallen," Smith said, sounding unconcerned.

"Fallen!" Joe gasped in revulsion at Smith's nonchalance.

"How did it happen?" Smith queried as a token gesture to the speechless patient.

"He can't talk!" Joe exclaimed, feeling that Smith knew that and was only asking for the sake of the other attendant who was standing quietly by.

"Oh, I don't know these patients on this ward very well."

Since there was nothing he could do until the stretcher came, Joe question the patients, but none, not even Jud, confessed that they had seen anything happen.

"I can't get a stretcher on the elevator," the attendant said as he returned ten minutes later.

"What?" Mrs. Suso said in surprise. "How are we going to take him to the medical ward without a stretcher?"

"How about if we stretch blankets under him and carry him that way?" Joe suggested.

"No, we will drag the mattress," Smith proclaimed as if it were final.

They lowered the mattress from the bed and started dragging the fearful hulk, feet first, toward the elevator. It looked to Joe as if having his feet higher than his head increased the patient's mouth bleeding, but Joe didn't mention it as he pulled.

"He probably had an epileptic seizure and hit his head on the bed," Mrs. Suso said as she made feeble gestures in an attempt to help the attendants. They all finally squeezed onto the elevator. On the first floor they swung the patient to the four wheel stretcher and he was taken away. Since quitting time was running close, Joe hurried back to his own ward and did the few morning chores. It did not take long however, because on this ward, the day crew released the patients from their rooms. At five minutes past seven, Joe made his way out into the deep snow his mind buzzing with the recent events.

"Mrs. Suso, sorry to bother you, but did you find out whether that injured patient, Onan, was an epileptic?" Joe asked as he walked into the supervisor's office the following evening.

"Epileptic?" Mrs. Suso repeated in a nervous voice, appearing to be at a loss for words. "No, he wasn't an epileptic."

"Could you find out what happened? Onan was pretty banged up and I know from working days on that ward that there must be at least one ruffian sleeping upstairs. Many mornings last summer we had to have patients stitched up. This patient should be separated from the rest so he won't hurt them."

Mrs. Suso shook her head in agreement. However she didn't look directly into Joe's eyes, and continued to sit quietly in her chair.

Joe continued, "I know those patients quite well, and if you give me a few days I will be able to tell you who did it."

"Yes, if you want to do that," Mrs. Suso said as she reached for the ringing telephone and wrote down the census that one of the wards was calling in.

"Want to go to ward 10M tonight?" she asked, hanging up the telephone and glancing at Joe. Then she paused as though considering whether to give Joe further instructions. "Guess you didn't hear that he died at ten this morning," she said, reaching for the ringing telephone again.

"What! he died?" Joe exclaimed, completely surprised.

She shook her head at Joe as she listened to the telephone.

"Oh, my God!" Joe exclaimed shocked. The blood rushed from his head, his vision narrowed and he had to fight a fainting spasm as he clearly pictured the horrible sight of that morning. "I'll find out who did it," Joe said as he started walking away, only to realize that ward 10M was at the other end of the hospital from 38M.

All night Joe pondered the slaying. He vowed to solve this murder himself and expose it, no matter what the hosiptal staff said.

Two days later, Joe came early to work.

"Mrs. Suso," he said excitedly as he quickly walked into the supervisor's office. "I found out who killed Onan. It was George Saul. Gore told me.

"He's a mental retardate and paranoid schizophrenic. It's hard for me to believe but two other patients confirmed it. George Saul is one of the good workers on that ward. He hardly ever says much and he did a lot of work for me, but he's the one," Joe related quickly before any interruptions could take her away.

"How can you be sure? You are taking the word of mental patients," she said.

"I know Gore and he isn't original enough to think up the story he told me. He said that Onan was wandering around during the night and then got into bed with Probity, who is a patient there. Gore said that Probity shoved him onto the floor and that George Saul got out of bed and started to hit Onan. Gore told me that Saul chased Onan back to Onan's bed and continued to beat and throw him on the floor for at least half an hour. Then Gore said that he shoved him under the bed, and that this all happened at four in the morning," Joe blurted out.

"What do you want me to do?" Mrs. Suso said defensively.

Joe was astounded at this.

"That man should be sent to the state mental hospital and put on a prison ward or at least put into maximum security."

"I agree that something should be done, but you must realize my position. The doctor's report said that Onan fell down and that's what the relatives of the man were told. If they were told that he was murdered, think of the lawsuit they could bring against me. They could get me for every cent I own and I am a poor old maid. I can tell you right now that if I told my superiors about it they would lose the report in red tape," she went on in alarm.

"I'll go with you to the higher ups. Or I can tell them myself and try and keep you out of it, but don't you think it should be brought to light?"

"I really do. Thank you for finding out. I'll do it and I'll tell the attendants to put Saul in one of the seclusion rooms. As of today we have two attendants for that ward anyway."

Joe was skeptical, but he gave the supervisor the benefit of the doubt.

Several days passed and as one week flowed into two, Joe realized that nothing would be done. But this time exams were approaching. Joe could only entertain himself briefly with the fantasy of going before the directors of the hospital because of the pile of unfinished studying he had to do.

It was several days since Joe had seen Mrs. Suso. On Friday, Joe made up his mind to confront her, but when he came to her office that night, he found her crying at her desk and didn't interrupt. On Saturday, the rumor flew around the hospital that Mrs. Suso had quit and a new supervisor was taking over the male service.

Sunday came and Joe made his usual trip to church before he slept. When the service was over he returned to his apartment and after quickly eating, went to sleep.

Later he found himself awake in his darkened room.

—I really must have slept a long time—wonder what time it is—where's the light—here—oh no, it's nine twenty already and I didn't get any studying done—oh well—I needed a good sleep— I'll be wide awake tonight—had a weird dream—let's see— there was a baby lying on the floor and people were gathering around it—it looked healthy but the people around said it wouldn't live so they called a doctor and he took a scalpel and opened the baby's chest and then everybody bent down with scissors and began cutting little pieces of the child's insides out—their hands weren't washed and they just seemed to be picking like vultures—the doctor then stood up and declared that the prognosis was death but he nailed the child's arms to the floor so that the baby wouldn't touch the wound and contaminate it—the dream reminds me of the intensive care ward where we had to tie the old man's arms down so he couldn't touch the incision that was made on his stomach—also reminds me of Onan who was lying there awake bleeding— wonder what it means—think I will write it down in my diary and try to figure it out—I never thought about it before but maybe Mrs. Suso was afraid that an attendant killed Onan or something—maybe the attendant came to get the patients up and was too rough because Onan wouldn't get out of bed— Smith said he saw another attendant beat a patient to death a few years ago—that would all the more reason to bring it before the hospital board—never thought but maybe the attendant told Gore to say what he did—no that's ridiculous. . .

Upon arriving at work, the new supervisor sent him to ward 39M.

—why that ward—it's chilly up there and I have so much reading to do—why have I been so compulsive lately and feel I must turn off every unnecessary light or not dirty the floor or eat the food—will God punish me for such little things—no—

216

God loves me—I know he does and I am so selfish and self centered—yes I even take haughty pride in my rights and keep building a haughtier pedestal with my good work but I really am not kind where it really counts—I don't love God and my neighbor the way I should—that sure was an inspirational sermon today—wish I could get up there in the pulpit and preach— simply being a minister must have its own intrinsic rewards— no—I am the biggest hypocrite going—how could I be sure that I would be preaching divine truths—it sure is dark here on these back wards—everybody is watching television—wonder if there will be two attendants assigned to the upstairs tonight—doesn't seem to be anybody in the downstairs office—if anybody is assigned with me—he is probably one of those watching television and will probably sleep downstairs on the bench—wish I could stay down here in the office and study on the desk— the ward doesn't smell too bad tonight—guess it's because there is no fresh crap lying around—oh—if only I could stay downstairs tonight and study—no—I have neglected my job too much— anyway my conscience would hurt me all night—guess the extreme stress of finals makes me so on edge and gives me this feeling that if I don't do things exactly right I will be punished or else punish myself by failing my exams—no I have slept on the job and done everything wrong—I am no better than anyone else—in fact I am worse because I pretend to be righteous and look down on those who do the same things that I do—no I can't punish myself for it—I have asked God to forgive me today and now I must forgive myself—yes—that's it—forgive myself—upstairs door—where's the key hole—here— sure is chilly in this stairwell—I should have brought a sweater with me to keep warm with—I'll wrap a sheet around me— the other door—this lock should open easier than this— it sure is cold up here—somebody must have opened the door—everybody's sleeping—hope Saul is locked in one of those rooms—oh no— there is someone in his bed—where's my flashlight—must see if that's him—oh no—it is Saul—they didn't do anything—I'll keep an eye on him tonight—there's Jud—he looks funny with his bare feet sticking beyond the bed—wonder if he gets cold that way—must be the strong medication. . .

Joe wandered among the aisles of sleeping patients to make sure everything was all right; then he unlocked the linen closet, turned on the light and, arranging two rocking chairs with blankets and sheets, fixed a comfortable seat by the door of the room so that he could view the ward.

Getting the snake-necked reading lamp out of the closet, he set it on a side table. Then he wrapped a sheet around himself and sat down to study.

—bet if I were working here for years and years I would sleep every night and do a lot of stuff and if somebody brought it to my attention I would tell them that I saw nothing wrong with it—and I would mean it—I must never stop trying to right my shortcomings—must live from day to day—dear God I want to thank you for accepting me at your table today and I am sure I was not completely acceptable but I also am sure you did forgive me and that you love me. I am not going to ask you for a lot of things in this prayer except that I may be acceptable in your sight and that I may some day be better able to reciprocate your love and in turn love my fellow man and not except or want anything in return. Please help me also to go from egocentrism to God-centrism and not want to take your place because of foolish ambition—well that's a lot to ask I guess—maybe I should say—yes that's it—please help me to put myself completely in your hands and help me be acceptable in your sight—please forgive my transgressions of this evening—this I ask in Christ's name amen—wish I could always think of the right words to pray—well—must study. . .

It was very chilly and Joe found his mind being distracted by the temperature. Once in a while a patient on the ward would get up and go to the bathroom and this also distracted Joe's attention, but he faithfully continued cramming into the night.

In the middle of the night, Joe felt his eyes becoming very heavy and lifted them from the page he was reading to glance at the dark ward in front of him. This was the first time tonight that he had really looked. Because he was near the light, Joe could not see the whole ward. He would look into one corner and see a form, but then it would blend with another. Things seemed to move in the darkness, but Joe could not tell whether the shapes were human or simply fictions of his imagination. Yes, it was dark, very dark and this gave Joe a reckless, light-headed feeling. It was not fear, because he knew all of the patients. It was as if blackness were shifting and at any

218

moment something could step into his midst unawares. Something could stand near and he would not perceive it. It was exciting and yet this numbness was not excitement. There was a horrible, beautiful quality to Joe's perception of this desolate land. The beds were dark, the blankets were blank and everything that moved in the shades was formless. It was the handiwork of the ages, the wretchedness of man, the blindness of his own eyes.

Examining the darkness intently, Joe broke out into a cold sweat. It seemed to him that the dark had receded and faces were staring at him. He could see the whites of eyes and open, hungry mouths. Many, many visages were crowded together staring, every eye directed at him. Joe knew that these appairtions were not real and they would flee with another blink of his eyes, but he didn't want them to go yet. They were not there to terrorize him. They were there to speak to him. They were talking silently, beckoning for air, calling for assistance. But who were they? They were not just the patients. There were no familiar faces; but then Joe blinked and the quiet illusion fled into the churning darkness and with it the answer.

The visitation had left and Joe now wished the phantoms had come to his chair and explained their purpose. It was as if this were the last time the darkness would bring torment and questions. No, it was uncanny, ridiculous. Joe felt himself in a different land or a different universe. It was not the same, it had different attributes, different meanings. It was clear, yet not entirely knowledgeable. It was fearsome, yet beautiful. Joe now knew that it was an internal world attributed to the outer, and this mixed quality heightened the emotions that was bubbling inside him. Turning his head upward, Joe looked at the light that burned over his head. Thin, golden threads streaked from it in every direction. It was hindering Joe's view. Reaching over, he flicked it off and turned the neck of his reading lamp to the table so that only a faint glow remained. Tearful and yet determined, Joe accustomed his eyes to the dark. He could see the raised forms of a few solitary figures outlined against their flat beds. Joe knew these were patients. He knew their faces as if he had shone the light on them. The darkness was now friendly, it covered but it did not deceive. All was real, the forms that moved were breathing. Looking at a far window, Joe saw that is was snowing. Filled with childish delight as he was years ago at the first snow fall of the year, he got to his feet and went to the linen closet window.

The fluffy flakes filled the air and silently came to rest everywhere. They made a gay procession to the earth, covering all, making homogeneous what was unsightly. It came down all across the sprawling land, nestled against stately trees and hiding the dead grass. It was a blessing to the earth that was beautiful but unasked for by man. It was a promise of purity that often is seen as a nuisance. The whiteness came into the circle of a streetlight below and each particle balanced a beam and carried it safely to the ground. Joe sat happily staring out the window with the darkness encircling him like a warm cloak.

"Could you give me a light?" came a familiar voice next to Joe. Completely startled, Joe backed from the window into a shadow.

—oh no—it's George Saul—what is he asking me for a light for—he ought to know. . .

"You know I can't give you a light until morning," Joe said authoritatively after regaining his composure.

"Oh," came a discouraged voice as the figure turned to go out the door.

—I'm going to find out once and for all. . .

"George, did you beat Onan?" Joe asked carefully selecting his words so that this patient wouldn't go mute. Everything was silent and Joe saw the darkened figure slowly turn toward him.

—it almost seems as if he is a different person tonight—in the day time he is so meek and cooperative—he always listened to me—he seems almost defiant now—maybe it's because he can't really see me nor I him—sure hope I don't have to fight him and drag him into seclusion by his neck—I better turn on the light. . .

Joe made a step forward to find the light switch and just as he did, he saw the figure reach for the lamp. Momentarily the lamp lit the room like lightning. Then Joe felt it gouge his eye and slash his face, throwing him back against a cabinet. Furiously trying to regain his feet, Joe shoved against the cabinet but it fell over and he sprawled on top as he felt blow after agonizing blow fall upon his helpless body.

—noise—I hear noise—something's happening—so cold in here —must roll up in a ball and then no one can hurt me—noise what is that noise—someone's in that room—someone's over there—someone's hitting something—did I hear my name being called—yes, I heard my name—it can't be—yes—I thought I heard it a third time—Jess is that you—Jess is that you is—that noise of pounding why is the door open—somebody must have broken into the room—it's none of my business—why is Jess talking to me—oh no he is here to punish me—I'm so cold— maybe take somebody else's blanket—must get warm and Jess will go away and I will be all right—somebody keeps pounding— I feel sick—oh this tooth is killing me—so cold—keeps pounding— wonder what somebody's pounding—stay away Jess—don't hurt me Jess— please don't hurt me—must get warm—am so sleepy— must get warm—tooth hurts bad—somebody keeps pounding for a long time—keep away Jess—must get warm—sleep—warm—sleep— noise—pounding—tooth—sleep. . .

"All right, you bastards, get your asses out of bed. Come on Gore, Saul, Jud, let's go, clean up all of this shit," came an attendant's voice in the morning as he turned on the lights.

Jud rolled over in bed and then edged himself into a sitting position.

"All right, which one of you bastards jimmied the lock of the linen closet?" the attendant said, walking to the door as the patients began to stir. "All right, who's been making a mess. . . Oh my God! *My God! My God. . .*" came screaming moans from the closet. A few patients, inquisitive as to the reason for the crying, journeyed to the door. Jud sat on the edge of his bed feeling unusually sick as he looked at the open door. "Get away! Get away!" came the scream of the frightened attendant as he bounced out of the closet and leaped down the hall and out the door, still screaming, as if spooked and fearful of everyone.

Getting up quickly, Jud walked over to the door. The patients got out of his way as he looked in. The room was in shambles and there were stains on the concrete floor. Taking a step into the room, Jud's eyes bugged as his stomach leaped into his throat. Behind the cabinet in a pool of blood lay a body. The arms and legs went everywhere in awkward directions and the clothes were torn and blood had dried on them, but worst of all was the face. Solid hunks of flesh were ripped so deeply on one side of the face that the cheek bone could be seen in one spot. The rest of the face was puffy and bashed and the nose was flattened. The hair was stuck together with lumps of coagulating blood. Feeling as if he would throw up, Jud edged his way closer. He felt he knew this vague countenance but he could not be sure. Coming nearer, he bent close to the face.

—Jess—it's you Jess—someone has killed you Jess—no Jess I didn't hurt you—I didn't kill you Jess—you are going to kill me Jess—I killed you Jess—Jess wake up Jess—I must think—I must —Jess—you aren't dead Jess—I must get you out of here Jess— I must get you somewhere where I can think.

Grabbing onto the two legs of the body, Jud began to drag it out of the clothes room. Just then he felt someone's strong arm around his neck, choking off his air.

Jud could hear a siren as he regained consciousness and found that he was in the downstairs seclusion room. Looking out of the winodw, he saw the back porch buzzing with attendants and others yelling information in the inside hall. A bed was quickly taken out of the ambulance and rushed upstairs. It was not very long before several atendant had hurried down, carrying the bed with the body, and shoved it into the ambulance. With flashing lights and a loud screaming noise, the white truck pulled away.

Jud huddled in the corner of the completely empty room and listened to the commotion on the ward. The window was open a crack and cold air from it blew goose bumbs over his nearly naked body, but he did not care. He knew he had done something bad, so he didn't care if air blew over him. It did not even make him uncomfortable or shiver. Occasionally he could see the faces peering at him through the window in the door and he could hear much discussion outside the room. Time passed and Jud did not move; he could hear the patients returning from breakfast and wondered why he didn't get breakfast. Finally he heard Goodman's voice coming toward his room. Upon hearing Goodman's keys rattle outside, Jud got up and started for the door in hopes that Goodman would let him out and give him food for his churning stomach.

"Stay there, Jud. Get over by the window," Goodman said in a pleasant sounding voice that was new to Jud.

Without a word, Jud backed to the window which was opposite the door as he noticed that there were several other attendants accompanying Goodman. Quickly the door opened and slammed shut.

"Drink it," Goodman said, looking through the wire screen again.

Looking down, Jud saw that there was a paper cup lying on the floor by the door. He walked over to it and picked it up. It was orange juice. As he started to drink, he realized that this was not ordinary orange juice. Mixed with the juice was the sharp pungent taste of Thorazine. There was Thorazine, but the dose he was being given seemed to be larger than he had ever had before. It seemed to burn his tongue.

Jud did not feel like talking, but he felt compelled to face Goodman who was standing at the portal.

"What's wrong?" he finally was able to gasp.

"Why did you attack Joe?" Goodman asked through the door.

"What?" Jud finally vocalized with much effort.

"Joe Mephibosheth, why did you do it last night?"

"Last night?" Jud said bewildered.

"Yes."

"Joe Mephibosheth, was that Joe?" Jud asked.

"Come on, confess and it will be easier on you," Barron said, making his face seen in the door.

"That was Joe?" Jud asked, feeling completely sober now.

"Why did you do it?" Barron said, showing only his good eye.

"I didn't," Jud said starting to feel nervous and shivery. "Is. . . Is he dead?" he forced out finally.

"Almost, you really did a good job on him. If he doesn't die it will be a miracle and even if he lives, he will probably wish he had died. He is a mess."

Jud felt himself too choked up to answer any more of the questions and the attendants finally went away.

Remembering the horrible sight that he had seen that morning, Jud became frightened.

—did I do it—did I kill Joe—maybe I did and don't know it—I didn't want to kill him—I didn't mean it—what will they do to me—they will kill me—they're talking about me out there—they want to send me to maximum security today and then to the state mental hospital—they say this room won't hold me—they're afraid of me—they're afraid to take me to ward 40 because I might fight—they're afraid of me—afraid—Jess I wish

223

you could help me—you would know what to do—did I kill him Jess. . .

Jud sat and listened to the ward outside and decided he would try to think. It was not long before Goodman's face looked in.

"Get away from the door, Jud," Goodman said in a kind voice.

Getting up was a great task because Jud felt very heavy, as if he would fall down and sleep. It was hard, very hard to think now.

Standing in the middle of the seclusion room, Jud caught glimpse of two new men who were working on the front of the door. Peeking outside, Jud saw they were putting two large bolts on the outside of the door and he knew that these bolts were to keep him from breaking the door down.

Jud did not care. He did not think. He was drunk. Staggering aimlessly around the square cubicle a few times, Jud saw the floor come up and, closing his eyes, he felt his numb cheek press against the hard concrete.

It was dark outside and the ward was very dim and quiet when Jud awoke and, looking around saw some food by his door dumped on a paper plate. Quickly he devoured the cold food and drank the coffee that was in a paper cup. This did not satisfy him.

"Attendant, attendant," he called. "Could I have a drink of water?"

Finally four attendants walked up; immediately Jud knew that this was the evening shift and the night shift had not started yet.

The attendants gathered around and looked at him as if he were an animal in a cage.

"What happened today?" came the voice of one of the attendants whom Jud had done much work for.

"Did I kill Jess?" Jud asked groggily.

"You sure did, Icarus. I called the hospital and they said he was putting up a hard fight but that he has been on borrowed time for hours," the attendant said.

"Could I have some water?" Jud asked, knowing he would be able to think straight after quenching his thirst.

"I'm not supposed to open the door, Jud."

"Please, I am very thirsty."

"I'm sorry I can't," the attendant said, "but you are supposed to take this pill." He handed him an orange pill through the screen.

"I can't swallow it without water," Jud pleaded.

The attendant looked at the other attendants and then turned to Jud. "All right, if I give you some water, will you swallow it?"

"Yes, and please give me two blankets. It's very cold in here."

The attendant left and returned.

"Now listen to me. Go over to the window. Keep your feet way back from the wall and lean forward and grab the window guard with your fingers. Stay like that until I tell you to move."

Jud followed instructions as he listened to the ring of the two latches and the sound of the key in the door. Quickly he heard the door slam.

"OK, you can turn around," the attendant said.

After turning around, Jud saw two wool blankets strewn in the middle of the floor and a cup near the door.

"Swallow that pill," the attendant said as Jud picked up the cup of water.

The attendant then went away. Jud took the pill out of his cheek and threw it out the window into the snow. His body longed for the rest of the water in the cup but he also threw its contents at the window in anguish and sat in the corner of the room, feeling tenseness increase all over his body.

He sat for some time. The cold increased along with his senses, but he did nothing about closing the window. His tooth ached and his body screamed, but he somehow welcomed this torment. Blackness shrouded his head as he contemplated a plan of action.

Finally, his thinking became louder and his depression more intense. As he sat he became fully aware of what he would do. He knew that he did not think of this himself. It was something that had been given to him. He had instructions to follow that he had not thought up.

Feeling for the blankets in the dark, he carefully and quietly began tearing them in strips. Someone had told him what to do. He did not know who.

He worked on into the night and carefully concealed his handiwork whenever he heard footsteps near his door. After he had torn one blanket into strips, he tied several of these strips to his toe and began braiding them.

As he worked he became more and more nervous and more panicky. The walls closed in on him and the floor oscillated as if trying to throw him all over the room. Huge tunnels formed in the corners of the room that threatened to swallow him alive, and giant cockroaches and wolves prowled in front of his eyes.

Frantically he worked. Feverishly, he threw the braids together. He knew he could not take much more. He knew something would happen if he didn't hurry. He was a murderer and he knew it. He must be punished. Blood was on his hands. His hands became numb and sore, but he worked on. Finally he was told that he had done enough and that he must hurry and tie the ends together. He did so. Then he took this strong rope and tied it into a hangman's noose. The walls and floor were transforming into monstrosities. They were becoming eternal torments for him. He must flee from them. Terror-stricken and shaking vehemently, he hurriedly dug his fingers into the window guard and pulled himself up.

He tied one end of the rope to the top of the guard as he balanced precariously on the window ledge. Giving a low grunt as he strained his arms to keep his position, he feebly placed the noose around his neck. Now the room was filled with all kinds of nameless black monsters and his head began to swim as he grasped firmly to the window guard to hang on to his life. At the same time a flash of light streaked into the room and he heard an attendant yell at him and then go running down the corridor for help.

Jud was caught and the noose tightened as he felt his fast weakening hands losing their grip.

The room turned over and the guard spun around and around trying to shake Jud from the window. He grasped, groped, strained and frantically fought for his life and air, but he felt his arms numb and disappear and then a sudden jerk of his head.

He tumbled onto the floor, his face painfully bouncing, causing rockets to brighten momentarily in his hypnotized brain.

Finally, writhing in the twisting, contorting room, he came to the realization that his rope had broken. Rolling over on his stomach, his eyes swelled and huge pools of water formed there as he vomited choking sobs in this forbidden cave.

Many footsteps could be heard running down the corridor to his room.